Pete and Myka watched as, one by one, members of the audience came forward to experience Princess Nefertiti's healing touch.

The football player, suffering from a potentially career-ending knee injury, tossed away his crutches. Disfiguring scars and burns faded away. Wheelchairs and walkers were abandoned. Pained expressions gave way to tears of joy.

Okay, Pete thought, *consider me impressed.*

The old lady with Parkinson's was finally getting her turn on the stage. "Let this gentle woman be healed," Nefertiti proclaimed as she laid her hands on the shaking senior citizen. Pete couldn't be sure, but he thought the healer's voice sounded slightly weaker than before. Dmitri, doing double duty as Nefertiti's assistant, stood close by. "Take away her trembling."

Cobalt sparks flashed, jolting the elderly woman. Dmitri caught her before she crumpled onto the stage.

Nefertiti seemed to need an assist as well. She tottered unsteadily on her feet. She was breathing hard. Sweat beaded her brow. She coughed and clutched her chest.

"Looks like all this healing is taking its toll," Myka observed. "A side effect of the artifact?"

"Probably," Pete guessed. There was almost always a cost to using an artifact. That was a big reason they needed to be taken out of circulation. He'd seen too many people get into serious trouble because they thought they could control an artifact's powers.

Like Princess Nefertiti?

WAREHOUSE 13

A TOUCH OF FEVER

GREG COX

POCKET BOOKS

New York   London   Toronto   Sydney

Pocket Books
A Division of Simon & Schuster, Inc.
1230 Avenue of the Americas
New York, NY 10020

This book is a work of fiction. Names, characters, places, and incidents either are products of the author's imagination or are used fictitiously. Any resemblance to actual events or locales or persons, living or dead, is entirely coincidental.

First Pocket Books paperback edition July 2011

POCKET and colophon are registered trademarks of Simon & Schuster, Inc.

For information about special discounts for bulk purchases, please contact Simon & Schuster Special Sales at 1-866-506-1949 or business@simonandschuster.com.

The Simon & Schuster Speakers Bureau can bring authors to your live event. For more information or to book an event contact the Simon & Schuster Speakers Bureau at 1-866-248-3049 or visit our website at www.simonspeakers.com.

Designed by Esther Paradelo

Manufactured in the United States of America

10   9   8   7   6   5   4   3   2   1

ISBN 978-1-4767-2547-5

WAREHOUSE 13

A TOUCH OF FEVER

CHAPTER
1

CHARLESTON, SOUTH CAROLINA

"Okay, I'm getting a seriously bad vibe here."

The Museum of Piracy was a cheesy waterfront tourist attraction designed to separate visitors from their hard-earned vacation dollars. It was well past closing time, however, and Pete Lattimer appeared to have the place to himself. A rugged, brown-haired ex-Marine in his midthirties, dressed casually in a dark sports jacket and slacks, he muttered to himself as he navigated quietly down a darkened corridor. The beam of his flashlight swept over the museum's various displays and decorations. A wooden steering wheel, salvaged from an old shipwreck, was mounted on one wall, next to a tattered black flag bearing the Jolly Roger. Pieces of eight were locked away under glass. A diorama depicted swarms of miniature buccaneers boarding a scale-model replica of a Spanish galleon. Informational plaques accompanied each exhibit. The nautical clutter made the place seem like a cross between a seafood restaurant and, well, a certain overstuffed Warehouse many hundreds of miles from here. . . .

His gaze darted from display to display, his alert brown eyes searching. None of these artifacts was the one he was looking for.

So why were the hairs on the back of his neck standing up?

Pete kept his guard up. He had a sixth sense when it came to trouble, and painful experience had taught him never to ignore his instincts. Paying attention to his "vibes" had served him well as a Secret Service agent, protecting the president. It was even more important now.

He hoped Myka was being careful too. What was keeping her anyway? In theory, his partner was checking out the upper levels of the museum while he explored the ground floor, but she should have caught up with him by now. They had split up to cover more ground quickly, but maybe that had been a mistake? He was used to Myka watching his back.

He listened for any sounds or disturbances coming from upstairs, but heard only the low hum of the air-conditioning. For a second he considered checking on Myka by phone, but decided it was probably too soon to worry about her absence. Myka was a pro; she could take care of herself. Chances were, she was just being thorough. Her keen attention to detail was what had made her such a great Secret Service agent—before they were both reassigned to other duties.

One of the "perks" of those duties? Having to prowl an empty museum in the middle of the night, in search of something that might or might not be here. And that could just get them killed.

What the heck, he thought. *It beats a desk job.*

An old woodcut illustration, enlarged and mounted on the wall, depicted a public execution. Pete winced at the sight of captured pirates dangling from the gallows before a jeering crowd. A caption informed him that the mass hanging had taken place right here in Charleston, back around 1718. Just looking at the illustration made Pete's neck hurt. His free hand went instinctively to his throat. He gulped.

Did they *have* to keep this place so dark after closing?

The grisly atmosphere was giving him the creeps. He quickened his pace, anxious to find the elusive artifact. Enough with the sightseeing. All he wanted to do now was snag it, bag it, tag it, and get out of here.

"Yeah, we should be so lucky," he muttered.

A black velvet curtain closed off the entrance to an adjacent wing. Ornate gold-painted letters above the threshold guided visitors toward the Hall of Infamy, while a smaller sign, dangling from a chain across the doorway, apologized that the exhibit was currently closed for renovations. He approached the curtain anyway. That tingly feeling was getting stronger.

Figures, he thought. The next stop on his tour of the museum would have to be something called the Hall of Infamy. *How come Artie never sends us to All-You-Can-Eat Cookies instead?*

Still, duty called. Pete took a deep breath, then unhooked the chain blocking the way. Drawing back the curtain, he stepped cautiously into the hall, which turned out to be a wax museum honoring the most notorious pirates of fact and fiction. Blackbeard, Captain Kidd, Black

Bart, Long John Silver, Captain Hook, Jean Lafitte, and about a dozen other legendary cutthroats and marauders were posed along both sides of a long, carpeted hallway, their molded features leering at Pete as he made his way down the carpet, past the still and silent buccaneers. Glass eyes and bloodstained cutlasses reflected the glow of the flashlight. Red fiber-optic fuses infested Blackbeard's bushy whiskers. A stuffed parrot perched atop Silver's shoulder. Treasure chests, cannonballs, anchors, and other props added to the maritime decor. Pete felt like he was running some sort of nautical gauntlet—or maybe walking the plank.

Yo, ho, ho, he thought wryly. *I'll pass on the bottle of rum.*

Doing his best to ignore the sinister figures, he finally stumbled onto his destination: a life-size replica of Charleston's most scandalous daughter: Anne Bonny.

The celebrated female pirate occupied a place of honor at the end of the hall. A tricorn hat topped a mane of wild red hair. A man's blue frock coat, a striped shirt, and canvas trousers failed to conceal her shapely figure. A red silk cravat, knotted around her neck, added a touch of color to her ensemble. A flintlock pistol was tucked into her belt. Striking green eyes gleamed with bloodlust and avarice. Her crimson lips were curled in a sneer.

"Hello, Annie," Pete whispered. He recognized her from Artie's briefing back at the Warehouse. The real Anne Bonny had been a bored young wife who had run off to sea to pursue a life of piracy nearly three hundred years ago. Along with her lover, "Calico" Jack Rackham, she had terrorized the Caribbean before being captured by the British navy way back in 1720. Legend had it that she had fought like a hellcat to the very end. Looking at her fierce expression, Pete could believe it.

He lifted his gaze. Anne's right arm was raised high, the better to deliver a fatal blow to the unlucky seaman cowering at her feet. There was just one problem: her wax fingers were empty. The bloody cutlass was missing.

Crap, Pete thought. *That isn't good.*

All of a sudden, his goose bumps had goose bumps.

"Where is the trader of London town? His gold's on the capstan, his blood's on his gown." A singsong voice, carrying an old sea chantey, issued from the shadows surrounding Pete. *"And it's up and away for St. Mary's Bay, where the liquor is good and the laddies are gay. . . ."*

What the heck? He spun around, searching for the source of the lilting voice, which echoed eerily off the walls of the spooky wax museum. His flashlight probed the darkness but could not immediately locate the unseen singer amidst the looming wax pirates. The chantey seemed to come from nowhere and everywhere at the same time.

"Farewell to Port Royal, the stink and the crowds. There's blood in the scuppers and wind in the shrouds. . . ."

"Hello? Is someone there?"

He reached instinctively for his Tesla gun, only to remember that it was Myka's turn to carry the high-tech sidearm. All he had was an ordinary semiautomatic. Damn.

"Myka? I could use a little help here?"

His vibe detector was on high alert. He could

practically feel hostile eyes scoping him out. Chills ran up and down his spine like an express elevator. His gut twisted itself into knots. Adrenaline primed him for action.

And none too soon. A rustling sound behind him alerted him to danger, and he dived for safety even as a dimly glimpsed figure charged from between a wax pirate and his booty. A gleaming cutlass sliced through the empty space Pete's head had occupied only seconds before. He rolled across the carpet and sprang to his feet just in time to see the polished steel blade connect with a waxworks version of Calico Jack instead.

Whoosh! In a blur of motion, the cutlass appeared to deliver fifty blows with a single swing. The air sounded like it was being churned up by a blender. One minute, Jack Rackham was striking a dashing pose in his brightly colored calico vest, the very picture of a rakish pirate captain; a second later the unlucky statue had been reduced to nothing more than a pile of shredded fabric and wax shavings. Paper-thin flakes wafted down onto the carpet. A glass eye rolled across the floor.

"Whoa!" Pete exclaimed. He scrambled backward, bumping into a rusty iron cannon. The beam of his flashlight swung upward, exposing his attacker: a blond woman clutching Anne Bonny's missing cutlass. He recognized her as Lainie Evers, a tour guide who worked at the museum. He and Myka had met her briefly when they were casing the place earlier today.

The formerly helpful guide was still dressed for work, looking like a theme-park version of a stylish female pirate. A plastic name badge was pinned to a ruffled white blouse. A laced red corset cinched her waist, above a black skirt and knee-high boots. A skull-and-crossbones motif was printed on the skirt. More like a Halloween costume than authentic pirate garb, in other words.

The cutlass, on the other hand, was the real deal.

Snarling, Lainie wheeled around to confront Pete, who put the cannon between himself and the sword-wielding guide. Crazed eyes and contorted features mimicked Anne Bonny's savage expression. She spit venomously at Pete.

"Fight like a man, you scurvy rogue, or die like a dog!"

Wow, Pete thought. *Somebody's swash is buckled a little too tightly.*

The cutlass was obviously messing with her head. As Pete knew too well, certain historical artifacts could become imbued with powerful tangential energies stemming from past owners and events—with bizarre, unpredictable results. Pete had hoped that he and Myka could get their hands on the cutlass before it stirred up any trouble, but clearly their timing sucked. The sword already had Lainie in its spell.

"Hey! Unshiver your timbers, lady!" He tried to talk her down. "You're not thinking straight. . . ."

"Belay that! A short life and a merry one, I say. Especially for you!"

She lunged at Pete, hacking wildly. The flashing cutlass struck sparks off the cannon as he ducked away from the multiplying blows. "Not really feeling the merry right now." He reached again for his gun, but reconsidered. Lainie was an innocent victim here; she wasn't herself. No way did he want to resort to deadly force.

Too bad she didn't feel the same way.

"Stand still, you villainous cur. Or I'll slip ye the Black Spot!"

Uh-huh, he thought. *Not going to happen.*

Dousing his flashlight, he retreated from the possessed guide, trying to blend in with Captain Kidd and the others. By now his eyes had partially adjusted to the dark, and he could dimly make out Lainie stalking up and down the red carpet, cursing profanely in a manner that would have seared the tender ears of any grade-school kids visiting the museum on a field trip. Pete assumed she didn't use that sort of language during business hours.

She slashed at the air, slicing it to ribbons. Whistling repeatedly with every swipe, the cutlass keened like a chorus of dying men. No doubt it had claimed the lives of many sailors during Anne Bonny's bloody heyday. Pete considered his options. Reasoning with Lainie appeared to be a lost cause; the cutlass's influence was too strong. He needed to get the sword out of her grip—and vice versa.

Ideally without getting turned into confetti in the process.

Moving as stealthily as he could, he circled behind her. Decorative cables and anchors threatened to trip him up, but he somehow managed to skirt around the edges of the exhibit without knocking anything over or getting tangled in the mock rigging. Creeping out from behind a painted wooden figurehead in the likeness of a busty mermaid, he snuck up behind Lainie, hefting his flashlight like a bludgeon. His eyes zeroed in on the back of her skull. All he needed to do was knock her out long enough to separate her from the cutlass and neutralize it. With any luck, she wouldn't remember any of this.

Lainie was only a few paces ahead of him. Her blond hair was tied back in a pigtail. He raised the flashlight.

Sorry 'bout this, he thought in advance. *The aspirin's on me.*

Before he could make his move, however, a harsh electronic buzz emanated from his jacket's inner pocket. Pete felt the Farnsworth vibrate insistently—at the worst possible moment.

Not now, Artie!

But it was already too late. The jarring signal alerted Lainie, who whirled about, swinging the cutlass in a deadly arc. Pete threw himself backward barely in time to avoid getting disemboweled. The tip of the blade shredded the front of his shirt, sending threads and buttons flying, but just missing the skin underneath. The close call sent his heart racing. Ignoring the persistent buzzing from his pocket, he took cover behind the carved wooden mermaid. He glanced down at the tattered fabric in shock. "Hey," he protested. "I *liked* that shirt!"

Lainie didn't care.

"Avast, ye filthy bilge rat! I'll feed your salty guts to the sharks!"

She came at him with a vengeance. The cutlass hacked away at the figurehead like a chain saw in disguise. Wood chips and splinters pelted Pete's face. The makeshift barricade was being whittled away right before his eyes. In seconds, there would be nothing left of the mermaid but a toothpick. He backed into the wall behind him. Lainie had him cornered.

He reached for his gun. Could he really bring himself to shoot an innocent victim?

"Sorry. That's my partner you're trying to turn into fish food," a familiar voice called out from the opposite end of the hall. Myka Bering appeared in the doorway. The tall brunette aimed an exotic-looking handgun at Lainie. The weapon looked like something from an earlier century, all polished brass and crystal, in contrast to her black blazer and slacks. Copper coils and batteries glowed inside its transparent barrel. Miniature gauges monitored its charge. Myka's stern tone made it clear that she meant business. "Feeding time is over. Hand over the cutlass."

"Never! I'll send ye down to Davy Jones's locker 'fore I surrender me blade, you poxy wench!"

Waving her cutlass, Lainie charged at Myka. Pete opened his mouth to warn his partner of the sword's rapid-fire capacity, but he needn't have bothered. A bolt of crackling blue electricity shot from the muzzle of the pistol, which had been designed and built by Nikola Tesla over seventy years ago. The galvanic blast stopped Lainie in her tracks. She stiffened in shock, her hair standing on end, toppling backward onto the carpet. The cutlass slipped from her grip.

Myka hurried forward and kicked the sword away from Lainie's limp fingers. She scowled at the prone tour guide.

"First off," she said, "I know exactly where Davy

Jones's locker is, and it's nowhere near the bottom of the ocean." She nudged Lainie with her toe to make sure she was down for the count. "Second, don't call me a wench."

Pete emerged from behind what was left of the mermaid. "Duly noted."

Myka eyed her partner with amusement. She was an attractive woman, only a few years younger than Pete, with curly auburn hair and dark brown eyes. She lowered the Tesla gun. Now that the immediate threat was over, her voice adopted a more teasing tone.

"'Bilge rat'?"

"Don't start." Pete brushed sawdust from his face and clothes. "What took you so long?"

"I stumbled onto a security guard upstairs. He was lying on the floor in the Sunken Treasure exhibit." She glanced at Lainie's unconscious form. "Our Anne Bonny wannabe here had got to him first."

"Eww." Pete imagined what the supercharged cutlass could do to a person. He grimaced at the grisly images flashing across his mind. "Was he . . . ?"

He pantomimed a chopping motion with his hand.

"What? No, no," Myka assured him. "He was just out cold. I figure he interrupted Lainie on her way to the cutlass."

Pete was glad to hear it. Sweeping up shredded security guard was nobody's idea of a good time. "Why do you think the cutlass latched onto her?"

"Proximity? Aptitude?" Myka shrugged. "Maybe she just spent too much time around the sword, and eventually it started invading her psyche? You know how it works. Sometimes artifacts can lie dormant for years before the right person—or the wrong one—comes into contact with them. Lainie probably just clicked with the cutlass for some weird metaphysical reason. After a while, she couldn't resist stealing it from the exhibit."

"And we all saw how well that worked out for her." Pete decided that he could skip any new pirate movies from now on. He nodded at the cutlass. "Let's neutralize this bad boy before Johnny Depp gets his hands on it."

"Better late than never," she agreed. "You care to do the honors?"

"Why not?"

Carefully following procedure, the agents donned specially treated purple latex gloves before handling the artifact. The last thing they wanted was for one of them to become possessed by the cutlass. Pete plucked the short, broad blade from the floor while Myka unfolded a lightweight metallic-silver evidence bag large enough to contain the cutlass. A small quantity of viscous purple fluid sloshed inside the bag; the concentrated "goo" could temporarily neutralize the arcane energies in certain artifacts. She held the bag open.

"All set?" Pete asked. He held the cutlass gingerly over the bag like it was radioactive.

Myka nodded. "Ready when you are."

"Okay. Watch your eyes."

Pete dropped the cutlass into the bag, then hastily looked away. A fountain of incandescent golden sparks erupted from the bag as the energized cutlass reacted with the goo. The pyrotechnic display faded quickly, but the flash was still bright enough to make Pete's eyes water. Glowing blue dots danced briefly in his field of vision. Myka was blinking too.

Wow, he thought. *That was a bright one.*

The sparks were a good sign, though. They meant that the cutlass really was the artifact they were looking for. An ordinary sword, with no supernatural properties, would not have triggered the reaction. Myka sealed the bag for safekeeping. In theory, the goo would keep the cutlass quiet on the way back to the Warehouse.

Pete's jacket buzzed again. Artie obviously wanted an update.

"You going to answer that?" Myka asked.

"Yeah. Hang on." He fished the insistent device from his pocket. Resembling an old-fashioned cigarette case, the Farnsworth was encased in a burnished bronze lozenge. He flipped open the lid to reveal a convex glass screen above a number of antique-looking knobs and dials. A video cell phone, the gadget was based on a prototype developed by Philo Farnsworth, the inventor of television, one weekend back in 1929. Completely off the grid of more conventional telecommunications networks, the Farnsworth provided the most secure line known to the Warehouse and its agents. Pete and Myka shared a single Farnsworth. A red light flashed in sync with the buzzing. Pete flicked a switch to accept the call. "Hi, Artie."

Preceded by a burst of static, the face of a grizzled older man appeared on the miniature TV screen. Bushy black eyebrows that looked like they were on steroids bristled above a pair of horn-rimmed glasses. Gray hairs infiltrated his frizzy black hair and beard. Artie Nielsen shoved his face forward. A fish-eye lens distorted the black-and-white image slightly, giving it the look of a funhouse mirror. A brusque voice emanated from the Farnsworth.

"Did you get it?"

"We're fine, thanks for asking," Pete replied. Artie could get a bit curmudgeonly where bagging artifacts was concerned. After being cooped up in the Warehouse for nearly four decades, his phone manners had grown rusty. "But, yep, we got it."

"Thank goodness." Artie sighed in relief. He relaxed visibly. "Run into any problems?"

Pete glanced around at the trashed museum. Calico Jack was nothing but shavings. The figurehead was kindling. Lainie Evers was sprawled upon the floor. Pete's best shirt hung in tatters, exposing his hairy chest. He carefully angled the Farnsworth so that his ventilated clothing was not visible.

"Nah," he answered. "Just the usual."

The funny thing was, he wasn't lying. Compared to some of their investigations, this had been a walk in the park. Nobody had blown up, spontaneously combusted, imploded, turned into glass, walked through walls, gone invisible, or been transported to another dimension. That kind of thing could really spoil your day. Chances were, Lainie Evers wouldn't even remember what had happened here tonight. The Tesla tended to scramble people's short-term memories.

"Good." Artie didn't ask for details. He'd review their reports later. "Now get that cutlass back here as soon as you can. But by coach, remember. Not first class. The Regents are on my case about the budget."

Pete bit his lip. You'd think a top-secret organization whose origins stretched back to antiquity wouldn't hold on to its purse strings quite so tightly, but by now he was used to Artie's chronic frugality. Coach it was. Pete's long legs cramped in anticipation.

Maybe there would be a good in-flight movie?

"Okay, Artie. See you soon. Say hello to Claudia and Leena for me."

"You can do that yourself, once you deliver that cutlass."

The transmission cut off abruptly. Pete put away the Farnsworth and took the silver bag off Myka's hands. The cutlass weighed it down. A gust of air-conditioning rustled the sliced-up shirt. He picked at the butchered fabric. "Aw, man . . ."

Myka smirked. "Maybe we can find you a souvenir T-shirt in the gift shop. Perhaps one with Anne Bonny on it?"

"Very funny," Pete said. "Next time, *you* search the Hall of Infamy."

Myka let him vent. "Deal."

CHAPTER
2

THE BADLANDS, SOUTH DAKOTA

Once a vast prehistoric ocean had covered the Great Plains, but that had dried up long before anyone was around to watch it gradually evolve into desert. Now the desolate scenery resembled a barren lunar landscape. Erosion had carved out thousands of acres of craggy hills, canyons, and cliffs. Gnarled rock formations cast weird, unearthly shadows upon the arid soil. Streaks of diversely colored stone laid bare the geologic history of the region, with each distinctive shade and hue serving as petrified evidence of a bygone era. Yucca, juniper, and other desert flora stubbornly set down roots. Patches of grass sprouted here and there. The Sioux Indians had named this place *mako sica,* or "bad land."

Warehouse 13 called it home.

It had taken Myka a while to appreciate the unique natural beauty of the Badlands. When she had first been reassigned here two years ago, she couldn't believe that she had been banished to some godforsaken wasteland in the middle of nowhere. But over time she had come to find the endless ochre hills and valleys both grand

and comforting. She relaxed into the passenger seat of a black SUV as she and Pete drove past the familiar landmarks. It had been a long trip, but soon they—and Anne Bonny's cutlass—would be back where they belonged.

"Here we are," Pete said from behind the wheel. "Home sweet home."

Warehouse 13 was located at the end of a long dirt road past several swinging metal gates. An enormous hangar-like structure built into the base of a secluded hillside, it had the entire valley to itself. No other buildings were in sight. The nearest town was miles away and didn't even have a name. No signs or markers pointed to the Warehouse. Even if you knew it existed, you might have trouble finding it.

Which was the whole idea.

Several stories high, the Warehouse's rusty façade loomed over the desert. Riveted steel plates, deceptively dilapidated in appearance, guarded its contents. Iron beams and girders, anchored by sturdy concrete foundations, buttressed the towering walls. Satellite disks pulled down data from the heavens. Angled tin roofs gave the building a roughly triangular shape, but what you saw from outside was only the tip of the iceberg. The Warehouse extended deep into the hills as well as several levels beneath the ground. Myka had worked here for nearly two years now, but she still had trouble grasping just how big the Warehouse really was. You could fit the Javits Center, the Louvre, and the entire Smithsonian inside the building and still have acres of room to spare. There were entire levels, galleries, and annexes she had yet to explore.

She wondered where exactly the cutlass would end up.

A cherry-red Jaguar roadster and a vintage El Camino pickup truck were parked in front of the Warehouse. "Looks like everybody's home," Pete observed. Braking to a stop beside the other cars, he killed the engine. His stomach grumbled audibly. "You think Artie's made cookies?"

"I wouldn't be at all surprised." Myka smiled at her partner. Pete's appetite was practically supernatural in its own right. "Remind me again how you keep your girlish figure?"

"Clean living, what else? Plus, lots of running for my life."

They stepped out of the car into the blinding glare of a hot August afternoon. The scorching heat came as a shock after the air-conditioned comfort of the car. Sunlight reflected off the Warehouse's tarnished metal walls. Myka was grateful for her tinted sunglasses, which were a necessity in this part of the country. It felt good to stretch her legs.

A solitary cow, grazing on a measly patch of grass, lowed in welcome. A hot breeze carried with it the distinctive aroma of a large heap of manure piled high a few yards away. Myka had once mistaken the heap for a small hill. She hadn't made that mistake again.

"Right back at you," Pete addressed the cow. He retrieved the cutlass, still securely bagged, from the rear of the SUV.

They approached the Warehouse. The front door was the same rusty metal color as the oxidized steel sheets around it, so that it blended in almost as though camouflaged. Myka clicked a button on a compact hand-held remote. Ancient hinges creaked as it swung open.

"After you," Pete said.

Myka strolled inside. Compared to the Warehouse's weather-beaten façade, the sterile white umbilicus looked like something designed by NASA. A flexible metal tube, barely wide enough to allow two people to pass through side by side, accordioned ahead of her for fifty yards or so. Fluorescent lights lit up the tunnel, which wobbled slightly beneath their tread like an enormous slinky. Explosive charges, mounted at both ends of the umbilicus, could be detonated if the Warehouse needed to be sealed off in a hurry. Myka wished the bombs weren't quite so visible. She had already seen them in action once. She knew how much firepower they packed.

Thank heavens nobody had died the last time the bombs went off. At least, not permanently.

The tube led to a locked white door. A metal box was attached to the wall next to the door. She opened its lid to expose a glowing blue retinal scanner. Myka positioned her right eye in front of the scanner. By now, the elaborate security measures were second nature to her.

An electronic chip confirmed that she was indeed herself. The door swung open.

"We're back," she called out.

Beyond the umbilicus was a cluttered office that resembled a cross between a musty old antique shop and the back room of a museum. Wooden file cabinets, shelves, and bookcases were crammed against the exposed brickwork. A bulletin board was covered with tacked-up index cards, photos, and newspaper clippings.

A pull-down map of the world occupied one wall, not far from an antique harpsichord. Overstuffed shelves and display cases sagged beneath the weight of various exotic relics and curios, including a Viking helmet, a fossilized dinosaur skull, a crystal ball, a gold record, a vintage Roy Rogers lunch box, a bedpan, and a monkey's paw. A suit of armor, that had once belonged to Richard the Lion-Hearted, stood guard in a corner. A news ticker, like the one in Times Square, offered an endlessly scrolling update on world events. Hanging lamps cast a warm glow over the office. A ratty Persian rug protected the floor. Shuttered windows at the far end of the office blocked her view of the mezzanine beyond, which looked out over the main floor of the Warehouse. A spiral staircase led to Artie's private quarters one floor up. Paperwork was piled high on the desks, which boasted a jarring mixture of high-tech computer screens and antiquated, retro-looking keypads. A souvenir snow globe was being used as a paperweight. Frost coated the outside of the globe. A micro-blizzard swirled inside it.

Myka barely noticed the eclectic decor, which was old hat to her. She looked instead to see who was waiting for her. Her smile widened as she saw that the whole gang was present.

"Hey! America's best-kept secret agents return!" Claudia Donovan sprang from an upholstered wingback chair, nearly spilling her laptop onto the floor. The teenage whiz kid was ten years younger than Myka, as evidenced by her funkier attire and style. Bobbed red hair was accented by a dyed blue swoop. A vintage biker vest was layered over her blue tank top. Novelty pins and buttons added flair to the vest. Her slim legs were tucked into a pair of skinny black jeans. She carelessly tossed the laptop onto the chair before rushing over to greet Myka. "What's up, girlfriend? How was ye olde pirate museum?"

"The staff was a little overly enthusiastic, but nothing we couldn't handle." Myka grinned back at Claudia before addressing the rest of her colleagues. "Hi, Leena, Artie."

"Welcome back." A slender young woman turned away from the card catalog, where she had been re-alphabetizing the files. A floral sun dress flattered her figure. A voluminous head of frizzy brown hair crowned her like a halo. Smooth skin was the color of caramel. Quieter and more composed than Claudia, she radiated a certain otherworldly serenity. Knowing brown eyes squinted at Myka, seeing more than just her physical appearance. "You look well," Leena said. "You, too, Pete."

"Just glad to be back." He followed Myka into the office, lugging the silver containment bag. The door clicked shut behind him. "Anybody order a bona fide pirate pigsticker?"

"Is that it?" Artie asked urgently. The grizzled agent looked up from his desk, which was strewn with index cards and yellow legal pads. A tan corduroy jacket was draped over his short, stocky frame. His rumpled black shirt needed ironing. His feet, in well-worn sneakers, rested flat on the floor. Behind the thick lenses of his glasses, shrewd brown eyes lit up like those of a kid in a candy store. "Was it damaged in any way?"

Ideally, they preferred to deliver the artifacts to the

Warehouse in one piece, but, sadly, that wasn't always possible. More than once, they'd had to sacrifice some precious historical relic in order to save innocent lives. Fortunately, that hadn't been the case this time around.

"It's fine," Pete assured him. "See for yourself."

He cleared off a space on the desk, then unsealed the bag. The cutlass spilled onto the desk, landing with a thud on the clear glass desktop. Leena, Claudia, and Artie moved in for a closer look.

"Anne Bonny's cutlass," Artie whispered in a hushed tone. "We've been looking for this ever since Anne escaped the gallows back in 1720 by pleading her belly—"

"Come again?" Claudia interrupted. "Pleading her whatsit?"

"She was pregnant," Myka translated. She had read all about Anne's infamous career while growing up in her father's bookstore. "With Calico Jack's child. The court delayed her execution until the baby could be born."

Claudia smirked. "That's one way to beat the rap, I guess. Better knocked-up than hung."

"Yeah," Pete added. "But your reprieve is only good for nine months, tops."

"As far as we know, the execution never took place," Artie said, picking up the story. "Some say her father, a wealthy merchant, managed to buy her freedom. Anne, her baby, and the cutlass all disappeared from history . . . until now."

He gazed reverently at the sword. For all its insidious properties, the cutlass was a genuine piece of history. Myka couldn't blame Artie for being excited to add it to the Warehouse's collection at last. He was a natural-born curator and historian, which made him the ideal person to manage Warehouse 13. Nobody knew the value of the artifacts, and just how much havoc they could cause, better than Artie Nielsen. He had devoted the better part of his adult life to the vital work of tracking down every weird and unnatural object that threatened to ruin the world's day.

The first Warehouse had been established by order of Alexander the Great, way back in the Bronze Age. Even then, it had been obvious that certain potent relics and talismans were too dangerous and unpredictable to be at large in the world; better for all concerned that they be kept locked away until such time, if ever, that their mysterious attributes could be fully understood and controlled. Subsequent Warehouses, in ancient Egypt, Rome, Mongolia, and elsewhere, had continued Alexander's work, hiding their preternatural prizes from those who might abuse their power. The current Warehouse, number thirteen, had gone into operation back in 1914. Thomas Edison, Nikola Tesla, and M. C. Escher had all contributed to its design. Artie himself had been recruited as an agent over forty years ago. By Warehouse standards, that was a remarkably long run. Most never lasted that long. . . .

Leena viewed the cutlass with distaste. "It has a very violent aura." She shivered and hugged herself. "Perhaps it belongs in the Dark Vault?"

The Dark Vault was the Warehouse's own Hall of Infamy, where the most sinister and dangerous artifacts were kept. Like an Aztec bloodstone, or Sylvia Plath's typewriter. The latter had nearly drained Pete's will to live last year. Anne Bonny's cutlass would fit right in.

Artie wasn't so sure. "I don't know. Pretty much all the artifacts are dangerous to some extent, or they wouldn't be here. And we can't keep *everything* in the Dark Vault. There are budget issues. Do you know how much it costs to maintain those high-intensity neutralizing fields?"

"More than our lives?" Myka asked.

"Let's try it out in the main collection first," Artie decided. "If it acts up, we can always move it to a more secure location later."

Leena frowned, but did not argue the point.

Neither did Myka. She was too tired to discuss it further. It had been a long trip.

Which Claudia wanted to hear all about.

"C'mon, dudes. Spill." She bounced around them like a hyperactive elf. "How was your latest road trip? Artie's had me cooped up here for days now, double-checking the inventory. I'm going stir-crazy."

"Maintaining an accurate inventory is vitally important," Artie began. "We've all seen what can happen when an artifact goes astray. . . ."

"Yeah, yeah. Spare me the lecture, Captain Bligh." Claudia had heard it all before. "Enough with the bagging and tagging. I want in on some primo snagging action."

"You're not a full agent yet," Artie reminded her. "Just an apprentice."

"But I've helped out in the field before!" She looked to Myka and Pete for backup. "Tell 'em, guys. Remember that time in Detroit? Or when Myka and I checked out that wrestling team in California?"

"You mean the time you fell into a vat of supercharged energy drink?" Artie said. "And almost spontaneously combusted?"

"That wasn't my fault. I was pushed."

Pete's stomach growled again. It sounded like a saber-tooth tiger newly escaped from the La Brea tar pits. A sound that, oddly enough, Myka was actually familiar with.

"Maybe we can table this discussion for later?" Pete suggested. "I've been driving for hours and I'm famished." He looked around hopefully. "Are there any cookies left in the pantry?"

As ever, Artie was on top of things. "I whipped up a fresh batch of snickerdoodles this morning." He glanced at Leena. "If you don't mind . . ."

"I'll go get them," she said, smiling warmly. Among other things, Leena ran a bed-and-breakfast in a nearby town. Hospitality was her speciality. "Be right back."

Myka settled into a comfy chair. A yawn escaped her. Pete could have his cookies, but she was more interested in calling it a day. Now that they had successfully delivered the cutlass to Artie, she just wanted to head over to the B&B and unwind with a good book.

Until their next investigation.

CHAPTER
3

LEENA'S BED-AND-BREAKFAST
"UNNAMED UNICORPORATED SETTLEMENT"

"What's a six-letter word for 'empty fingers'?"

Myka squinted at a half-finished crossword puzzle as she and Pete enjoyed a relaxing brunch on the patio. A plate of fresh scones with raspberry jam rested on the elegant wrought-iron table between them, alongside a pitcher of hot coffee. Elm trees, their leaves already changing colors, offered shade from the sun. Graceful white columns framed the patio. Potted plants and flower boxes added life to the setting. A rose garden offered a fragrant bouquet. The morning paper was dismembered atop the table. As usual, Myka had claimed dibs on the crossword, while Pete chuckled over the comic pages. Her pencil was poised above the empty squares of the puzzle. She was not so arrogant as to use a pen.

"Beats me," Pete mumbled through a mouthful of scone. His eyes remained glued to the funnies. "Okay, so why is it that Dilbert can't find a better job?"

Myka assumed that was a rhetorical question.

A trace of jam leaked from the corner of his mouth.

She resisted an urge to reach out and wipe it away with a napkin.

Maybe later.

She took a moment to enjoy the morning. Leena's bed-and-breakfast was an oasis of tranquillity in their often tumultuous lives. The elegant Victorian Gothic edifice was located in "Univille," the officially unnamed township just down the road from the Warehouse. Painted white walls and a pitched blue roof gave the B&B a much tidier appearance than the seemingly ramshackle Warehouse. Steep gables crowned the arched windows. Ivy climbed the walls. A widow's walk topped the uppermost turret. Myka, Pete, and Claudia all had rooms at Leena's place, giving them someplace cozy to go home to at the end of the day. Only Artie preferred to bunk down at the Warehouse full-time. He didn't know what he was missing.

Or maybe he did.

A back door banged open and Claudia rushed breathlessly onto the patio. "Sorry I'm late, amigos, but I was up late kicking butt on the intertubes. Would you believe some troll actually thought he knew more about quantum processing and fuzzy logic than yours truly?" She snorted at the very idea before her gaze alighted on the remaining scones and jam. "Ooh! Raspberry goodness!"

She plopped herself into an empty chair and helped herself.

Artie arrived a few minutes later, about ten after twelve. A brown accordion folder, stuffed with notes, was tucked under his arm. Myka guessed that the folder held the details of their next assignment. She put aside her unfinished puzzle. She couldn't wait to find out what sort of bizarre, unearthly mystery Artie had turned up now.

"Good morning," he greeted them, then consulted his wristwatch. "My mistake: Make that 'Good afternoon.'" He placed the bulging folder down on top of the open newspaper. His eyes were also captivated by the tempting spread Leena had provided. "Are those scones?"

Claudia shot him a warning look. "Go easy on the jam and butter, old man. Just because the universe is expanding doesn't mean you have to."

"Devil child." He peeked sheepishly at his slight paunch before joining them at the table. Under Claudia's watchful gaze, he applied just a dollop of jam to a scone. "Just wait until your own metabolism slows down."

"Not going to happen, gramps. My candle burns at both ends, you know."

"Actually, Edna St. Vincent Millay's candle was snuffed by a Warehouse agent decades ago," Artie informed them. "Heaven help us if either end is ever lighted again."

He was a font of arcane lore and history, with a tendency to ramble on sometimes. "An interesting woman. Did you know she went by the name 'Vincent' in her early years, and also wrote prose as 'Nancy Boyd'? But it was her poetry that really stirred things up. . . ."

Myka saw a lengthy digression coming on and tried to head it off. She nodded at the folder. "What's up, Artie?"

The older agent made a habit of scanning news reports, police bulletins, government databases, classified ads, advice columns, human interest stories, auction listings, obituaries, scientific journals, book reviews, message boards, blogs, and other ephemera in search of freak events and patterns that might indicate the influence of a rogue artifact. Specialized computer filters and algorithms helped sort through the ceaseless flurry of data, but could never truly replace the keen eye of a veteran Warehouse employee. Tracking down artifacts was an art, not a science, and Artie was the reigning maestro.

"Yeah, Artie." Pete lowered the funny pages. "You got something for us?"

"Possibly." Artie finished off his scone before launching into today's briefing. "I got a ping regarding a string of supposedly 'miraculous' healings associated with a traveling carnival that's working small towns along the eastern seaboard."

Rummaging through the folder, he extracted a garishly colored flyer promising *Rides! Games! Amazing Acts and Performers!* Clowns, carousel horses, and grinning children crowded the artwork, beneath the image of a towering Ferris wheel. *Fun for All Ages! The Whitman Bros. Family Carnival!* A bright golden starburst that looked as though it had been recently added to the design of the flyer extolled *The Magical Touch of Princess Nefertiti, the World's Greatest Psychic Healer!*

Myka had never heard of her.

Princess who?

Artie slid the flyer across the table toward Myka and Pete. "Every one of the healings took place at this carnival sometime over the last three months."

"I don't know, Artie." Myka peered dubiously at the

paper, which reminded her of any number of colorful circus and carnival posters she had seen displayed on telephone poles and barbershop windows over the years, each touting some fly-by-night caravan of thrill rides, rigged games, and greasy food. This just looked like more of the same. "Sideshow charlatans and snake-oil peddlers are a dime a dozen," she said, playing devil's advocate. "How can we be certain there's an artifact involved?"

"Right," Pete agreed. "Maybe the whole thing's just hype? Or a hoax?"

"Or perhaps there's some kind of placebo effect involved," she suggested. "People feel better because they *think* they've been healed."

Artie shook his head. "No, that's not it. I've looked into this and the claims appear to be legitimate." He pulled more documentation out of the folder, including copies of confidential medical records and insurance claims. "We're talking broken limbs healed in record time, tumors disappearing, incurable illnesses reversing themselves . . . even at least one case of an Alzheimer's victim who suddenly regained her faculties." He held an X-ray up to the light. "I'm seeing all sorts of red flags here."

That was good enough for Myka. Artie had been doing this for a long time. His hunches almost always paid off.

"All right," she said. "If you think you're onto something, we need to check it out."

"Yes! It's carnival time." Pete punched the air, clearly psyched at the prospect. "And you know what that means? Funnel cakes!"

"I'm more of a caramel apple girl myself," Claudia chimed in. "But to each their own. Maybe we can squeeze in a couple rounds of dart tossing? I'm warning you, I have 'mad skillz' when it comes to popping balloons. . . ."

"You're on," Pete said, accepting the challenge. "Loser has to carry the giant stuffed panda . . . and buy the winner a ride on the Ferris wheel."

Artie cut short the playful banter. "Sorry, you're not going anywhere," he informed Claudia, popping her balloon more effectively than any feathered dart. "Those inventory reports are not going to update themselves. Well, technically, they could—but that's never a good idea."

"But, Artie . . . !" Claudia protested. "I never get to go on any of the really fun jaunts."

"This isn't about having fun," Artie said sternly. "It's about tracking down a possible artifact whose true nature and potential remain unknown. There are way too many variables here, and I'm not sending you into the field when I have no idea what sort of jeopardy might be waiting. This is a job for Myka and Pete, not a bored teenager." His gruff voice softened somewhat. "Trust me, it's for your own good."

Claudia got the message, even if she didn't want to admit it. "Party pooper."

"Tough luck, little buckaroo," Pete consoled her. "I'll bring you back a goldfish or something."

"Just watch out for those midway games," Artie grumped. "They're all rigged."

"We'll keep that in mind," Myka promised. "So where is this carnival's next stop?"

"West Haven, Connecticut." Artie starting tucking the evidence back into his folder. Myka made a mental note to review the files during the flight to the East Coast. Artie wrapped up the briefing by looking gravely at both Pete and Myka. "Just be careful, you two. As I was saying before, we don't know what exactly we're dealing with here."

"Do we ever?" Myka quipped.

CHAPTER
4

WEST HAVEN, CONNECTICUT

The Whitman Bros. Carnival had set up shop in a vacant field outside town. A galaxy of twinkling electric lights lit up the night, washing out the starry sky overhead. High-pitched squeals and laughter competed with raucous calliope music. Excited throngs crowded the midway, scoping out the gaudy attractions. Tattooed carnies urged gullible visitors to try their luck at the ring toss and water gun race. Shrieking men, women, and children rode the Tilt-a-Whirl, the Matterhorn, and bumper cars. The humid August night smelled of popcorn, cotton candy, and fried-dough pizza.

Pete's mouth was already watering.

"Man," he exclaimed, eagerly soaking in the festive sights, sounds, and atmosphere. "Does this ever take me back." He tilted his neck back to check out the glittering Ferris wheel rotating above the other rides. "I can't re-member the last time I rode one of those."

"Focus," Myka said. "We're on the job, remember."

They strolled down the midway. Dating couples, happy families, and packs of roving teens packed the carnival, impeding the agents' progress. Sawdust muffled their footsteps. A cow mooed over by the petting zoo. Pete didn't know where to look first.

"I know," he replied. "But c'mon, you have to admit this is pretty cool. Didn't you ever want to run away to the circus when you were a kid?"

"Sure. But let's think about taking a spin on the merry-go-round later, *after* we've located and neutralized whatever artifact might be lurking in the vicinity."

"If there's even one to be found," he pointed out. "We don't know that for sure."

On the surface, the small-time carnival, with its slightly seedy glitz and glamour, seemed unlikely to be hiding a genuine historical artifact, let alone one of supernatural power, yet he knew better than to jump to any assumptions. Experience had taught him that dangerous relics could be found almost anywhere. A construction site, a prison, a New York fashion show, a Las Vegas casino . . . you never knew where the next artifact might turn up.

Maybe even a carnival sideshow?

"Let's find out," Myka said. "Then maybe you can win Claudia a prize . . . if I don't beat you to it."

"Fair enough." He was amused, but not too surprised, to see that his partner was not entirely immune to the lure of the midway. When he and Myka had first started working together, she had struck him as a real by-the-book type, with a stick the size of the Washington Monument up her butt. But she had loosened up a lot since then, revealing the real Myka Bering: a smart, funny, resourceful woman he could always count on to watch his back, no matter what. He couldn't ask for a better partner. "You ready to check out the world-famous Princess Nefertiti?"

"Lead the way."

Bypassing the rides, games, and concession stands (for now), they made their way to the sideshow at the far end of the midway. A striped canvas tent about the size of a merry-go-round was set up in front of a caravan of parked trucks and trailers. Garishly painted banners festooned the tent, the lurid illustrations promising a variety of human oddities and performers: the Fat Lady, the Strong Man, the Sword Swallower, the Alligator Boy, and so on. The usual carnival staples. But one attraction clearly took star billing. A huge banner, larger and less faded than the others, was stretched above the entrance to the tent, where nobody could miss it.

Now Appearing!! PRINCESS NEFERTITI, Healer Extraordinaire!!

Unlike the other performers, there was no portrait of Nefertiti outside the tent. To create an aura of mystery about her? Or was her name alone enough to draw an audience?

It seemed to be working. A long line was snaking into the tent, egged on by the barker, who called out to the crowd from his podium. Greasy muttonchops blended with his five o'clock shadow. He had the ruddy, veined nose of a hard drinker.

There but for the grace of AA, Pete thought.

"Step right up, ladies and gentlemen! Don't miss your chance to see six of the most amazing acts ever assembled beneath a single tent! All for the price of a single ticket! You can't see anything like this on TV, folks. It's all real . . . including the incomparable Princess Nefertiti, whose miraculous gifts are truly a blessing in these troubled times." He lowered his voice before adding the obligatory disclaimer. "Presented purely for entertainment purposes, of course."

"Of course," Myka echoed, a skeptical expression on her face. She scanned the line before them. "Say, Pete, is it just me, or does this crowd look better suited to a hospital than a sideshow?"

Looking more closely, he saw what she meant. Many of the ticket buyers appeared to be suffering from some sort of ailment or infirmity. An older gentleman in a wheelchair sucked on bottled oxygen. A teenage jock wearing a maroon football jersey hobbled forward on crutches. Concerned friends and relatives assisted sick people who seemed too weak to make it on their own. Skullcaps and obvious wigs hinted at the ravages of chemotherapy. Drawn, anxious faces contrasted sharply with the carefree crowds patronizing the rest of the carnival. Unlike the folks riding the carousel, these people didn't appear to be out for a good time.

"It's not just you," he confirmed. "Looks like Princess Nefertiti's reputation precedes her."

"I spotted a lot of out-of-state license plates in the parking lot, too," Myka noted, observant as ever. "You think these people came all this way just to check out a sideshow healer?"

"Why not? We did."

An elderly woman, dressed rather too warmly for the temperature, approached the barker. "Is it true?" she asked urgently. A telltale tremor in her limbs suggested that she was afflicted with Parkinson's. "Can Princess Nefertiti really heal the sick? Even when doctors can't?"

"See for yourself, madam." The barker steered her toward the growing line. "Trust me, you won't be disappointed."

Pete found himself hoping that the healer was the real deal, if only for the sake of all these ill and disabled people. It would be a crime to raise their hopes like this and not deliver. If this was just a scam, he might need to have words with these carnies. "For entertainment purposes only, my ass."

Making their way to the front of the line, he bought tickets for both him and Myka. Pete asked for a receipt, so he could expense it later, but the sallow-faced carnie manning the entrance just snorted in derision. "Seriously, dude. A receipt? At a sideshow?"

"Never mind."

Sorry, Artie, he thought. *I tried.*

They stepped past a drawn canvas flap into the stuffy interior of the tent. Bleachers, erected on both sides of a central walkway, faced a low wooden stage. Curtains at the rear of the stage provided a backdrop for the performers. A single white bulb, hanging overhead, was supplemented by lambent footlights. Canned music played from a pair of loudspeakers. Sawdust carpeted the floor.

"Don't say I never take you anywhere classy," Pete joked.

"Tell me about it," she replied. "From the looks of things, people are practically dying to get in here."

The bleachers were packed, and a veritable obstacle course of wheelchairs and walkers was parked in front of the stage, but the two agents managed to find a couple of seats in the back row. The show, which appeared to be on a continuous loop, was already in progress. A young knife thrower, identified by a wooden sandwich board as the Dazzling Dmitri, demonstrated his eagle eye by hurling shining silver blades at a spinning star-shaped target while the *William Tell Overture* played tinnily in the background. A wiry youth with wavy blond hair, he wore a spangled gold tunic and tight blue trousers. A crimson sash girded his slender waist. The crowd clapped politely as, one by one, he planted a knife at each tip of the star, plus one more in the bull's-eye.

"Not bad," Pete commented. "Reminds me of a would-be assassin I tackled in Portland once. Of course, her target was breathing."

"The audience doesn't seem all that impressed," Myka observed. "Or interested."

She was right again. All around them, audience members squirmed with varying degrees of impatience, as they waited for the star attraction.

"Enough with this bullshit!" a grumpy-looking dude in the front row exclaimed. His florid complexion made Pete wonder just how high the man's blood pressure was. "We want Nefertiti!"

Others in the bleachers took up the chant.

"Nefertiti! Nefertiti! Nefertiti!"

They stomped their feet in rhythm with the chant, shaking the bleachers. Pete's seat vibrated beneath his butt. He hoped the bleachers were solidly constructed.

"Uh-oh," Myka said. "Looks like the natives are getting restless."

Pete whistled. "Talk about a tough crowd. You've got to be pretty nervy to heckle a knife thrower."

"Or desperate."

In any event, the Dazzling Dmitri got the message. He hastily wrapped up his act, took a bow, and retreated from the stage. A stagehand dragged the knife-studded target away. A moment later Dmitri reemerged from behind the curtain. A chorus of boos started up, but the young performer raised his voice to be heard over the protests.

"And now, ladies and gentlemen, what you've been waiting for." He gestured dramatically at the curtain behind him, which rustled provocatively. "Without further ado . . . Princess Nefertiti!"

A hush fell over the crowd. They leaned forward expectantly. Pete caught himself doing the same. Forget the Sword Swallower and the Alligator Boy. *This* was what they were all really here for.

The music switched tracks. An ethereal, faintly Middle Eastern air emanated from the speakers. Incense wafted from the wings. The footlights dimmed, the curtains parted, and a petite figure stepped onto the stage. Her hooded white robe was belted at the waist by a delicate silver chain. The shimmering fabric seemed to glow in the footlights. Her head was bowed, hiding her face. Gloved hands were tented before her as though in prayer. Wide sleeves drooped beneath them.

Her sandaled feet strode gracefully across the stage. A gleaming silver ankh hung conspicuously from a chain around her neck.

Pete's eyes zeroed in on the ankh. "What do you think?" he whispered to Myka. "A souvenir from King Tut's tomb? Or Cleopatra's favorite bit of bling?"

"Maybe not Cleopatra. Her pet asp is already preserved in a jar on Level 12, Aisle 343, of the Warehouse." She playfully punched him in the shoulder. "You really need to familiarize yourself with the inventory more."

Pete had heard it before. "So you keep telling me. But give me a break. I could study night and day for a year and still not make a dent in the inventory. We're talking over two thousand years of wacky knickknacks, you know." A mental image of the Warehouse's endless aisles and shelves flashed across his mind. "Besides, there's no rule that a person can't produce more than one artifact. Cleo probably had enough mojo to power a whole wardrobe of artifacts. I mean, look at how many movies she's inspired."

"I suppose," Myka conceded as Princess Nefertiti's show got under way.

After a dramatic pause, the supposed healer raised her head. Her gloved hands reached up and drew back the hood, revealing the bronzed face of an attractive young woman who looked barely out of her teens. Kohl shadowed a pair of striking green eyes. Her black hair was cut short, Theda Bara style. A ruby was glued to the center of her forehead like a third eye. A serene expression conveyed a seriousness and wisdom far beyond her years.

"Welcome, brothers and sisters," she intoned in a posh English accent. "Blessings upon you all, and on the celestial providence that brings us all together this fine evening. Before we begin, let me tell you something of myself—and from whence my humble gifts derive."

"This ought to be good," Myka muttered.

"I am descended from a long line of healers, medicine men, and wise women dating back to the bygone days of the pharaohs. It is my privilege and my sacred calling to ease the suffering of my fellow travelers, as much as it is within my ability to do so." She gazed out at the rapt audience. "Now, then, who among you is in need of healing?"

Hands shot up like a Whac-A-Mole. Anxious voices cried out, competing to be heard.

"Over here! Please!"

"Me! Me first!"

"Help me! Help my baby!"

Pete couldn't be sure, but he thought Nefertiti looked a little overwhelmed by the vehemence of the crowd's reaction. She faltered slightly, taking an involuntary step back, before regaining her composure. She held out her arms to quiet the throng.

"Please! One at a time. I promise, I'll do my best to minister to as many of you as I can." She waited for the audience to settle down before singling out a little boy near the front. "You there, the handsome young man in the *Iron Shadow* T-shirt. Come forward, child."

Overcome with shyness, the boy hesitated until his mother took his hand and led him from the bleachers.

No more than ten years old, he looked winded just step-ping onto the stage. His tiny fingers clutched a plastic inhaler. In the hushed atmosphere of the tent, Pete could hear the kid wheezing all the way in the back. His pale skin suggested that he didn't get outdoors much. You didn't need a medical degree to diagnose his problem.

"Asthma?" Nefertiti guessed.

The mother nodded. Worry lines and puffy violet pouches under her eye testified to sleepless nights. "We've tried everything, but it just keeps getting worse. You're our last hope."

"I understand." Nefertiti knelt before the boy so that she could look him in the eyes. "What is your name, sweet child?"

"Brian," he wheezed. "But the kids at school call me Squeaky, 'cause of the way I breathe."

"Not anymore they won't." She raised her eyes to the heavens. Her voice took on a more imperious tone. "Now, by the sacred blood that flows within me, let this innocent child breathe freely once more!"

Taking a deep breath, she laid her hands upon Brian's trembling shoulders. Bright blue sparks crackled around her fingertips, and Brian stiffened as though zapped by a Tesla gun. Tiny hairs stood along the back of Pete's neck. Suddenly the atmosphere inside the tent seemed charged with static electricity. He sniffed the air. A cloying sweetness invaded his nostrils.

He nudged Myka. "Do you smell that?"

"Yep," she verified. "Fudge."

The chocolaty aroma was often associated with artifact activity. Nobody had ever really been able to explain why.

Looks like Artie was right on target, he thought. *As usual.*

Down on the stage, Brian gasped and collapsed against Nefertiti, who deftly caught him before he fell. "Brian!" his mother cried out in alarm. "Baby!"

"Fear not," Nefertiti assured her. "All is well." She cradled the boy in her arms. "He'll be all right in a moment."

Sure enough, a few seconds later Brian lifted his head from the healer's shoulder. "Mommy?" He looked around in confusion. "Where am I? What happened?"

"A certain amount of disorientation is normal," Nefertiti explained. She placed Brian back on his own feet. "How do you feel now, Brian? Breathe for me."

"Mommy?"

His voice already sounded stronger. He didn't seem to be wheezing anymore.

"Go ahead, baby," his mom pleaded. "Breathe for Mommy."

"Okay." Hesitantly at first, he inhaled. His eyes widened as he sucked in a deep breath, perhaps his first in who knew how long. A delighted grin broke out across his face. "Mommy, Mommy, I can breathe! Listen!"

"I hear you, baby!" Overcome with emotion, Brian's mom dropped to her knees and hugged her child. Tears of joy flooded her cheeks. She gazed adoringly at Nefertiti. "I can't thank you enough!"

Pete's throat tightened. He couldn't help being touched by the joyous scene. Glancing at Myka, he saw her dab at her eyes.

Nefertiti appeared to be the real deal, and doing nothing but good.

"I don't get it," he whispered. "Where's the down-side?"

CHAPTER 5

LANCASTER COUNTY, PENNSYLVANIA

Calvin Worrall kept off the main roads.

Behind the wheel of a luxury Lincoln Town Car, he drove north past miles of moonlit countryside. Acres of cornfields and leafy tobacco plants provided most of the scenery. Amish farms advertised fresh eggs and homemade root beer, but not on Sunday. A horse-drawn buggy, trotting slowly along the shoulder of the road, forced the car to slow to twenty miles an hour. Worrall sighed impatiently but reminded himself that this sort of delay was to be expected, given the route he had selected. The main highway would have been faster, true, but there were good reasons to stick to the back roads.

More privacy. Fewer witnesses.

Gloved hands gripped the steering wheel. Despite the humid weather, the windows were rolled up and he wore a dark turtleneck sweater to keep warm. He was pushing thirty, but he looked much older. His gaunt face was pale and drawn. Swollen veins wormed beneath his shaved scalp. Sunken gray eyes were streaked with red. Classical music emanated from an expensive sound system.

He drove alone, the backseat of the car filled with luggage. He had been on the road for weeks now, covering hundreds of miles a day. Home was a fading memory. He glanced at his watch. It was already after eight. Soon he would have to start looking for another motel, unless he felt like driving all through the night, which he was doing more and more often, health permitting. The northbound road called to him like a drug.

He was getting closer. He could feel it.

An open straightaway gave him a chance to pass the buggy. Hitting the gas, he left the clip-clopping horse and its burden behind. *About time,* he thought. Maybe now he could finally make some progress toward . . .

Where?

Ah, that was the rub. He had no idea where his final destination was, only that he was getting closer with every mile. Soon, very soon, his search would be over.

I know it's out there, he thought. *It's pulling on me.*

A billboard advertised a roadside diner a few miles ahead. His stomach growled, reminding him that he hadn't eaten for hours. He scowled at the inconvenience. The last thing he wanted to do was stop driving, not when he could feel his prize somewhere up ahead, but apparently his treacherous body had another idea. What's more, he could feel a headache coming on. Acid churned in his gut. His jaw clenched.

All right, he groused. *Maybe just a quick stop.*

The diner was a low steel structure that resembled a boxcar. A neon sign promised *All-American Eats.* Only a handful of vehicles were parked out front. The Lincoln pulled in beside them.

He stepped out of the car into the cool night air. Gravel crunched beneath his feet. He had to admit, it felt good to stretch his legs after all that driving. But then the migraine caught up with him, just like it always did. Pressure started building in his temples, squeezing his skull like a vise. Throbbing eyes felt hard as marbles. A sudden wave of nausea swept over him.

Already? he thought. *Again?*

A queasy stomach drove all thought of food from his mind, but he didn't get back in the car. There was no point. Pretty soon he would be too sick to drive anyway.

Unless . . .

He dragged himself toward the diner.

An annoying bell announced his arrival. He winced at the chime. Bright interior lighting stabbed his eyes and he hastily put on a pair of designer sunglasses. "Seat yourself," a solitary waitress called out to him. "Be with you in a jiff."

He glanced around the diner, which was decorated in nostalgic 1950s kitsch. A jukebox, mercifully silent, occupied one corner. Vintage Coca-Cola signs were mounted on pink walls the color of Pepto-Bismol. A transparent display case held slices of fresh shoofly pie. A jar by the cash register collected change for the March of Dimes. Seating was available at the counter or in booths with molded plastic seats. Only one of the booths was occupied, by a family enjoying a night out. A trio of high school girls were seated at the counter. They whispered and giggled amongst themselves. Everyone seemed to be happy, healthy.

Damn them.

Their carefree chatter grated on his nerves. These stupid people had no idea how lucky they were. They took their sound, healthy bodies for granted. They hadn't spent their whole lives sick and miserable.

It's not fair, he thought bitterly. *Why should I be the only one to suffer?*

Invisible ice picks jabbed his brain. Resentment bubbled over inside him, like the acid climbing up his throat. He choked on the reflux, coughing violently into his right fist. The noise drew anxious looks from the other customers. A teenager spun around on her stool. She wrinkled her nose in disgust. The parents in the booth turned their heads and covered their mouths to keep from catching anything.

Like that was going to do them any good.

He dropped into the nearest empty booth. Ragged breaths shook his bony form. He massaged his temples, but the trembling fingers brought little in the way of relief. It was all he could do to keep from vomiting. Even the slightest movement sent a fresh jolt of agony through his aching head. He considered taking a pill, but why bother? It wouldn't do any good. It never did.

Only one thing helped.

The waitress, a middle-aged floozy wearing an apron, approached him. A plastic name badge pegged her as Marjorie. She handed him a menu. "You okay, hon? You're looking a little green around the gills."

He could believe it. There was no turning back now.

"I will be," he rasped. "At least for a while."

He seized her arm with his left hand. An oily gray haze flowed from his fingertips. Misty tendrils seemed to sink into Marjorie's skin. A sour, gangrenous odor clung to the haze.

She swooned and grabbed onto the seat to keep from falling. Her order pad slipped from her fingers. All the color bled from her face. Her lips took on a grayish tint.

"W-what did you do to me?" she stammered weakly. "I feel sick. . . ."

She fainted onto the floor.

"That's odd," he said archly. "I'm starting to feel much better."

One of the teenagers screamed out loud. Over at the other booth, the mom and dad put their arms protectively around their kids. They gaped at Worrall. "Listen, mister," the father began, "I don't know what's wrong with you, but . . ."

Worrall ignored the man's pointless babbling. He rose from the booth, moving less painfully than before. His head was still pounding, but not for much longer. He stood in the aisle, blocking the exit. He coughed again to clear his throat, then raised his arm like a conductor facing an orchestra. A grayish fog spread throughout the diner.

The lights flickered overhead. A chorus of groans and coughs greeted his ears.

His stomach began to settle. The pain in his temples receded.

He made a mental note to grab a slice of pie for the road.

WEST HAVEN

Little Brian, formerly Squeaky, was just the beginning. From the bleachers, Pete and Myka watched as, one by one, members of the audience came forward to experience Princess Nefertiti's healing touch. The football player, previously suffering from a potentially career-ending knee injury, tossed away his crutches. Disfiguring scars and burns faded away, leaving smooth, unblemished skin behind. Wheelchairs and walkers were abandoned. Pained expressions gave way to tears of joy. A fudge-like aroma overpowered the incense.

Okay, Pete thought, *consider me impressed.*

The old lady with Parkinson's was finally getting her turn on the stage. "Let this gentle woman be healed," Nefertiti proclaimed as she laid her hands on the shaking senior citizen. Pete couldn't be sure, but he thought the healer's voice sounded slightly weaker than before. Dmitri, doing double duty as Nefertiti's assistant, stood close by. "Take away her trembling."

Cobalt sparks flashed once more, jolting the elderly woman. Dmitri caught her before she crumpled onto the stage. Judging from his smooth move, he'd had plenty of practice.

Nefertiti seemed to need an assist as well. She tottered unsteadily on her feet, almost as though she were on the verge of collapsing. She was breathing hard. Sweat beaded her brow. She coughed and clutched her chest.

"Looks like all this healing is taking its toll," Myka observed. "A side effect of the artifact?"

"Probably," Pete guessed. There was almost always a cost to using an artifact. That was a big reason they needed to be taken out of circulation. He'd seen too many people get themselves into serious trouble because they thought they could control an artifact's powers.

Like Princess Nefertiti?

The healer's debilitated state did not escape her assistant's notice. "That's enough for tonight!" After escorting the dazed old woman back to her seat, Dmitri bounded back onto the stage. He threw a protective arm around her shoulders. "Princess Nefertiti needs her rest."

Disappointed cries and protests erupted from the audience.

Nefertiti wavered, clearly reluctant to let down her petitioners. "Perhaps just one more?"

"No." Dmitri was emphatic. He hustled her back toward the curtain while shushing the crowd. "Show's over, folks. Please come back tomorrow!"

For a moment Pete feared a riot, but the audience proved more civilized than that. Perhaps the touching scenes they had witnessed had brought out the better angels of their natures? Or was it just that the grumblers were too sick to make a fuss? Or unwilling to risk offending the healer? In any event, the crowd shuffled out of the tent, leaving Pete and Myka alone on the bleachers. They waited until the audience had entirely cleared out before heading backstage. Pete drew back the curtains.

They found themselves in a small prep area crammed with props, seating, and a cooler full of iced drinks. A sturdy wooden pole, driven through a hole in the stage, held up the tent. Dmitri was fretting over Nefertiti, who had collapsed into a folding director's chair. He handed her a bottle of water while shaking his head. "You shouldn't push yourself like this. You're making yourself sick."

"It will pass," she assured him. The English accent had

vanished with the audience, replaced by the less elevated cadences of New Jersey or Long Island. Her voice was hoarse. "It always does."

Pete cleared his throat to get their attention.

Dmitri noticed the intruders for the first time. He scowled and stepped in front of Nefertiti. "Didn't you hear me before? The show's over . . . and this area is off-limits. No townies allowed."

"I've got a backstage pass." Pete flashed his badge and ID. "Secret Service."

The badge caught them both by surprise. Nefertiti sat up straight. "Secret Service?" She blinked in confusion. "Is the president coming here?"

You wish, Pete thought. *That would be pretty good publicity for your little tent show.*

Not that he would let the POTUS come within a hundred miles of a suspected artifact.

"I'm afraid not," Myka clarified. "We're here on a different assignment." She presented her own ID. "My name is Myka Bering. This is my partner, Agent Lattimer." She eyed the young healer skeptically. "And I'm guessing your name isn't really Princess Nefertiti, is it?"

"Nadia Malinovich," the girl confessed. "From Long Island."

Backstage, without all stage dressing and ballyhoo, she seemed a lot less mystical and more like a worried young woman wondering what had brought the Feds to her door. She nervously fingered the ankh around her neck.

"And all that business about being descended from a long line of healers?"

"Just patter. Although my mom and pop used to do a mind-reading act back in the eighties." She shrugged. "I'm third-generation carnie."

"What's this all about, anyway?" Dmitri demanded. "Why are you bothering her?"

Pete got the distinct impression that the young knife thrower was more than just Nadia's assistant. "And you are . . . ?"

"Jim Doherty," he divulged. "And you still haven't answered my question. What are you doing here?"

"We watched your act," Pete said. "We want to know how you managed to heal all those people."

"Why?" Jim protested. "She's not hurting anyone."

"Except maybe herself." Myka squeezed past Jim to speak to Nadia directly. "Is that it, Nadia? Does healing others make you sick?"

"It's a gift," the girl insisted. "I just want to heal people. What's wrong with that?"

A fair question, Pete admitted. Nadia struck him as sincere.

Myka tried to explain. "It may not seem obvious to you now, but trust me on this, what you're doing is not safe. There are bound to be negative consequences down the road. Serious ones. My partner and I have dealt with this kind of thing before. Power like this always comes with a heavy price tag. More than you may want to pay."

"Stop harassing her," Jim said. "Do you know how many people she's helped?"

Like little Brian and everybody else tonight? Pete recalled all the heartwarming moments he had just beheld. He couldn't deny that Nadia had made a lot of people's lives better. Artifact or not, she seemed to be doing more good than harm. Just ask Brian and his mom.

He felt uncomfortable cracking down on Nadia. To be honest, it wasn't the first time he'd felt this way. James MacPherson, Artie's former partner, had once tried to convince Pete that some artifacts were too valuable to be locked away in the Warehouse, where they couldn't do the world any good. MacPherson had been a murderous creep, of course, but maybe, just maybe, he'd had a point?

He pushed the doubts out of his head in order to get the job done. "My partner is right," he said, backing Myka up. "You need to tell us how you're doing this."

Nadia kept toying with the ankh. "I—I don't know what you mean."

His spider-sense tingled. "I'm getting a real vibe here," he informed Myka. He looked pointedly at the ankh. "You thinking what I'm thinking?"

Myka nodded. She slipped on a pair of purple gloves. "Hand over the ankh, please."

"Why?" Nadia asked. "It's just a prop. I picked it up at a dollar store."

Myka held out her hand. "Then there's no harm in showing it to me, is there?"

Jim pushed forward. "You can't do this. You have no right!"

"Easy, buster!" Pete got between Jim and the women. He had a few inches and about twenty pounds of muscle on the younger man. "Don't make us do this the hard way."

"It's all right, Jim," Nadia called out. "It's no big

deal." She removed the ankh and handed it over to Myka. "I'm not sure why you want this."

Was she truly unaware of the ankh's special properties? Pete couldn't be sure.

"Keep back," he warned Jim before fishing a silver bag from his pocket. He held it open for Myka, then turned his head away. "Bombs away."

Myka dropped the ankh into the goo. Pete braced himself for the usual fireworks.

But nothing happened. Not even a fizzle.

"What the heck?" He shared a surprised look with Myka. "Did I miss something?"

She plucked the ankh from the bag and wiped it clean with a tissue. Holding it up to her eyes, she squinted at the small hooped cross. "False alarm," she declared. "Look at this."

She held up the ankh for his inspection. He spotted a tiny inscription:

Made in China.

Oops!

Nadia and Jim stared at the agents in bewilderment. "Is that it?" he asked. "Are you happy now?"

"Not really, no." Pete scratched his head. "Okay, so if it's not the ankh, what is it?" He looked Nadia over. The bright red gemstone on her forehead caught his eye. "Maybe that ruby thingie?"

"It's just a cheap piece of costume jewelry," Nadia insisted. She peeled it off her brow and tossed it to Pete. "Take it."

He caught it reflexively, then held it up to the light. On close inspection, he had to admit it didn't look all that impressive. Polished glass, maybe, or crystal. Then again, that didn't mean much. Sometimes the most innocuous of objects could turn out to be artifacts. Like a rubber dodgeball or an old can of tuna fish.

"What do you think?" he asked Myka.

His partner had another idea. "Her gloves," Myka said, giving Nadia's hands wear a closer look. "I was distracted by the ankh before, but those gloves don't really go with the rest of her costume. They don't fit with the whole 'Egyptian high priestess' look she's going for."

Pete looked at the gloves. They were wrist-length and made of white kid leather. Decorative stitching adorned their backs. Delicate ivory buttons held them tight about her wrist.

"Good call." He tended to defer to Myka on matters on women's fashion, but he saw what she meant. Unlike the rest of Nadia's outfit, the gloves looked better suited to Queen Victoria than Cleopatra. "And it's not exactly cold in here."

Myka made up her mind. "Let me see the gloves."

"No!" Nadia yanked her hands back, reacting much more strongly than before. "You can't have them. They have . . . sentimental value."

Pete didn't buy it. If anything, Nadia's outburst proved they were on the right track. He stuck the phony ruby in his pocket, although it was probably worthless, just like Nadia had said. The gloves had moved to the top of their to-do list. "Sorry. I think those gloves are coming with us."

"Please." Nadia held her hands tightly to her breast, one over the other. "You can't—"

"Leave her alone!" Jim lunged to her defense. "I won't let you—"

"Okay, that's enough." Pete grabbed the young carnie by the shoulders and roughly steered him away from Nadia. Jim struggled to break free, but Pete had years of Secret Service training on his side. He strong-armed Jim toward the curtain. "I know you're just trying to stick up for your girl, pal, but it's time for you to clear out of here. This is between us and those gloves."

He shoved Jim out of the backstage area, then waited to see if the carnie was going to come back swinging. He hoped it wouldn't be necessary to zap Jim with the Tesla. He felt enough like a storm trooper as it was. Too bad the artifact wasn't being misused by some crook. That always made this easier.

Surprisingly, Jim got the hint. Pete heard the youth storm out of the tent. "That's better." He turned away from the curtain and joined Myka in front of Nadia. "All right. Let's get this over with."

"But you can't just take them," the girl begged. "They belong to me."

"Sorry," Pete apologized again. Her pleas stung his conscience, even though he knew they were doing the right thing. "Believe it or not, this is for your own good."

"Who are you to decide that?" Nadia asked bitterly. "What gives you the right?"

"The U.S. government," Myka said, simplifying things somewhat. In truth, the agents answered to a secretive board of Regents whose relationship to the federal government was . . . complicated. But that was more than Nadia needed to know. "This is our job."

"Just give us the gloves, Nadia," Pete said. "We're not leaving until we get them."

Outnumbered and overwhelmed, Nadia finally gave in. She pulled off the gloves and practically threw them in Myka's face. "Fine. Do what you have to do."

"Thank you." Myka politely ignored the attitude. She quickly examined the gloves, just to avoid another embarrassing "Made in China" moment, then beckoned to Pete. "Shall we try this again?"

"Sounds like a plan." Pete recycled the silver retrieval bag. "Go for it."

Into the bag went the gloves. This time he kept his eye on the reaction, which was only marginally more pyrotechnic than before. The goo fizzed a little, and he caught a glimpse of a few flickering sparks, but it was hardly the usual blinding flash.

"Okay," he commented, "I don't think that was fully neutralized."

"Didn't seem like it," Myka agreed. Her brow furrowed as she tried to puzzle it out. "Maybe we're dealing with another two-part artifact, like Poe's quill and journal, or Robert Louis Stevenson's bookends? In that case, we'd need both items to neutralize them."

No surprise that she recalled those incidents. Poe's notebook had nearly killed Myka's father, before they had managed to track down the quill as well.

"But don't we already have both gloves?"

"Maybe not." She rescued the gloves from the bag and gave them another once-over. "Hmm. The stitching on the left glove looks a little too uniform, almost like it was done by a modern sewing machine. The stitching on the right glove seems like it was done by hand." She turned toward the gloves' owner. "Nadia?"

"The left glove is a copy," the girl admitted. "I had a costumer whip it up to match the right glove."

"Which came from where?" Pete asked.

"A thrift store near Gettysburg. It was just lying there, in a bin of mismatched items. I guess somebody must have cleaned out an attic or something." She paused, remembering. "I don't know what it was about the glove, but it just . . . called to me somehow. Like I was meant to find it."

Sounds plausible enough, Pete thought, believing Nadia's story. He wondered how long the glove had been sitting dormant—and who had it originally belonged to. Mary Todd Lincoln? Charlotte Brontë? Catherine the Great? Maybe Artie could figure it out.

In the meantime, there was a more pressing question.

"So where is the *real* left glove?"

"I wish I knew." Nadia looked hopefully at the right glove. "Does this mean I get them back?"

"Sorry," Pete said. They needed to hang on to the glove until they found its mate. "No can do."

"But you don't understand!" She grabbed for the glove, but Myka yanked it away from her, beyond her reach. Nadia burst into tears. "I have to heal people! I *have* to!"

Whoa, Pete thought, taken aback by her outburst. *Talk about a drama queen.* Was there more to this than just an understandable desire to do good? She sounded out of control, almost like she was under some kind of compulsion. *Maybe we're taking that glove away from her none too soon?*

"Hey, rube!" an angry voice intruded. "You need to listen to the lady."

The curtain was yanked open from the outside, exposing the stage. Jim Doherty had returned—with reinforcements. His sideshow cronies glared at the two agents. A snake charmer cradled a hissing python. A scowling strong man flexed his muscles. The fat lady crossed her slab-like arms atop her capacious chest. The alligator boy, his body covered in scales, bared his teeth, which were filed to points. A full set of throwing knives was tucked into Jim's belt.

Crap, Pete thought. *This could get ugly.*

Myka held up her badge. "I'm going to have to ask you all to vacate the tent. We're on official business."

"No way, toots," the strong man rumbled. A poster outside had hyped him as *The Mighty Atlas!* Leopard-print trunks left most of his imposing frame exposed. His muscles had muscles—and big, bulging ones to boot. His sinews stood out like steel cables. A thick skull rested atop a neck wide enough to serve as a pedestal. A handlebar mustache framed his jowls. His deep bass voice made James Earl Jones sound like a castrato. "Nadia's one of us. We look after our own."

"Yesss," Ophidia the snake charmer hissed. Sequins glinted like scales on her tight sheath dress. A forked tongue showed just how far she was willing to go for her act. The python flicked its own tongue in unison. "Ssshe's helped usss all."

She got a little too close to Atlas, who shot her a

disgusted glance before putting some distance between them. He clearly wasn't a fan, not that Pete really cared. The agent was more concerned with shutting down this sideshow before someone got hurt.

Like maybe him and Myka.

"Everyone needs to calm down here." He drew his Tesla from beneath his jacket and swung its muzzle from left to right and back again, trying to keep the entire crew in his sights. "And leave the tent immediately."

"You got that backwards, rube," Jim shot back. "You and your partner are the ones who are leaving." He nodded at Myka. "Without the glove."

"No way." Myka stuffed the glove into her pocket, then pulled out her own sidearm, but the knife thrower was quicker on the draw. Moving faster than the proverbial eye, he flung a blade at the gun, knocking it from Myka's grasp. The gun skidded across the dirt.

"Myka!" Pete decided that Jim was the primary threat. He swung the Tesla at the youth even as Atlas and the alligator boy charged him from opposite sides. A bolt of polyphase energy burst from the gun, but struck the alligator boy instead. Electricity lit up his scaly body and flung him backward across the stage, nearly colliding with Jim, who jumped out of the way just in time. He hurled a second knife at the Tesla, but the commotion threw off his aim. Pete felt the blade whoosh past his hand as he lurched away from the knife—right into the arms of the oncoming strong man.

Herculean arms caught him in a bear hug, pinning his arms to his side. The Mighty Atlas lifted Pete off his feet so that his legs dangled above the ground. The arms

squeezed tightly, crushing him like an implosion gre-
nade. Pete gasped for breath.

"M-maybe we can just shake hands instead?"

A few feet away, Myka had problems of her own. She
watched in dismay as her gun flew from her fingers, leaving her empty-handed. Ducking her head, she started to
dive for the weapon, only to hear the snake lady hissing
at her pet.

"Sssic her, Sssussie-Q!"

Susie-Q? Myka barely had time to register the python's
name before the snake charmer tossed the reptile at her.
Over fifty pounds of squirming serpent came flying at
Myka, who threw up her hands to protect herself. She
grabbed the coils with both hands, trying to keep them
from wrapping around her throat. That was the major
threat, she knew. No matter what, she had to keep the
python away from her windpipe.

Not getting bit would be good too.

The python snapped and hissed at her, its fangs only
inches away from her face. Myka struggled to hold on to
the thrashing reptile; it was like wrestling with a whip-
ping water hose. The snake's lower coils wrapped around
her waist, squeezing tightly, but there was nothing
she could do about that now. She couldn't let go of the
snake's throat for a moment.

The serpent's scaly body was cool and dry to the
touch. Myka fought an instinctive sense of revulsion.
She had to stay cool and keep her wits about her. Thank
goodness snakes were not among her phobias.

"That'sss it, sssugar!" Ophidia cheered on her pet. "Show that nasssty lady who'sss bosss!"

Myka wished the woman had trained poodles instead.

A hand wriggled past the snake to dig around in her pocket. "Yes!" Nadia exclaimed as she reclaimed her glove and slipped it back onto her right hand. "I've got it!"

She darted for the exit, taking the artifact with her. "Run, Nadia!" her boyfriend urged her. "Get out of here!"

She hesitated in the doorway. "Aren't you coming with me?"

He shook his head. "I'll catch up with you later. We'll hold on to these losers while you get away!"

"Nadia, don't!" Myka called out. Caught up in the coils of the python, she could only watch in frustration as the artifact slipped away from them. "You don't know what you're messing with!"

None of them did, really.

But Nadia ignored the agent's orders. The fat lady scooted the young healer out of the tent, then planted herself in front of the exit. "Don't worry," she assured Jim and her fellow carnies. "Nobody's getting past me."

The python squeezed her ribs. Myka's hold on its neck slipped for a moment, and its fangs came closer to her face. A forked tongue licked her cheek. Grimacing, she shifted her grip on the writhing coils and shoved the snake's head back. Its gaping jaws offered her a clear view down its gullet. It was a visual she could have done without.

Remind me to make sure that asp is safely bottled up, she thought, *if and when we make it back to the Warehouse.*

Where was Pete? She glanced away from the snake's fangs long enough to spot her partner in a tight squeeze of his own. The strong man had Pete in a bear hug, and it didn't look like he was planning to let him go anytime soon. Myka wondered which of them was in the most trouble.

Given a choice, she thought, *I think I'd prefer the muscle man.*

The snake snapped at her again.

Pete's ribs and arms felt like they were in a vise. He tried to break from the strong man's grip, but it was like straining against iron girders. The rugged agent liked to think he had plenty of muscle, too, but the strong man made him feel like a ninety-pound weakling. All he needed was sand kicked in his face.

What the heck were they feeding this guy?

"Good job, Atlas!" Jim urged the strong man. "Don't let him go."

Despite his current predicament, Pete noted that the knife thrower had yet to put his blades to lethal use, despite plenty of opportunity to do so. This told him that Jim Doherty wasn't actually out to hurt them. He just wanted to let his girlfriend get away—with that darn glove.

Pete wasn't going to let that happen.

Years of hand-to-hand combat training proved useless against the human behemoth squeezing the breath out of him. He tried to hook his leg around Atlas's and yank him off his feet, but it was like trying to uproot a redwood. A head butt just bruised his own brow. The strong man had a skull of concrete.

"Try that again," Atlas snarled, "and I'll crack your ribs."

His breath reeked of tobacco and alcohol. Pete turned his face away to avoid the stench.

"Sorry 'bout that," Pete gasped. "My mistake."

Dangling above the ground, it was difficult to get any leverage. All he had managed to do was hang on to the Tesla, not that it was doing him much good right now. He and Atlas were just a little too cozy at the moment. There was no way to blast the strong man without zapping himself as well. Electricity was a bitch that way.

What about Myka? Out of the corner of his eye, he spotted his partner wrestling with an upset python while the snake charmer egged the serpent on. Myka appeared to be holding her own for the time being, but in the meantime Nadia and the glove were getting farther and farther away.

There had to be some way out of this mess.

Pete noticed that Myka was still wearing her protective purple gloves. A wild idea occurred to him. His arms remained pinned to his sides, but he could still move his wrist slightly. Maybe enough to aim the Tesla . . .

"Myka!" he shouted. "Can you unwrap yourself a little?"

She risked a peek at him. Her eyes widened as she spied the Tesla's transparent barrel recharging. She nodded back at him, getting the message. Her right hand let go of the python's throat, leaving only the left hand to hold its head—with its gaping mouth and fangs—away from her, and grabbed the snake's tail. Agent and serpent danced awkwardly across the backstage area as she forcibly unwound the coils around her waist. It didn't look easy, and she grunted with exertion, but she briefly managed to extricate herself from the python's embrace. "Hurry!" she yelled, holding the writhing snake at arm's length from her body. "It's getting loose!"

"Hang on!" He bent his wrist back as far as it would go, pointing the Tesla toward her. There was no way to read the gauges on the weapon, but he hoped that it still had enough of a charge to take out a snake. "Here goes nothing!"

He squeezed the trigger. Cobalt lightning sizzled through the air to strike the python, which twitched and sparked like a high-voltage cable. Myka turned her face away from the crackling electricity, relying on her gloves to insulate her. Ozone tickled Pete's nostrils.

The python went limp in Myka's hands.

"Sssusssie-Q!" Ophidia shrieked sibilantly. "Sssweetie!"

Her leathery face contorted with rage, she ran at Myka, who dropped her with a spinning kick to the jaw. The snake charmer joined her pet in unconsciousness.

"Next time, keep your 'sweetie' on a leash," Myka advised, her hands still full of stunned reptile. She turned toward Atlas. "Hey, big boy. You like snakes?"

Had she also noticed the strong man's aversion to the serpent earlier? Of course, Pete realized. This was Myka, after all.

Atlas backed away from her. "Get that slimy thing away from me!"

"Trade you," she said. "Catch!"

She lobbed the sagging serpent at the strong man, who let out a surprisingly high-pitched squeal. Panicked by the sight of the snake flying toward him, he let go of Pete and threw himself backward—right into the central pole supporting the tent.

A couple hundred pounds of pumped muscle collided with the pole, which cracked alarmingly. Heavy canvas heaved and tore loose from its moorings. The rippling fabric crackled like thunder. Pete looked up in dismay, as did everybody else under the tent.

"Oh, for crying out loud," the fat lady said.

Jim dived for cover. More poles snapped.

"Timber . . ." Pete groaned.

An avalanche of canvas came down on their heads.

CHAPTER
6

WEST HAVEN

Everything was dark and stuffy. Pete felt like a princess looking for a pea as he wriggled beneath the heavy canvas toward a narrow sliver of light. *Just a few more inches,* he thought, as a meaty hand closed on his ankle. "Forget it, slick," the fat lady huffed. "You're not going anywhere."

He gave her a taste of his shoe leather. He felt bad kicking a woman in the face, but maybe the extra padding in her cheeks would soften the blow? In any event, the pudgy fingers came loose long enough for him to scramble out from beneath the collapsed tent into the open air of the midway. The bright electric lights came as a jolt after the suffocating darkness. Squinting, he jumped to his feet. He kept a tight grip on the handle of the Tesla. Artie would kill him if he lost it.

"Myka?"

"Right here." His partner emerged into the electric glow a few yards away. He ran over and helped her to her feet. "You okay?"

"I'm fine." She brushed the dirt from her knees, then looked up and down the midway. "Where is Nadia?"

"Hell if I know." He joined her in scanning the bustling carnival. Unfortunately, her sideshow buddies had given the fleeing healer plenty of time to vanish into the crowd. She could be anywhere by now, and they didn't have time to search the entire show on foot. Glancing behind him, he saw more bodies burrowing under the canvas. Jim and the others would be crawling out soon. Anxious carnies and random lookie loos came running to check on the fallen tent. Pete and Myka blended into the spectators like they had nothing to do with the accident.

"We can't let her get away with that glove," Myka said urgently.

"Tell me about it."

The Ferris wheel rotated above them. High-spirited shrieks and laughter spilled from its swinging cars. Pete's gaze climbed to the top of the wheel, which was at least 150 feet above the carnival. There had to be quite a view from up there. . . .

"Hey!" he announced. "I just had the greatest idea ever."

A nearby souvenir stand hawked cheap plastic toys and doodads. Pete dashed over to the stand, squeezing past a milling pod of schoolkids. Toy swords, rubber snakes, helium balloons, inflatable cartoon characters, whistles, pennants, and posters competed for his attention, but he ignored them in favor of a pair of flimsy plastic binoculars. "Put it on my tab," he told the vendor as he snatched the binoculars and made tracks for the Ferris wheel, which was several yards away. He bulldozed through the crowd while a confused-looking Myka rushed to keep up with him.

"Pete?"

He tossed her the Tesla.

"Take this! You might need it!"

He skidded to a halt in front of the Ferris wheel and pointed to the topmost cars. "Maybe I can spot her from up there," he explained, while cutting to the front of the line. He flashed his badge at the ride operator. "Secret Service, bub. I'm commandeering this ride."

The operator looked understandably baffled. "'Commandeering'?"

"You heard me, mister." Pete took possession of a bottom car, over the protests of a teenage Romeo and his date. He barked orders at the carnie. "Take me up and don't bring me down until you hear me yelling. This is a matter of national security!"

That might be stretching it or bit, or maybe not. Who knew what the full potential of Nadia's glove was? Not too long ago, Charles Atlas's workout trunks had nearly destroyed Detroit. . . .

"Okay, okay," the cowed operator complied. "Whatever you say, man!"

The carnie worked a lever and the wheel resumed its turning. Pete called out to Myka as his car lurched forward. "I'll let you know if I spot her. Stand by!"

"Good luck!" she shouted back.

The wheel's leisurely rotation wasn't nearly fast enough. He tapped his feet impatiently against the floor of the car while he waited for the ride to carry him upward. As soon as he cleared the roofs of the surrounding snack bars and ticket booths, he started scanning the carnival grounds through the toy binoculars. The cheap lenses weren't exactly government issue, but they were better than his naked eyes . . . barely. Pete found himself wishing that he had borrowed George Reeves's eyeglasses from the Warehouse before heading east. He could really use some super-vision right now.

The car shuddered to a halt at the top of the wheel. It rocked beneath him, even as he checked out the bird's-eye view before him, which was just as breathtaking as he had imagined. The entire carnival was spread out beneath him. Tiny figures paraded amidst the brightly lit rides and attractions or crowded around the collapsed sideshow tent. Dozens of feet below, Myka looked like The Incredible Shrinking Agent. She waited tensely at the foot of the ride.

Pete wished he had time to enjoy the spectacular vista, but spotting Nadia took priority. He swept his gaze over the sprawling carnival, searching for the fugitive healer. At first he didn't see anything, and he started to wonder if this was such a bright idea after all. He lowered the binoculars to try to take in more of the scene. How was he supposed to spot one lone girl in all the glittery hustle and bustle below?

Come on, come on, he thought. *Where are you?*

Just as he considered giving up, a small white figure snagged his eye. Unlike the other miniature men, women, and children strolling the carnival, taking their time to enjoy its gaudy sights and sounds, this figure was zigzagging frantically through the crowd, making a bee-line away from the fallen tent.

A surge of excitement quickened Pete's pulse. Who else could it be? Lifting the binoculars to his eyes again, he zoomed in on the Lego-size figure.

Bingo! A clear shot of Nadia came into view. She was still wearing her Princess Nefertiti getup, making her stand out from the ordinary carnival-goers around her. The healing glove fit snugly onto her right hand. Pete took a moment to track her headlong path before ringing Myka's cell phone. She picked up right away. "Yes?"

"Got her!" He wished they both had Farnsworths so she could see for herself. "Looks like she's heading for the parking lot by the southern exit!"

"Roger that! Meet you there!"

Myka hung up abruptly. Pete watched from above as she took off toward the parking lot. Was there still time to catch Nadia before she got away? Pete crossed his fingers and wished Myka luck.

Go get her, partner!

Anxious to join the chase, he hollered down to the ride operator.

"Hey, buddy! Bring me down—pronto!"

Myka couldn't wait for Pete to touch down on terra firma again. Leaving her partner behind, she sprinted across the carnival. "Out of the way!" she shouted, waving her badge above her head. "Coming through!"

Startled civilians cleared a path for her. A photographic memory helped her navigate the carnival's confusing twists and turns as she remembered the route back to the parking lot. Her arms pistoned at her sides, and she silently thanked every minute she had spent jogging along the Warehouse's never-ending catwalks. Nadia might be younger than she was, but Myka doubted that she was faster. This wasn't the first time she'd pursued someone on foot. If she hurried, maybe there was still a chance to catch Nadia before she escaped with the glove.

Watching intently for the other woman, Myka missed the fallen snow cone lying in her way. Her foot slipped on the spilled ice, wrenching her ankle. "Damn!" she cursed, recovering her balance before hitting the dirt. Her ankle stung like blazes, but she couldn't afford to favor it. She kept on running, albeit with a painful limp. Every step jabbed her like a red-hot knife.

Where was a healer now that she needed one?

Myka spotted the exit ahead. A carnie stood by the gate, stamping the wrists of customers who might want to return later. Beyond the exit, a grassy field had been converted into an ad hoc parking lot. Cars and trucks were lined up in rows. Glowing headlights heralded new arrivals and departures.

But where was Nadia? Deprived of Pete's bird's-eye view, Myka didn't see the healer right away, but then she spotted the younger woman racing toward the exit, on the other side of a spinning carousel. Painted wooden horses galloped between Myka and her quarry, creating a strobe-like view of the healer. Nadia still had a decent head start on her. Myka realized there was no way she was going to intercept Nadia.

Unless . . .

She jumped onto the moving merry-go-round and grabbed onto the back of a mock wooden sleigh to keep from being thrown from the ride. A pair of passengers yelped in surprise, but Myka ignored them. She let the carousel carry her halfway around until she was in front of the exit, then jumped directly into Nadia's path. The impact sent throbbing spasms through her ankle, but she managed to stick the landing without falling over.

Yay me, she thought.

"End of the line!" she barked at Nadia, who froze before her like a bronzed bad guy. Myka aimed the Tesla at the wide-eyed healer. The aching ankle added a definite edge to her voice. "It's over, Nadia. Give me the glove."

The agent's ambush had obviously taken Nadia by surprise. She looked around anxiously, unsure of what to do. "Please." She guarded her gloved hand with her left, holding it close. "I just want to help people."

"I know." Myka's voice softened somewhat. She limped toward the girl. "Believe it or not, so do I."

Nadia backed away fearfully, her eyes glued to the muzzle of the Tesla. Chances were, the weapon needed more time to recharge after zapping the snake, but Nadia didn't know that. "No, you don't understand. I can't give it up. I *can't.*"

The carnie at the gate lumbered toward them. "Hey, what's going on? This lady bothering you, Nadia?"

"Don't even think about it," Myka growled, turning the gun in his direction. She'd had enough carnie solidarity tonight, thank you very much. "Stay out of this."

The pivoting motion twisted her injured ankle. Myka winced.

"What's the matter?" Nadia asked. She stepped

forward meekly, like she was finally ready to surrender. A concerned look came over her face. "Are you hurt?"

"It's nothing." Myka appreciated the girl's improved attitude. She hoped she could get some aspirin soon, *after* she had the elusive glove in custody. "Just my ankle."

"Let me help."

Too late Myka realized what the healer intended. Nadia reached out and placed her gloved right hand on the agent's wrist.

"Wait!" Myka blurted. "Don't—"

Bright blue sparks ignited where the glove touched her. An electric shock jolted Myka's nervous system, surging from her wrist to her wounded ankle. Her body convulsed. Her eyes rolled backward until only the whites were visible. The whole world dissolved into static.

Myka crumpled to the ground.

"Myka!"

Pete found her sprawled near the exit. Rushing to her side, he feared the worst until his voice roused her. She sat up clumsily, looking woozy and disorientated. Wide brown eyes blinked rapidly before focusing on her partner. "Pete? Wh-what happened?"

For a moment he wondered if she had accidentally zapped herself with the Tesla, but no, that didn't make sense. She'd still be out cold. Something else must have knocked her for a loop. Like maybe Nadia's glove? Pete recalled the way her "patients" had collapsed before.

"Don't look now," he told her, "but I think you got healed. With extreme prejudice."

Myka looked down at her ankle, which she wiggled

experimentally. Pete could see the pieces coming together in her mind. "Nadia!" she blurted, snapping back to business. "She's getting away." She gestured urgently toward the exit. "You've got to go after her!"

Pete hesitated, reluctant to abandon his partner. "Are you sure?"

"I'm just a little dizzy," she assured him. "Go!"

Taking her at her word, he ran through the exit into the parking lot. Rows of stationary vehicles obstructed his view while he searched for Nadia. His earlier sympathy for the distressed young healer was eroding fast. She had decked his partner, sort of. That made this personal.

He took off down the center corridor, figuring that was her most likely escape route. Did Nadia have a car parked here? Probably not, he figured; this lot was for the paying customers. Which meant that hopefully she was still on foot.

A young couple approached the carnival from the outer reaches of the parking lot. Pete ran up to them. "Excuse me, folks. Have you seen a runaway Egyptian priestess?"

"You mean that hot chick in the white robe? She went that way," the guy volunteered, before casting a nervous glance at his date, who appeared less than amused by his powers of observation. He gulped. "Er, not that I really noticed. . . ."

"Thanks!" Pete left the poor guy to dig himself out of whatever hole he was in. "Good luck, dude."

Heading off the way the man had indicated, he cut through a line of parked cars to reach an open corridor one row over. His efforts were rewarded by the sight of Nadia herself at the far end of the fence. A barbed-wire fence cut off the parking lot from an adjacent pasture, blocking her escape. She paused, visibly uncertain which way to go next.

"Nadia!" Pete sprinted toward her. He made a mental note not to let her lay hands on him until he took that glove off her. He had a touch of heartburn at the moment, probably from that chili dog he had munched on the way here, but nothing that needed healing *that* badly. "Stay right where you are, okay? We don't want any more trouble."

She spun around. Pete noticed that she was sweating and out of breath. Her face was flushed. Perhaps she hadn't recovered from healing all those people yet? No wonder she hadn't been able to shake their tail. She looked like she was at the end of her rope.

Pete hoped there was no more flight in her. He was anxious to get back to Myka and make she sure she was okay.

"You don't need to run anymore." He walked toward her in what he hoped was a nonthreatening manner. "We're the good guys. Really we are."

The roar of a powerful V-twin engine drowned out his words. A motorcycle zoomed past Pete, then braked in front of Nadia. "Hop on!" Jim Doherty shouted. The determined knife thrower must have gotten out from beneath the sideshow tent. "Hurry!"

Nadia didn't need to be asked twice. She jumped onto the chopper behind her boyfriend and threw her arms around his waist. He wore a leather jacket over his spangled costume. No helmet protected his skull. He shot Pete a dirty look.

"Wait!" Pete hollered. This whole operation was going south on them again. He rushed toward the bike, but Jim wasn't sticking around. Gunning the throttle, he pulled a wheelie, then peeled out parallel to the fence. Pete guessed that he was heading out of the parking lot toward the open road. The bike's exhaust hung in the air.

So much for chasing Nadia on foot. Pete tried to remember where his car was parked. Retrieving his keys from his pocket, he remote-activated the locks. An answering beep led him back to a rented Subaru and he jumped behind the wheel. Honking madly to clear a path, he sped out of the lot after the bike. He yanked his seat belt into place.

The lights of the carnival receded in his rearview mirror. A winding country road lined by low stone walls and drooping elms and oaks led him away from West Haven. Keeping his eye on the motorcycle, Pete hit the gas to eat up the distance between them. Irritated drivers honked at him as he passed them in pursuit of the fleeing carnies. An oncoming pickup truck came around a corner fast, and he yanked hard on the wheel, barely making it back to his own lane in time. The close call left his heart pounding.

This would have been easier in the Badlands. . . .

His wild driving made him impossible to miss. Jim and Nadia looked back over their shoulders. It was obvious they had made him.

The chopper accelerated, trying to shake him, but Pete stuck to them like Sticky String, something he'd had plenty of gooey experience with. The bike wove reck-lessly through traffic, tempting fate. Did having a healer aboard encourage Jim to play daredevil, or was he just determined to keep Nadia out of the agents' nefarious clutches?

Probably the latter, Pete guessed.

They shredded the speed limit, turning the moonlit road into a racetrack, as Pete floored it to keep up with the bike. His brain was racing, too, trying to figure out how to end this chase safely. Running the chopper off the road was not an option; as much as he wanted that glove, he wasn't going to risk getting the two carnies killed in the process. Nor could he call for backup; he really didn't want to involve the local constabulary in this. All he could do now was keep on top of the fugitives until they gave up or ran out of gas. Losing them now would suck big-time.

A stop sign warned of an approaching intersection. The Harley didn't even slow down, despite an oncoming station wagon with the right of way. The wagon slammed on its brakes as the bike cut in front of it, risking a colli-sion. The driver honked his horn in protest. Pete gave him an apologetic wave as he blew through the crossing after the bike.

The problem with high-speed chases was that they always endangered any innocent drivers sharing the road. Pete's temper heated up. Jim and Nadia weren't risking just their own skins now.

An open straightaway gave him a chance to zoom past the cars between him and the chopper. He pulled in behind the bike, which was right ahead of him, hammering down the road. Pete honked and flashed his headlights to try to get them to pull over. Too bad the rental car hadn't come with a siren. Or a tractor beam.

The riders ignored his signals. Instead, to his surprise, Nadia stood up behind Jim and *climbed over* her boyfriend's shoulders even as he scooted backward to make room for her up front. The daring high-speed acrobatics were like something you'd see in a circus—or a carnival. Pete's jaw dropped. Nadia and Jim traded places atop the speeding chopper. She grabbed the handlebars, taking control of the bike. It swerved wildly for a second but then got back on course. The bike kept on rolling.

"What the hey?" Peter muttered. He couldn't figure out what they were up to.

The answer came in the form of a flashing blade. With Nadia now steering the bike, Jim's hand was free to pluck a throwing knife from his belt and hurl it back at Pete. The blade caught the gleam of the Subaru's headlights. Pete ducked involuntarily, but Jim wasn't aiming at him. Instead of striking the windshield, the knife plunged toward the car's front tires instead. The knife struck the driver's-side wheel with a jarring bump. Air hissed from the punctured tire.

More knives followed, one after another. Both front tires blew. White knuckles gripped the steering wheel as Pete lost control of the car. He hit the brakes, and the car swerved to the right, clipping a mailbox and crashing into a ditch. An air bag inflated explosively, swallowing his face. Abused metal crunched noisily before falling silent. The Subaru came to rest nose down in the ditch. Broken glass tinkled across the mangled hood. Smashed head-lights went black.

Pete guessed he wouldn't be getting his deposit back.

Over the ringing in his head, he heard Nadia open up on the throttle.

The chopper sped away into the night.

Artie didn't like what they had to tell him.

"You lost the artifact? It got away?"

"I'm afraid so," Myka admitted. She and Pete shared their Farnsworth while, a few yards away, a tow truck extricated the battered Subaru from the ditch. A second car, which she had "borrowed" from the carnival park-ing lot, was parked nearby. Unfortunately, she had not arrived in time to keep Nadia and Jim from escaping with the glove.

On the brighter side, her ankle felt good as new.

"At least we know what we're looking for now," Pete pointed out. His face was scratched and bruised from the crash, but otherwise he seemed to be in one piece. His hair and clothes had looked better. "If not where it came from."

"That's progress," Artie conceded. "A glove, you say? Of antique design?" He scratched his beard thoughtfully, sounding intrigued. "Hmm. Let me look into that. In the meantime, you two need to get a lead on that girl. What about her fellow carnies?"

Myka shook her head. "They're not talking. Turns out the Mafia has nothing on the sideshow code of si-lence. Plus, they all seem to regard Nadia as a genuine saint. She's been using the glove to relieve their aches and pains for weeks now. They're not going to flip on her."

Pete squirmed uncomfortably. "Speaking of which, Artie, I've gotta ask: Are you sure we're doing the right thing here? Nadia really does seem to be helping a whole lot of people."

"Are you serious?" Artie acted surprised by the question. "How long have you been working here, again? Since when do we leave unidentified artifacts at large?"

"You weren't there, Artie," Myka said. She understood where Pete's doubts were coming from. To be honest, the same reservations had crossed her mind. "You didn't see how happy those people and their families were after Nadia healed them."

"But at what cost?" he said sternly. "I'm sure that this Nadia person means well. People who find an artifact, or are found by one, often do. But we absolutely, positively cannot let this go. That kind of thinking never ends well." A grave look came over his bewhiskered face. "Look what happened to MacPherson."

James MacPherson's schemes to exploit the power of the artifacts had ultimately gotten him killed, along with plenty of innocent people. And it had all started when he used a dangerous artifact to save one woman at the expense of others. That had been the end of his career as an agent—and the beginning of a tragic tale of death and betrayal.

"Point taken." Myka wished it was otherwise—that they could just let Nadia keep on healing people—but she'd been an agent long enough to know better.

So had Pete.

"Don't worry, Artie," he sighed. "We'll track her down, just like we always do. It just kind of sucks sometimes, you know?"

Artie smiled sadly. "Do I ever."

Pete tried to lighten the mood. He peered into the Farnsworth, trying to see around Artie's head. "Is Claudia around?" He fished the cheap plastic binoculars from his pocket. Miraculously, they had come through the wreck unscathed. "I got her a souvenir, just like I promised."

Oh, boy, Myka thought. She could just imagine Claudia's excitement . . . or lack thereof.

"Sorry," Artie said. "She and Leena are doing inventory."

In other words, they could be busy for a while. . . .

CHAPTER
7

WAREHOUSE 13

"Queen Victoria's wedding cake?"

"Check."

The Warehouse seemed to go on forever. Aisle after aisle of overstuffed shelves and storage areas stretched further than Claudia could see. Wooden crates, metal drums, cardboard boxes, steamer trunks, Tupperware bins, plastic coolers, picnic baskets, and other containers were piled several stories high. Labels, ranging from handwritten index cards to sophisticated electronic video units, attempted to impose order on the sprawling collection, which threatened to fill up every nook and cranny of the vast, cavernous space. The sheer size of the Warehouse could take one's breath away. Claudia had been apprenticed here for over a year now, and she was still stumbling onto new areas and artifacts she had never seen before. Maintaining an accurate inventory was a Sisyphean task, despite her continuing efforts to update Artie's stubbornly antiquated records and filing systems. Like, a card catalog . . . seriously?

"D. B. Cooper's parachute?"

"Check."

She rode a rolling metal ladder along the towering shelves, calling out the artifacts in front of her, while Leena strolled down the aisle below, checking the items off on a clipboard. They had been at this for hours now, but had yet to find anything out of place or missing. Claudia fought a yawn. If it were up to her, she'd be on the road with Pete and Myka rather than stuck here doing scut work, but Artie had been insistent. Given recent security breaches by the likes of MacPherson and H. G. Wells, he wanted to make sure everything was exactly where it was supposed to be. A reasonable precaution, she had to admit, even if that didn't make the job any less mind-numbingly tedious.

"Sigmund Freud's cigar." Claudia paused. "What does *that* do?"

Leena made a face. "You don't want to know."

"Okaaay. Moving on . . ."

It was hot, thirsty work, especially since there was no air-conditioning on the main floor of the Warehouse (which, granted, would be a budget buster). The musty, dusty atmosphere seemed unusually stuffy today, like she was stuck in the world's biggest sweatshop. Her mouth was dry and she kicked herself for not bringing along a can of soda. There was a small fridge back in Artie's lair, but that was umpteen aisles, half a dozen stories, and at least a thirty-minute hike away.

Maybe after they finished this shelf?

She tried to focus on the task at hand. Leaving the skeevy cigar behind, she checked out the next item: a battered tin pot resting right side up. A faded paper label identified it as once belonging to John Chapman (1774–1845), a.k.a. "Johnny Appleseed."

Right, she thought. A storybook illustration of a scruffy, barefoot wanderer planting an orchard in the wilderness popped from her memory banks. *Dude used to wear his pot as a hat.*

Talk about a bold fashion choice!

But that wasn't all the pot was good for. Intrigued by the description pinned to the shelf beneath it, Claudia couldn't resist lifting the pot from its perch. As she brought it toward her face, the interior of the pot magically filled with swirling golden-brown liquid. The enticing aroma of fresh apple cider tickled her nose.

Her mouth watered. She licked her lips.

She lifted the pot to her lips. One little sip couldn't hurt, right? It was just like using the snow globe to cool her drinks back at the office. . . .

"Claudia?" Leena called out from below. "Everything okay up there?"

She blushed guiltily. On second thought, maybe she should pass on the cider. Messing with artifacts was seldom a good idea. Look what happened that time she tried to use Volta's lab coat to change a lightbulb. . . .

"We're copacetic," she assured Leena, a little too quickly. She lowered the pot from her lips, hoping that Leena hadn't seen. "Strictly professional all the way."

She started to put the pot back where it belonged. Just then, a burst of azure energy flashed into existence farther down the aisle. Crackling like ball lighting, the thunderous discharge threw off spidery blasts of electricity as it came racing toward her.

"Holy moley!" She had seen this before. Sometimes the sheer accumulation of tangential energy in the Warehouse kicked up a little static, as Artie liked to put it, which could be extremely hazardous to your health. "Duck and cover!"

The roiling electrical storm rattled the shelves. The metal ladder turned into an elevated lightning rod. Grasping the danger just in time, Claudia leaped off a rung and grabbed onto the edge of the nearest shelf right before the energy bolt struck the ladder, sending it spinning across the aisle away from her. Sparks cascaded down the ladder's length as the grounded energy dispersed into the floor. Within seconds the crisis was over.

Except, of course, that Claudia now found herself dangling some ten feet above the floor, hanging on by her fingertips. Her feet searched for purchase but couldn't quite reach one of the lower shelves. Gravity tugged on her legs. Not for the first time, she wished she were a few inches taller.

"Er, Leena? A hand, please?"

The other woman had thrown herself facedown onto the floor, her hands over her head. She lifted her eyes cautiously and looked around to make sure the coast was clear. Then she jumped to her feet and ran over to the displaced ladder. Playing it safe, she pulled on a pair of protective purple gloves before taking hold of the ladder and wheeling it back under Claudia. "Here you go," she said. "You okay?"

"I think so." Claudia lowered her feet onto a metal rung, which felt reassuringly solid compared to empty air. She let go of the shelf. Her aching fingers thanked her. "You?"

"Just a little dusty." Leena smoothed out the wrinkles of her dress. She had worked at the Warehouse longer than any of them except Artie. It took a lot to rattle her. "Nothing I haven't seen before."

Claudia scrambled down the ladder, grateful to set foot on the floor again. Her heart was still pounding from her near brush with electrocution. She was too young to go to the great chat room in the sky just yet. Ozone lingered in the air, along with a faint aftertaste of fudge. That soda back in Artie's office was sounding better and better.

"I don't know about you," she said, "but I think I'm ready to call it a day."

Leena didn't disagree. "After all that, I think we deserve a break." She recovered her clipboard from the floor. "We can tackle the rest of this section tomorrow."

"That's what I'm saying." She glanced down the long corridor, which held enough relics, curios, and knickknacks to crash eBay for good. No way was she up to taking on another mile of shelves right now. "It's not like all this junk is going anywhere."

"Knock on wood," Leena teased.

Claudia rapped a shelf before they headed back toward the office.

The women's footsteps receded into the distance. Forgotten in the confusion, and toppled by the violent shaking, John Chapman's pot lay on its side several shelves above the floor. Apple cider crept toward the lip of the pot, then began to spill onto the shelf. A small puddle slowly formed and cider started to seep through the wooden slats. Cider dripped onto the shelf directly below, but no one was around to notice.

Drip, drip, drip . . .

CHAPTER
8

FAIRFIELD, CONNECTICUT

"Thank you so much for taking us in like this."

"Oh, please." Their hostess waved away Nadia's gratitude. "It's the least I can do after the way you cured my arthritis. *I* should be thanking *you* for finally giving me a chance to repay you."

Nadia sat at a kitchen table in a comfortable suburban home. Jim sat beside her, digging into a home-cooked meal. They had changed out of their carnival garb into fresh clothes provided by their benefactor, a retired high school principal named Judith Noggle. A steaming mug of coffee was cupped between Nadia's palms. Although she had discarded the rest of her costume, she still had on her gloves. After nearly losing *the* glove to those Secret Service agents, she couldn't bear to be parted with it again.

"Just the same, we really appreciate this. Especially on such short notice."

She and Jim had literally e-mailed Judith from the road after ditching those Feds yesterday. The older woman was just one of several grateful "patients" who had expressed a fervent desire to do whatever they could for Nadia someday, pressing their business cards and contact information upon her after being healed. Nadia had an entire shoe box full of cards and thank-you notes back at the carnival. Some, like Judith, had even friended her online. Nadia had used Jim's phone to reach Judith after they went on the run. Thankfully, her home was only a short drive from West Haven.

A doorbell rang.

"That must be them," Judith announced. "I'll go let them in." She patted Nadia on the shoulder. "Feel free to finish your coffee, dear. There's no rush."

She exited the kitchen, leaving Nadia alone with Jim. He took advantage of the momentary privacy to check on her. "How are you holding up?"

"Okay enough." She squeezed his hand. "I'm feeling a lot better now."

He looked her over, obviously concerned. "You positive about that?" He scowled. "I don't like this. I mean, now we've got the government after you? Maybe it's time to get a new act."

"It's not just an act!" she blurted, more vehemently than she intended. "I'm sorry. I didn't mean to snap at you. It's just that . . . this means a lot to me, you know?"

How could she make him understand? She'd spent her whole life conning rubes with carnie tricks, or risking her neck doing acrobatic stunts. Carrying on the Malinovich family tradition. But now she was finally doing something important with her life. Something real. She wasn't just putting on a show. She was *helping* people.

How could she give that up?

"Yeah, I know," he grumbled, trying to sympathize. "But it's making you sick. We both know that. Hell, even those Feds could see it."

"It doesn't last," she insisted. "I just feel a little shaky afterwards, that's all."

"Really? 'Cause it seems like it's getting worse the more you do it."

She looked away from him, unable to meet his eyes. Deep down inside, she was afraid he might be right. What had that woman, Agent Bering, said before? That power like this came with a hefty price tag? What if she and her partner knew what they were talking about? To be completely honest, sure, she had her own doubts sometimes about where the glove came from and what it was doing to her—not that she ever wanted to admit that to Jim. He already worried about her too much.

Which was sweet, really. But she couldn't let that stop her from doing what she was meant to. What she *had* to do.

"I can handle it, okay?" She smiled and squeezed his hand again. "Trust me on this."

Jim knew better than to argue with her. "All right. But I still think we should head for Canada first chance we get. We need to put a border between you and those Feds."

"No." They had already discussed this. "That's . . . the wrong direction."

"Wrong how? I don't understand."

Neither do I, she admitted silently. She couldn't explain

it. It was like there was an invisible force pulling on her . . . or the glove. Her palm itched and she scratched at it through the soft white leather. "I just want to keep heading south, like we were before."

"But why? What difference does it make?"

Judith's return spared Nadia from confessing that she had no idea. "Excuse me, dear. They're ready for you now."

"Of course." Nadia got up from the table, grateful for the interruption. Jim frowned. Clearly this conversation wasn't over, but right now she'd settle for an intermission. "Let's not keep them waiting."

Judith led them into a tastefully decorated living room, where a middle-aged Asian couple was waiting for her. Nadia could tell right away the wife was the sick one: she looked frail and haggard. According to Judith, Linda Ogawa had been fighting leukemia for years. Obviously nervous, the couple eyed her with a familiar mixture of hope and apprehension. Nadia didn't blame them for their doubts.

A few months ago, I wouldn't have believed in me, either.

"Nadia, these are my friends the Ogawas. I've told them all about you."

They weren't the only ones. A steady stream of pilgrims had been flocking to the house since Nadia had arrived, lured by Judith's enthusiastic endorsement. There was even talk of staging some sort of public event at a local high school later this week. The former principal had missed her calling, Nadia reflected wryly. She should have been an agent or carnival barker.

"Is it true?" Ken Ogawa asked. "Can you really help my wife?"

The naked desperation in his eyes and voice tugged at her heart. He clung anxiously to Linda's hand. How could she possibly disappoint them?

Jim came up beside her and whispered in her ear. "You sure you're up to this?"

Absolutely, she thought. Her fingers flexed within the glove, eager to begin. All her doubts and fears evaporated. Those scary government agents were wrong. There was a reason the glove had come into her life. This was always meant to be.

"Please," she said. "Make yourself comfortable."

She held out her hand.

PENNSYLVANIA

Worrall followed the road north. Clouds drifted across the horizon.

Today had been a good day so far. His head wasn't torturing him. His gut was not on fire. He'd even managed to get a decent night's sleep in a motel last night. By his own pathetic standards, he actually felt halfway healthy.

Too bad the same couldn't be said of those unlucky souls he had run across at the diner the other night. He'd left them sprawled on the tile floor, moaning pitifully. By now they knew what he'd been going through all these years.

Tough. He couldn't afford to feel sorry for them. Making other people sick was the only thing that made him feel better, if only temporarily. If strangers had to suffer to ease his misery, so be it. *Why should their well-being be more valuable than mine?*

He wasn't concerned about getting caught. He'd done this before. Plenty of times. Past experience had taught him that they would all be too dazed to remember exactly what had happened to them. Their memories had been scrambled by the awesome power of his glove. Chances were, they would blame the diner's greasy food.

For however long they survived.

Just one thing worried him. It used to be that infecting just one person would give him relief for days, but lately it seemed as though he needed to afflict more and more people to get the same effect. It was like an addiction.

Just the one glove wasn't enough. He needed the other one too. The one that could cure him forever. No matter what the cost.

The road called to him. "Aïda" sang from the speakers. Mile after mile fell behind him. His left hand itched.

He was getting closer.

The sky cleared up ahead, letting more of the sun through. The light reflected off the blacktop before him, hurting his eyes. He put on his shades, but it was too late. That same damn pressure started building in his temples. His eyes watered. Nausea twisted his stomach in knots. His jaw clenched. Shaking hands gripped the wheel.

Damnit, he cursed. *It's too soon.*

There was nothing to be done about it, though. Except find someone to share his misery with.

Or, better yet, several someones.

The outskirts of a small farming town struck him as a promising hunting ground. Worrall's throbbing eyes searched for a likely venue. Scorching bile climbed up his throat. He retrieved a roll of antacids from his pocket and chewed down on several of them. The chalky tablets provided only minimal relief. Fairly soon, he knew, he wouldn't be able to keep anything down at all. Medication couldn't help him.

But he knew what could.

A modest-size church appeared alongside the road up ahead. The parking lot out front was full. Visitors bearing gifts flocked toward the church entrance. They had all dressed up for the occasion. Ushers in rented tuxes greeted people at the door. A sign at the curb read: *Congratulations, Nick and Shelly!*

It seemed a wedding was in progress.

Worrall smirked at his good fortune. He pulled over to the side of the road.

Checking himself in the mirror, he straightened his clothing and joined the procession toward the church. A few curious looks were cast his way, but nobody challenged him. He forced himself to maintain a smiling countenance, despite the pain and nausea driving him onward. His swollen veins pulsed horribly. His teeth ground together.

Worrall entered the church, gratified to discover aisles of unsuspecting people. The bride and groom were not yet in evidence, but he had no doubt that they were nearby. He had his own gift to bestow on the happy couple.

A helpful usher who couldn't have been more than seventeen approached him. "Are you here for the bride or the groom?"

"All of the above," Worrall said.

CHAPTER
9

WAREHOUSE 13

Claudia and Artie were in full search mode.

Scattered notes, files, and printouts were strewn across their respective desks as well as large portions of the floor. A whirring fan rustled the documents, which were held down by assorted oddball paperweights. Claudia was glued to her keyboard, scouring the Internet, while Artie went old-school, leafing through various dog-eared dossiers, catalogs, and history books in search of some clue to the glove's provenance—and Nadia's possible whereabouts. They had been going at it all day without a break. Leena had headed back into town to check on the B&B. Claudia figured she'd catch up with her later. Right now, the game was on.

"Gloves . . . gloves." Artie muttered to himself. A neglected mug of herbal tea went cold. He repeated the refrain like an incantation, as though trying to summon up some stray scrap of knowledge from his voluminous memory. Frustrated, he slammed shut yet another volume. "But *whose* gloves? That's the question. If we can just pinpoint their origin, we might be able to predict where they will turn up next."

"Not sure I can help you there," Claudia said. "But I might be onto something."

"What is it?" His interest piqued, he rolled his chair across the office to join her. "Anything interesting?"

She scooted over to give him a better look at the computer screen. "I was prowling hospital and emergency databases, looking for more cases of people being cured inexplicably," she explained. "Just in case there really is another glove out there."

"And did you find any?"

"Just the opposite, actually." She nodded at the glowing monitor. "There's been a chain of freakishly sudden, unexplained illnesses popping up all along the East Coast, more or less in sync with Nadia's recent spate of healings. We're talking perfectly healthy people suddenly coming down with typhoid fever of all things . . . for no apparent reason. Several people have died already, and the rest are still hospitalized. The last outbreak was a few hours ago, at a wedding in Pennsylvania. The whole production—bride, groom, guests, et cetera—had to be hospitalized before they even got to the cake."

Artie lifted his glasses to squint at the screen. His eyes weren't what they used to be. "Typhoid?"

"Yeah. Weird, right? And that's not all." Her fingers danced over the keyboard, calling up a map of the eastern seaboard. "I plotted the epidemic's vector against Nadia's magical mystery tour." She stabbed a macro key. "Check this out."

On the map, a green line charted the southward progression of the Whitman Bros. Carnival as it made its way from Rhode Island to Connecticut. Blinking dots marked documented healings along the route. A red line, connecting each of the bizarre fever outbreaks, meandered north from Florida to Pennsylvania.

"They're on an intercept course," Artie realized. A theory instantly formulated in his brain. "The two gloves, separated for who knows how long, are being drawn back to each other."

The same notion had crossed Claudia's mind. "But are we sure there's a connection? Maybe these two patterns are unconnected?"

"Not on your life," he said confidently. "There's no such thing as coincidence where artifacts are concerned. This is all starting to make sense now."

At least by Warehouse standards, Claudia thought. "So how does this work, then? One glove heals people, the other one makes them sick?"

"Exactly! Complementary forces. Yin and yang. Left and right. Sickness and health . . ." The words came tumbling out of his mouth excitedly. Claudia could tell he was onto something. He lurched from his chair and started pacing back and forth across the carpet. "Healing, disease . . . typhoid fever . . ."

"Maybe Typhoid Mary?" she suggested.

"Unlikely. Mary Mallon never healed anyone, and she didn't wear gloves, although she probably should have." He smacked his palm against his forehead. "Of course! How could I have missed it before? Clara Barton!"

Claudia didn't get it. "Can I have the bonus commentary, please?"

"Clarissa Harlowe Barton, 'the Angel of the Battlefield.'" He pulled a heavy tome from the bookshelf. It landed with a thud onto the desk. "During the Civil War, she nursed thousands of wounded and dying soldiers, her tireless efforts bringing her to many of the war's bloodiest battlefields. Fredericksburg. Richmond. Bull Run. Antietam."

Artie blew a thick layer of dust off the book's cover. Claudia coughed and fanned the cloud away with her hand. He flipped through the pages until he came to a sepia-toned photo of a somber, matronly-looking woman wearing a Red Cross medallion around her neck. An army tent formed the backdrop for the photo. Artie rummaged atop the desk until he found a magnifying glass. He held the glass over the photo, then beckoned to Claudia. She peered through the lens at a pair of elegant white leather gloves—just like the one Pete and Myka had described.

"Along the way, her gloves must have absorbed both the blessing of healing . . . and the deadly curse of the war. During which, it should be noted, disease and infection killed far more soldiers than bullets ever did."

"Diseases like typhoid fever?" Claudia asked, catching on.

Artie nodded. "Nadia is healing people with Clara Barton's right glove. I'm sure of it."

Claudia took his word for it. She glanced back at her computer screen, where the red line continued to pulse ominously. Over two dozen people had already died of fever, and who knew how many others were on the verge of death?

"So who has the bad glove?"

"That's what we need to find out," Artie said grimly. "After we bring Pete and Myka up to speed."

He reached for his Farnsworth.

Drip, drip . . .

Cider trickled from John Chapman's pot, raining gently on the artifact one shelf below: an ornate marble bathtub whose claw feet resembled demonic talons. Reinforced steel rods supported the weight of the tub, which had once belonged to Elizabeth Báthory, the infamous Blood Countess of Hungary. Over four hundred years ago, the countess had bathed in the blood of hundreds of murdered young women in the belief that such sanguinary cosmetic treatments would preserve her youth. Walled up inside her own castle for her crimes, Elizabeth had been outlived by her tub. Ancient brown stains discolored the once-pristine marble.

Drop by drop, the cider filled the bottom of the tub. The spicy amber juice grew saltier, and began to take on a disturbing crimson hue. . . .

Artie was pacing again. Claudia didn't stop him. She figured he could use the exercise.

"All right," he said, thinking aloud. "We have two gloves, both in the wind. How do we track down Nadia Malinovich . . . and the other glove?"

Claudia leaned back in her chair, the heels of her

sneakers resting on the desk. She spitballed ideas off the exposed brick walls, while chewing distractedly on a ballpoint pen. "I don't know. Maybe there's some way we can take advantage of the fact that the gloves are being drawn back to each other?"

"Hmm. Not a bad idea." He crossed the office to the large roll-down maps hanging on one wall. He pulled down a map of the eastern seaboard, covering the world map underneath. Working from memory, he charted the converging paths Claudia had plotted before. An easy-erase grease pencil defaced the map.

"You know, you could just use my computer," she suggested.

"Quiet," he shushed her. "I think better this way." After marking up the map, he stepped back to absorb the picture. "Let's see. The right glove is heading south. The left glove is traveling north." He applied the marker once more, connecting the dots. "From the looks of things, they're due to come together somewhere around . . ."

Claudia raced him on the computer.

"Fairfield, Connecticut," they said in unison.

Artie shot her a bemused look. "All right, genius. Where in Fairfield? And when?"

"Already on it." She fired up multiple search engines, all of which came back with the same answer. A rush of adrenaline woke her up faster than caffeine. "Eureka!"

"The town?"

"No. You having a senior moment or something? Stay with me." She gloated over her discovery. "Wanna take a wild guess where a 'celebrated psychic healer' is appearing tomorrow evening?"

Artie hurried over to check out the links. "Fairfield?"

"Bingo. Give the old guy a prize."

"I'll take Nadia's glove," he said, "now that we know where she's going to be."

And where one glove was, could the other be far behind?

CHAPTER
10

FAIRFIELD, CONNECTICUT

"Okay, this could be a problem."

A large crowd had turned out for Nadia's latest public appearance, which had taken over a local high school gym for the evening. The bleachers were packed with people who had found out about the event from announcements on the Internet. Pete thought he recognized a few faces from the audience at the carnival. According to Claudia, "Princess Nefertiti" already had several fan Web sites devoted to her. Her abilities and appearances were much buzzed about in chat rooms and message boards—which made the agents' job both easier and harder.

Easier because Nadia's growing fame made her easier to locate. Harder because they were obviously not the only ones eager to see her.

"And then some," Myka agreed. "How are we going to get to her with all these people around?"

The agents lurked at the rear of the gym, trying to keep a low profile. A stage had been erected at the opposite end of the gym. Pete spotted Jim Doherty peeking out through a curtain at the crowd. He guessed that Nadia was waiting backstage for her introduction. The strong man, Atlas, stood guard near the base of the stage. Having shed his leopard-print trunks for a tight gray T-shirt and slacks, he looked more like a bodyguard or bouncer than a sideshow attraction. Arms crossed atop his chest, he scanned the crowd for any potential troublemakers.

Pete made sure to keep out of the strong man's line of sight. His ribs were still sore from that bear hug back at the carnival. "We can't just rush in without a plan," he said. "The big guy there isn't going to give Nadia up without a fight. And he's not the only one who isn't going to take kindly to us barging in. We try to confront Nadia in front of her fan club here, we could be talking a riot." His face remained bruised from the free-for-all at the carnival and ensuing car crash. "Personally, I'd prefer a little less excitement this time around."

Myka considered their options. "I suppose we could wait until after the show and try to catch her when she leaves?"

"Nah," Pete said. It was tempting to let Nadia heal a few more people before they shut her down, but they still didn't know enough about what the glove was doing to her. Or where the mysterious second glove fit in. "Artie's right. We need to get that glove out of commission as soon as possible, if only so we can concentrate on finding the other one."

He inspected the audience. Was the second glove already here? According to the gang back at the Warehouse, it was heading this way.

"All right," Myka said. "So what's our game plan?"

Pete scoped out their surroundings. He spied a fire alarm mounted to a wall by the front entrance. Exit signs glowed at both ends of the gym. There was even one over by the stage.

He pointed it out to Myka. "Head around back and be ready. I'll be right with you."

She nodded and headed for the door. "Give me five minutes."

"Make it six, just to be safe."

The alarm switch was only a few yards away. He casually eased toward it while she exited the gym, squeezing past the latecomers pouring into the facility. Reaching the alarm, he leaned against the wall and waited for Myka to get into position. Minutes ticked by.

The lights dimmed, signaling that the show was about to begin. Dozens of murmured conversations fell silent. A local dignitary whose name Pete didn't catch walked onto the stage and approached a microphone.

"Welcome, friends and neighbors," the emcee greeted the crowd. A squawk of feedback interrupted her remarks and she paused to adjust the mike. "Thank you all for showing up on such short notice, and thanks to the good folks at Mohegan High School for generously allowing us to rent this facility for the evening. I suspect that most of you have already heard something of our guest's astounding gifts, or you wouldn't be here, but perhaps there are some skeptics in the audience too?" A handful of people hesitantly raised their hands. "Well, I'm here to assure you that everything you've heard is true . . . as you are about to discover for yourself." She gestured grandly toward the curtain behind her. "You may know her as Princess Nefertiti, but tonight you will meet the real woman behind the miracles that have brought relief and wellness to so many people. Ladies and gentlemen, let's give a warm welcome to . . . Nadia!"

An enthusiastic round of applause greeted the healer, who appeared to have shed her sideshow trappings and stage name for this slightly more dignified venue. The former carnie wore a tailored beige dress suit and skirt that nicely matched her gloves. Her makeup was more conservative too. Tastefully applied eyeliner and mascara had replaced the exotic kohl-eyed look she had sported before. No ruby baubles adorned her forehead. She was ready for prime time.

Not if I can help it, Pete thought.

All eyes were on Nadia, giving him the anonymity he needed. With no one looking, he seized the handle on the fire alarm and yanked it down.

An ear-piercing siren blared, cutting off the applause. Confusion and anxiety shot through the audience. People scrambled to their feet and started heading for the doors. Up on the stage, Nadia froze in bewilderment, interrupted before she could say a single word. Jim rushed out from behind the curtain and herded her toward the nearest exit—just as Pete had hoped. Atlas followed closely behind them.

"Everybody out!" Pete shouted above the siren. "Nice and orderly!"

Beating the exodus to the front door, he dashed out of the gym and raced around to the back, where he found Myka waiting for him. His partner was staked out in a courtyard behind the gymnasium, facing a rear door that, if Pete's mental geography was correct, corresponded to the fire exit behind the stage. It was early evening, and the stars were just starting to come out. A clear sky promised perfect weather for artifact snagging. Twilight painted the horizon in shades of red and purple. Elevated lamp poles lit up the paved yard. There was no way Nadia could slip past them unseen.

The agents didn't have to wait long. The back door swung open. Nadia, Jim, and Atlas hurried out of the gym—to find themselves face-to-face with Pete and Myka.

"End of the line, kids."

Jim reached beneath his jacket for a knife, but Pete already had the drop on him.

"Uh-uh." He kept his Tesla aimed at the trio. "No sideshow tricks this time. Hands up in the air."

"And keep that glove where we can see it," Myka added.

Atlas shoved his way in front of his two young charges. "You again?" he rumbled. Loyalty to his fellow carnies, or perhaps steroids, overcame his sense of self-preservation. He charged at Pete like an enraged bull. "I going to cram that toy ray-gun up your—"

A galvanic bolt turned him into the Amazing Electric Man. He hit the pavement like a slab of meat. Pete was inclined to leave him there. Moving him would probably require a forklift.

"So much for Atlas the Mighty," Pete said. He turned the gun back toward Nadia and Jim. "I'm hoping you two are smarter than Mister Muscle here. Don't make me use up all my batteries."

In fact, the Tesla was going to need some time to recharge after downing Atlas, but Jim and Nadia didn't know that. And Pete wasn't about to tell them.

"Now, then," Myka said. "Where were we?"

She approached Nadia warily, not wanting a replay of last time's electroshock treatment. Pete covered her as she donned a pair of purple gloves and held out her hand. "You remember the drill. Give me the glove, Nadia. Slowly."

"I don't believe this!" Jim glared furiously at the agents. He, too, had ditched his carnival garb for more casual attire. His fists clenched at his sides. "Don't you people have better things to do than hassle innocent people?"

"Can it, easy rider. We've heard it all before." Pete made a mental note to have Myka frisk Jim for knives after she was done with Nadia. "And hey, thanks for the flat tires the other night. Nothing I like more than crashing my car into a ditch. I'm fine, by the way."

Jim spit at the ground. "Too bad."

Pete reminded himself that the kid was just defending his girlfriend. "Don't make this any harder than it has to be, chum." He brandished the spent Tesla like it still had some juice in it. "Or I might forget I'm a professional."

Nadia was giving Myka a hard time too. "Please, not again." Tears leaked from her eyes, smearing her makeup. "You don't understand. This is my calling. It's what I was meant to do."

Pete could tell she meant it. A shame that didn't make a bit of difference.

"This isn't up for discussion," Myka said firmly. "The glove, Nadia. Now."

"No! You can't have it!"

The girl lunged forward, hoping to "heal" Myka, again, but the agent was ready for her this time. Myka deftly sidestepped the attack, spinning into a round-house kick that swept Nadia's legs out from under her. The young woman fell forward onto the pavement. Before she even knew what was happening, Myka had her wrists pinned.

"Sorry about that," the agent said. She knelt on top of the prone healer. Her knee dug into Nadia's back, holding her down. She twisted Nadia's right arm behind her back. "Did I mention that my ankle is much better now?"

The expert takedown knocked the wind out of Nadia, or maybe she just realized she was hopelessly outmatched. She put up little resistance as Myka forcibly pried the glove from the girl's right hand, then rose to her feet.

"Got it," she informed Pete. "Finally."

"That's one down." He relaxed a little. "Now we just need to find the other one."

She placed the glove in a silver bag for safekeeping. Once again the goo visibly failed to neutralize it. She stepped away from Nadia, freeing the girl to get off the pavement. Myka glanced at the lights of the city, visible beyond the parking lot. "In theory, it should be on its way here."

Pete started thinking ahead. "Maybe we can use this glove as a compass . . . or bait?"

"Worth a try," Myka said. 'I'll bet Claudia has some ideas along those lines."

Sobbing gently, Nadia climbed slowly to her feet and sought refuge in her boyfriend's arms. She stared with naked longing at the bag holding the confiscated glove. Pete half expected her to start mumbling about "her precious," like Gollum in *The Lord of the Rings*.

Jim spoke up instead. "Other glove?"

Pete didn't bother to explain. He wondered if it was worth interrogating the couple, or if he and Myka should just let them go. He didn't see any point in handing them over to the authorities. There were no laws against using rare historical artifacts to heal people, at least as far as he knew.

"I don't suppose you know anything about Clara Barton?"

Before either Jim or Nadia could answer, a hoarse, raspy voice interrupted.

"Excuse me, miss. Can you help me?"

A bald-headed stranger emerged from the rear of the gym, looking badly in need of Nadia's services. Hollow cheeks and sunken eyes gave the man's face a distinctly cadaverous appearance. His papery skin was dry and colorless. He walked stiffly, as though every movement pained him. A tan trench coat was draped over his bony frame. Pete could hear the man's ragged breathing from yards away. The guy looked like death warmed over.

Pete thought he recognized the newcomer from the audience before. A bad vibe played chopsticks on his spine. He covered his mouth to avoid catching whatever the poor guy had while still keeping one eye on Jim and Nadia.

"Sorry, buddy." He tried to send the stranger on his way. "Now is not a good time."

The man kept on coming. "Please, I've come such a long way. If I could just have a few moments with Nadia?"

He grimaced and clutched his gut. Pain contorted his face.

Pete felt sorry for the guy, who had showed up too late. He lowered the Tesla and took out his badge. "Official business, sir. Please move along."

Neither the gun nor the badge discouraged the desperate stranger, who continued to shamble toward them. Watery, bloodshot eyes were fixed on Nadia, like she was the only thing that mattered. Veins pulsed beneath his hairless scalp.

"Back away, mister." Pete didn't want to get rough with some poor sick dude, but the guy wasn't leaving him any choice. "Don't force us to have you removed."

The weather, which been perfectly calm before, took a turn for the worse. Churning black clouds rolled in from nowhere, darkening the sky. A sudden wind whipped up the candy wrappers and cigarette butts littering the courtyard. The temperature took a nosedive, shedding degrees faster than Gypsy Rose Lee had ditched her veils before they ended up in the Warehouse. The wind chilled Pete to the bone. He shivered beneath his jacket. Goose bumps pebbled his skin.

"Myka?" He glanced over at his partner. "I have a really bad feeling. . . ."

She was staring intently at the stranger, who had just stepped into the glow of an elevated lamp. Her eyes widened in alarm.

"Pete!" She pointed at the stranger. "His hand! Look at his hand!"

A white kid glove, just like Nadia's, sheathed the man's fingers.

Holy cow, Pete realized. *It's the other glove.*

The one that makes people sick.

The stranger snarled. Glaring at Nadia, he noticed for the first time that her right hand was bare. "Where is it?" he demanded. "Give it to me!"

He reached out with his left hand. An invisible force yanked Myka's arm up. She struggled to hold on to the silver bag containing Nadia's glove, which appeared to have been seized by a powerful magnetic pull. She grasped it with both hands, fighting against the attraction. "Pete! The glove! I can barely hold on to it!"

The weather went nuts. The sky turned into a mass of seething storm clouds. Fierce winds nearly knocked Pete off his feet. Airborne dust and grit pelted his face. His breath frosted before his lips.

The stranger felt the pull of the gloves as well. He spun toward Myka. "You! You have it!" His arm outstretched, he stumbled toward her. "It's mine! Give it to me!"

That sounded like a bad idea to Pete. He squeezed the trigger of the Tesla, but the gun only sputtered; Pete kicked himself for wasting its charge on Atlas. The stranger lunged at Myka, who was too busy hanging on to the bag to defend herself. His gloved hand groped for her. That was the bad glove, Pete recalled. It wasn't going to heal Myka.

"Stay away from her, Typhoid Barry!" With no time to lose, he tackled the stranger, slamming him into a lamppost. The man grunted out loud. Pete hoped he hadn't hurt the guy too bad. For all he knew, it was the glove that had driven the stranger crazy—just like that pirate wench back in Charleston.

"That's enough, pal." Pete grabbed the man's left wrist, holding the bad glove away from him. He had no intention of getting zapped like Myka had back at the carnival . . . or worse. "Cool down and this will all be over in a jiffy."

"Unhand me!" The stranger thrashed like a crazy person. "You asked for this!"

He spit a mouthful of phlegm into Pete's face. "Yecch!" the agent sputtered. Repulsed, he tried to wipe his face with his sleeve, briefly loosening his grip on the stranger, who proved stronger than he looked. With a burst of manic energy, he tore his wrist free and grabbed Pete's shoulder with his left hand. A swirling gray haze flowed from his fingers before sinking through Pete's jacket.

It was like being hit by a speeding plague wagon. Pete staggered backward, clutching his shoulder. A hot, feverish sensation spread all over his body. His skin threw off heat like a furnace. His head swam and he leaned against the side of the car to steady himself. He coughed hoarsely. His stomach ached.

What had this creep done to him?

"Pete!" Myka cried out. "Oh my God, Pete!"

A few feet away, Jim Doherty tugged on Nadia's arm. "This is our chance. Let's get the hell out of here."

"No!" Nadia protested. "Not without my glove!"

The stranger shoved Pete aside. He advanced on Myka, moving noticeably more smoothly than before. He no longer seemed quite so infirm. "Give me that glove!"

"Not on your life!" Myka said, even as she clutched the rebellious bag with all her strength. It flapped frantically in her grip, hanging parallel to the ground. Straining against the pull, she managed to take a few steps backward, putting more distance between her and the stranger. "What did you do to my partner?"

A sneer curled his lip. "Let me show you."

Before he could get any closer to her, however, blaring sirens raised a deafening racket. Fire trucks and police cars, their lights flashing brightly, zoomed toward the courtyard. They were only moments away from arriving.

"Damnit!" the stranger cursed. His gaze darted back and forth between Myka and the oncoming emergency vehicles. He hesitated, obviously torn between his lust for the other glove and the need to escape the authorities. Greedy fingers clutched at empty air. "Not now!"

A squad car speeding into the yard made up his mind for him. Swearing, he turned his back on Myka and rushed past Nadia and Jim, who scrambled to get out of his way. He raced from the scene, taking the other glove with him. Within seconds he had disappeared into the shadows beyond the gym.

"I don't understand," Nadia gasped. "Who was that?"

Myka wished she knew. She let out a sigh of relief. The silver bag went limp in her grasp, and she briefly considered chasing after the stranger but decided to cut her losses instead. Pete was leaning against a lamppost, gasping for breath. She needed to make sure he was okay before pursuing the fugitive. They could track down the second glove later. Right now, her partner took priority.

At least we have Nadia's glove, she thought. *That's a start.*

"Pete?" She started toward him. "Are you all right?"

More cars and trucks zoomed into the yard. Spinning gumball lights strobed the scene. The lead patrol car squealed to a stop. Its door slammed open and a middle-aged police officer stomped toward them. A graying crew cut hinted at a military background. His unsmiling face was deeply furrowed. A star-shaped badge identified him as the county sheriff. His name, Pitts, was inscribed on the star. His expression darkened further at the sight of Atlas lying sprawled upon the pavement. He knelt to make sure the strong man was just unconscious before rising to confront Myka and the others.

"All right," he demanded gruffly. "Somebody tell me just what's going on here."

Other officers provided backup. Firefighters in full gear hurried to check on the gym, while a paramedic attended to Atlas. The weird weather settled down abruptly. Overhead, turbulent clouds dispersed almost as quickly as they appeared. The frenzied winds quieted. Myka figured that meant that the stranger was long gone. Nature, it seemed, was much happier with the gloves apart.

Not that she expected the sheriff to understand that.

"Agent Bering, Secret Service," she identified herself, presenting her badge. "Sorry for the excitement."

He squinted suspiciously at the badge, then turned to Nadia and Jim. "You two okay?" His voice softened. "These strangers giving you trouble?"

"Can't you see? They shot my bodyguard!" Nadia

dragged Jim toward the sheriff while pointing accusingly at Myka. "And she stole my glove!"

Pitts scowled at the female agent. "Is that true?"

Huh? Myka was slightly taken aback by the sheriff's tone. What was this all about? She didn't get vibes the way Pete did, but even she could tell that something was off here. Why was this guy treating her like a suspect?

"Excuse me, Sheriff." She tried again to take charge of the situation. "These individuals are persons of interest in a federal investigation. My partner and I will be happy to brief you later," she lied, "but right now I would appreciate your full cooperation."

"Oh, you would, would you?" He sneered at her badge. "How do I know that thing's not a fake?" A smirk lifted the corners of his lips. "You know, now that I think of it, that looks plenty counterfeit to me."

Myka couldn't believe this. "Seriously?" she asked, not bothering to conceal her growing exasperation. Local authorities frequently gave her and Pete a hard time about invading their turf, and questioned the agents' involvement in whatever bizarre occurrences were going on, but she wasn't often accused of impersonating a Secret Service agent. She reached into her pocket and offered Pitts a business card bearing a Washington phone number that was routed directly to the Warehouse. "Feel free to contact my superiors if you don't believe me, but right now I don't have time for this." She started to push past the sheriff and the other cops. "I need to check on my partner."

"Not so fast." He blocked her path. "You're not going anywhere until we sort this out."

Myka found herself facing not just Pitts but several of

his officers. Behind her, the alarms in the gym fell silent. A fireman approached the sheriff. "Looks like a false alarm, sir," the man said. "No sign of an actual fire."

"A false alarm, eh? That's a criminal offense." He looked Myka over. "You have anything to do with that?"

"It was all a trick," Jim piped up, "to lure us into an ambush!"

"Is that so?" Pitts made up his mind. "I think you and your partner need to come down to the station with me. We take false alarms, and armed robbery, pretty seriously around here."

Myka didn't back down. "Sheriff, you are making a serious mistake. You have no idea what's going on here."

"Listen." Pitts placed a protective arm around Nadia's shoulders. "All I know is that this special young lady has helped plenty of good people, including my own boy. That gives her the benefit of the doubt in my book." He stepped forward and confiscated the silver bag from Myka. "And I'm sure as hell going to believe her before I take orders from a couple of so-called Secret Service agents."

"We're for real and you know it," Myka said coldly, although she knew she was wasting her breath. This whole encounter made sense now. Just their luck: the sheriff was another member of Nadia's growing fan club. "You're obstructing federal agents in the line of duty."

"Oh, yeah? Last I heard, the Secret Service didn't go around robbing innocent people at gunpoint." He handed the bag over to Nadia. "Here you go, princess. Don't you worry about a thing. I've got this under control."

Nadia acted positively overjoyed to be reunited with her glove. "Thank you so much, Sheriff George!" she squealed, the familiarity making it crystal-clear that this was not the first time they had crossed paths. She tore open the containment bag like a crazed toddler on Christmas morning. Traces of purple goo clung to the glove, but she eagerly pulled it back onto her hand anyway. Her fingers flexed inside the glove. She choked up. "Oh, God, that was close. I was afraid I'd lost you forever."

Jim tugged on her arm again. "C'mon. Let's get out of here before anything else crazy happens." He appealed to Pitts. "Is it okay if we take off, Sheriff?"

"Go ahead. I've got this covered."

Nadia gave Pitts a grateful hug before finally letting her boyfriend drag her away. Myka experienced a fully explainable case of déjà vu as she helplessly watched Clara Barton's glove elude them one more time. Fuming silently, she longed to snatch it back, and even flirted with the notion of going for her gun, but she was frustrated, not crazy. Assaulting several legitimate police officers and firefighters singlehandedly was not really a viable plan. Not even Pete would try something so reckless.

Pete . . .

"Pete?" She peered past the phalanx of uniformed police types between her and her partner. From what she could see, he was still on his feet but holding on to the lamppost for support. Maybe whatever that stranger had done to him was wearing off already? He put up no fight as a wary cop relieved him of his Tesla. Myka called out to him. "Can you hear me? How are you feeling?"

Pitts had other things on his mind. "That's enough. You two can hold each other's hands back at the station."

He placed his hands on his hips. "Now, are you going to come quietly, or do I have to break out the handcuffs?"

Disgusted, Myka reached into her pocket and took out her own cuffs. "Here. Have mine." She tried to squeeze past the cops again. "*Now* will you let me check on my partner?"

Pitts didn't have a chance to answer. Pete let go of the lamppost and staggered toward Myka unsteadily. A recovered alcoholic, he hadn't touched a drop in years (at least, not in his own body), but he wobbled like a drunk on a bender. His face was gray. He clutched his gut, grimacing in pain. His agonized groan tore at Myka's heart. He gasped for breath. Blood trickled from his nose.

"Myka? I don't feel so good."

He collapsed onto the pavement.

CHAPTER
11

WAREHOUSE 13

Drip, drip, drip . . .

In the lonely aisle, observed only by its fellow artifacts, Elizabeth Báthory's bathtub began to overflow. The crimson spillover, which no longer bore the slightest resemblance to apple cider, streamed down the smooth marble sides of the tub. Viscous red droplets slipped through the metal rods supporting the artifact. Blood fell like rain.

A shrunken head rested on the shelf below the tub. Its shriveled features were dry and leathery, like old beef jerky. A mop of wild black hair clung to its scalp. Its sooty eyelids were squeezed tightly shut. The protruding lips were tightly pursed. Tiny beads were strung in its hair. A bone pierced its nose.

A warm red shower pelted the hideous relic. The first few drops of blood seeped between its lips. At first the head did not react, but then the dark, mummified flesh twitched. Stirring upon the shelf, the head rocked backward, turning its grotesque face up toward the falling droplets. It licked its lips. Its eyes opened. Blazing bloodred orbs gazed out at the Warehouse.

Shrunken lips parted. Piranha-like fangs caught the light.

The head smiled.

"UNIVILLE"

"Howdy, Leena. Beautiful afternoon, isn't it?"

Bert the grocer greeted her warmly as he swept the sidewalk in front of his store. Downtown consisted of a single broad avenue that was home to pretty much all of the local businesses. Bert's groceries shared the main drag with the barbershop, the hardware store, a Chinese restaurant, the drugstore, the bank, the florist's, a video rental place, a bakery, a doctor's office, and other small-town fixtures. All were locally owned: the big chains had yet to discover "Univille," possibly because they didn't even know it existed.

"I'll say," she agreed. A basket of fresh vegetables from the farmer's market hung from her elbow. "I couldn't ask for a nicer day."

The sun shone down on Main Street. Elm trees shaded the wide sidewalks. Patriotic flags and bunting added color to the storefronts. Cars were parked on the curb. People wandered in and out of the various shops and offices. Leena was happy to see that her neighbors' auras all seemed to be in alignment today. She had known most of them for years.

"How's things at the B&B?" Bert put away his push broom and wiped his hands on his apron. "Those IRS goons giving you any trouble?"

As far as the townspeople knew, Pete and Myka and Claudia all worked for the Internal Revenue Service, and

the Warehouse itself stockpiled every tax return ever
filed. Alas, while this cover story served to discourage
any locals from looking too closely at what went on at
the Warehouse, it hadn't exactly endeared the agents
(and apprentice) to their neighbors. Most of the folks in
Univille wanted as little to do with them as possible.

"They're nice people, Bert. Really."

She had it easier than the others. Nobody knew she
worked for the Warehouse. They just thought she put
them up at her bed-and-breakfast.

"Sure they are," he said dubiously, "until you find
yourself being audited to the last dime." He shrugged.
"I guess their money's as good as anyone else's, and I'm
sure you appreciate their business, times being what they
are. But me? I'm not sure I'd be comfortable sleeping
under the same roof as the IR-fricking-S."

"Don't worry about me," she said, smiling. "I sleep
just fine."

Except, perhaps, when Pete or Myka or the entire
world was in danger.

"Well, better you than me." He changed the subject.
"You coming to the big bash this weekend?"

A canvas banner stretched above Main Street hyped
the town's annual "UnFounders Day" celebration, which
was being held on Saturday. Leena was looking forward
to it.

"Of course. You know me: I wouldn't miss it for the
world."

"Great. See you there." He headed back inside his
store. "You take care, Leena."

"You, too, Bert."

She continued on her way, exchanging more greetings with old friends and neighbors. Old Mrs. Lozenko was out walking her dog. Dr. Stevens, the dentist, was picking up his dry cleaning. The Brubaker twins were racing their bikes down the sidewalk. Claire and Janice, who ran the coffee shop, were pushing a baby stroller. Deputy Joe was checking the parking meters. Dave the UPS guy was dropping off a package at the thrift store. Crazy Vic was sleeping it off on a bench. Leena smiled at them all. She petted the dog.

"Hello, Lola. You enjoying your walk?"

A warm breeze rustled her hair. She took a moment to appreciate the relative peace and normalcy of the town, especially compared to the frequent crises and craziness of Warehouse 13. She had lived in Univille for years and years now. It was more than just her base of operations. It was her home. She couldn't imagine living anywhere else.

"Be careful not to overexert yourself," she advised Mrs. Lozenko, whose aura was shading weak. "Just a short walk today. And don't forget to take your vitamins."

"I will," the old woman promised. "It's so nice of you to care."

Bidding good-bye to the dog and its owner, Leena cut across a small park near the center of town. An unusual-looking modern sculpture consisting of several hollow metal tubes pointing at the sky had been installed over a small reflecting pool. A flexible rubber hose connected the tube array to the pool. A robin perched on top of the artwork.

She paused to admired the sculpture, which had been

donated to the town by an anonymous benefactor many years ago. A private joke lifted her lips.

If only that bird knew what the "sculpture" could really do . . .

She checked her to-do list. Most of her errands had been taken care of, but she still needed to swing by the pet store to pick up some ferret chow for Myka. Humming to herself, she started to cross the park when her cell phone buzzed in her purse. She took it out and held it to her ear.

"Hello?"

"Leena?" Artie's somber tone immediately alerted her that something was wrong. She didn't need to read his aura to know that he was calling with bad news.

"It's Pete," he said. "He's sick."

FAIRFIELD

The sheriff unlocked Myka's handcuffs. "Sorry for the misunderstanding, Agent Bering."

"Yeah, I'll bet." She didn't buy his phony apology a bit. Massaging her chafed wrists, she resisted the temptation to arrest *him* for obstruction of justice. Instead she simply took back her badge and Tesla. "Now that Nadia is long gone, along with the suspect who assaulted my partner."

"That's too bad what happened to him," Pitts allowed. "Maybe you can explain exactly what went on back—"

"Thank you, Sheriff," Mrs. Frederic interrupted. A stern black woman whose braided brown hair was stacked in an old-fashioned beehive, she had arrived at the hospital via a chauffeured limousine. A tailored wool business suit gave her a conservative, professional appearance. She peered at Pitts over the rims of her glasses. Her inscrutable expression made the Sphinx seemed like a chatterbox. "We'll let you get back to your duties now."

Her imposing presence was practically a force of nature. Just by showing up, she had turned the sheriff's hostile attitude around and gotten the charges against her agents dropped. Myka could tell that Pitts still had plenty of unanswered questions, but he knew when he was being dismissed . . . and that Mrs. Frederic was not somebody to be crossed.

"All right, ma'am. I hope your man comes through okay." Heading out, he took a parting shot at Myka. "Next time, just let me know when you're pursuing an investigation in my county. As a matter of professional courtesy."

Myka bit her tongue. With any luck, there wouldn't be a next time.

The sheriff departed, leaving the two women in a bustling corridor outside Pete's hospital room. Following Pete's collapse at the high school, Pitts had at least had the decency to rush them both to the nearest hospital instead of a jail cell, even if he had insisted on treating Myka like a felon throughout. She doubted that he had been serious about locking her up; he had simply wanted to give Nadia and Jim plenty of time to make a clean escape—with Clara Barton's right glove.

"Thank you for bailing me out," Myka said. "I still can't believe that jerk pretended to think I was an impostor!"

"You're welcome," Mrs. Frederic replied. An enigma

in pearls, she had personally recruited both Pete and Myka and kept a close watch over all things related to Warehouse 13. Nobody really knew how old she was. Even Artie was intimidated by her. "I couldn't afford to have you hamstrung by the local constabulary, not when there are more urgent matters at hand."

Like Pete.

Pushing the sheriff's infuriating conduct out of her mind, Myka hurried into Pete's room. She tried not to react at the sight of her partner lying sick in bed. An IV was hooked up to his arm. Blinking medical apparatuses monitored his vital signs, which appeared distressingly weak. His face was chalky and drenched in sweat. Rosy splotches blemished his exposed neck and collar. He was running a fever. Wet, raspy breaths whistled from his lungs. His eyes were lidded. He appeared only semiconscious. Myka hated seeing him like this.

A blond woman was leaning over him, applying acupressure to his face and chest. It didn't seem to be helping. He groaned in discomfort.

Mrs. Frederic followed Myka into the room. "How is he faring, Doctor?"

"Not good, I'm afraid."

Vanessa Calder turned away from her patient. An attractive woman in her late fifties, she wore a stylish blue jacket and turquoise necklace. Wavy yellow hair fell to her shoulders. She had personally doctored Warehouse agents and the Regents for many years now. Myka didn't know her well, but she knew that Pete was in good hands.

"How so?" Mrs. Frederic asked.

Before Vanessa could answer, a portly physician wearing a white lab coat stormed into the room. His florid complexion and potbelly did not exactly set a healthy example for his patients. He yanked Pete's chart away from Vanessa.

"Excuse me," he demanded, "what are you doing with this patient? I don't believe you have privileges at this hospital."

Vanessa retained her composure. "And you are . . . ?"

"Dr. William Vertue," he huffed. "I'm in charge of this hospital—and this patient."

"Pleased to meet you, Doctor." She extended her hand. "Dr. Vanessa Calder, Centers for Disease Control. My apologies for not consulting you earlier, but we have an urgent situation here."

Her calm authority, and supposed affiliation, took the wind out of his sails. "The CDC?"

"Agent Lattimer here is Patient Zero," she declared ominously, lowing her voice. "We need to establish an immediate quarantine. Nobody is to be allowed in this room except with my express permission." She clucked at him. "To be honest, I was rather alarmed to discover that such measures had not already been implemented."

Vertue went on the defensive. "Well, um, we were still assessing the situation." He glanced worriedly at Pete. "Patient Zero? Quarantine? What precisely are we dealing with here?"

"It's best that we keep that under wraps for now." She gestured at Myka, who made a production of closing the door to discourage eavesdroppers. "I cannot stress too highly the importance of keeping this case out of the press, in order to avoid a national panic. I trust we can count on your full cooperation—and discretion."

"Yes, yes. Of course." He tugged at his collar. Without being too obvious about it, he sidled away from Pete's bed, putting more distance between himself and the infected agent. "My lips are sealed."

"Thank you." Vanessa gave him an approving nod. "I'll be sure to mention your help to the surgeon general."

The funny thing was, Myka didn't know whether Vanessa was conning the other doctor or not. The Regents had all sorts of connections and resources. For all Myka knew, Vanessa really did have pull with the CDC and the surgeon general.

"Now, then, if you could see to that quarantine, I need to attend to my patient."

"Certainly." He handed the chart back to Vanessa. "This hospital is at your disposal."

He shut the door behind him on his way out.

"Nicely handled," Mrs. Frederic complimented Vanessa. "So, you were saying about Agent Lattimer?"

Vanessa beckoned the other women away from Pete's bedside. "I've never seen anything like it," she said in a hushed tone. "Pete appears to have come down with some strange, exceptionally virulent version of typhoid fever."

"Typhoid?" Myka echoed.

"Of course." Mrs. Frederic sounded unsurprised by the diagnosis. "One of the greatest killers of the Civil War." She shook her head before turning to Myka. "It's vital that we locate that other glove, Agent Bering. Clara

Barton was a remarkable woman." She spoke almost as though she had known her personally. "She would not want her legacy to bring pain and suffering to the present."

At the moment Myka was more interested in preserving Pete's future. She looked anxiously at Vanessa. "Can't you do anything for him?"

"I wish I could," the doctor said. "Nowadays typhoid is treatable by antibiotics and rehydration therapy. But so far Pete's fever is resisting both conventional and alternative treatments. The disease also appears to be progressing at a preternaturally accelerated rate." She did not mince words. "If it can't be halted, he'll die soon of fever and peritonitis."

Myka couldn't keep from gasping. Her hand went to her mouth.

Mrs. Frederic appeared troubled as well. Myka wondered if she blamed herself for recruiting Pete in the first place. "Is he contagious, Doctor?"

"Not excessively so. Under ordinary circumstances, typhoid is spread by food and water that has been handled by carriers of the disease."

"Like Typhoid Mary," Myka recalled. "She was a cook. That's how she managed to infect so many people."

"Exactly," Vanessa confirmed. "As long as Pete refrains from cooking for us and takes a few reasonable precautions, we should be okay." She glanced at the door. "That 'quarantine' business was to keep Dr. Vertue out of our hair—and this whole situation under wraps."

Mrs. Frederic nodded. "What about Agent Lattimer? How long does he have?"

"I'll do what I can," Vanessa promised. "But . . . days. Three or four at best."

Myka refused to accept that. "We need to find Nadia's glove. The one that heals people. It might be able to save him."

"Possibly," Mrs. Frederic said. "But at what cost?"

Myka didn't know how to answer that.

CHAPTER 12

TRENTON, NEW JERSEY

Worrall kept an eye on his speedometer as he drove north. The last thing he needed was to get caught by some local speed trap. That had been a close call back at the high school. Too close. As far as he knew, the police were not looking for his car, but why press his luck? He had come too far, and been traveling too long, to risk running afoul of the law now.

Not when he was so close.

How long had this endless quest been going on? For years, really. Born to wealth, his body had always been his enemy. Weak and sickly, he had spent much of his childhood in bed or at doctors' offices. While the rest of the world went about its business, enjoying life, he had been lucky to be able to function at all. Migraines. Ulcers. Allergies. Insomnia. His so-called life was a never-ending litany of discomfort and affliction. An intolerable situation, to say the least.

He had even been too sick to attend his parents' funeral after that car accident. Not that he had been too broken up about their untimely passing. It was their damn genes that were responsible for his misery. A three-car pileup on the highway served them right.

Besides, he had his own problems to worry about.

Modern medicine had always let him down, so over time he had been forced to look elsewhere. Over the years, he had squandered much of his inheritance acquiring rare objects and talismans reputed to possess miraculous healing properties. Imported water from Lourdes. A silver grail that had supposedly once belonged to Prester John. Potions derived from bits and pieces of dozens of endangered species. Even a scrap from Florence Nightingale's handkerchief.

But nothing had worked. They had all been fakes or disappointments.

Until one of his suppliers got a line on Clara Barton's glove. It had cost him a fortune, but he still remembered the surge of excitement he had felt when he had first slipped the glove onto his left hand. A tingling sensation had raced like blood poisoning from his fingers to his brain. The smell of black powder had tantalized his nostrils while the echoes of bygone cannons had reverberated in his ears. He had known at once that it was the real thing.

It was only later that he'd realized that it was the *wrong* glove.

He had been searching for the good glove, the healing glove, ever since. It had been a long, exhausting search, but at last he knew where it was. That stupid girl had it.

But not for long . . .

His hand itched and he scratched at it irritably. He was stiff and sore from driving all day. A vein throbbed behind his ear. He could feel another sick headache coming on. Waylaying that federal agent at the high school had only eased his pain for a brief spell. If only there had been time to infect those other people as well. Maybe he should have tried to sicken the whole lot of them, cops and firefighters as well. Or would that have been too risky?

He frowned at the memory. Worry aggravated his ulcer, causing acid to eat away at his stomach lining. He searched his pocket for some Tums.

Where had those gun-toting agents come from anyway? Running into them outside the gymnasium, where they had apparently been trying to take custody of the glove, had been an unpleasant surprise. Who else was after Clara Barton's glove? Granted, he had already taken care of the man, but that female agent was still out there, along with whomever she worked for.

That complicated matters. He didn't like having competition.

The mounting pressure on his skull made it hard to think. Bile curdled at the back of his throat. He was already getting nauseous.

Time for another rest stop.

A community park offered the perfect solution. Dozens of people were crowded into the bleachers of an open-air football stadium, cheering on the local team. They rose to their feet, bellowing like baboons, as some disgustingly fit small-town hero scored another touchdown. Their full-throated cheers could be heard even through the rolled-up windows of the Lincoln. Worrall admired their spirit.

Too bad it couldn't last. . . .

WAREHOUSE 13

The shrunken head awoke with a ravenous hunger. The blood dripping down on it from Elizabeth Báthory's tub was not enough. Beady crimson eyes fixed on an electrical cable affixed to one of the shelves' sturdy vertical supports. Jaws snapping, it scooted across the shelf and started gnawing on the insulated cable. A warning label posted next to the cord read DANGER. HIGH VOLTAGE.

Sadly, English was not the head's native tongue.

Razor-sharp fangs sliced through the rubber insulation. Sparks erupted between the head's clenched jaws. Its wild black mane stood up straight. Its red eyes rolled in their sockets. Smoke rose from its shriveled scalp. Its bloody lips sizzled and flaked off. An aroma not unlike fried bacon mixed with the smell of burnt hair. The shrunken head vibrated like a jumping bean.

A final jolt of electricity flung the charred head across the room. It knocked over Groucho Marx's honorary Oscar before crashing to the floor several shelves below. Blackened and smoking, it landed at the foot of a tall metal vault. The head twitched a few more times, then stopped moving. It was scorched inside and out. All the blood in the world couldn't reactivate it now.

But the damage had already been done. The chewed-up wire sputtered and short-circuited. The aisle lights flickered on and off. A digital display on the steel vault blinked out and its locking mechanism disengaged. Rusty gears squeaked loudly as the vault door swung open, releasing a gust of stale air. Erratic lighting exposed the contents of the vault.

A Native American totem pole faced the aisle. Over

twenty feet tall, the pole consisted of three carved wooden beasts stacked on top of each other. A grizzly bear, poised upon its hind legs, formed the base of the pole. A mountain lion, with chiseled fangs and claws, rested atop the bear, while a fierce-looking thunderbird crowned the pole, which had been painted according to tradition. Large black eyes gazed out from the vault. Bright red mouths and a jagged beak added splashes of color to the weathered timber pole, as did the streaked black and red feathers on the thunderbird's wings. The entire pole had been carved from a single huge log. At least two thousand pounds, it filled the entire vault.

At first, the pole stood still and silent, like every other totem pole on display throughout the country. But then the flickering overhead lights seemed to create the illusion of animation, as though the timber limbs and jaws were gradually stirring. Any visitor observing the pole could be forgiven for assuming that its apparent movements were just a trick of the light.

But they would be wrong.

The bear growled.

The lion gnashed its fangs.

The thunderbird spread its wings. . . .

CHAPTER
13

FAIRFIELD

Pete felt like crap.

His body was burning up. Hot and sweaty, he kicked off his covers in a vain attempt to cool down. The sudden movement proved to be a mistake. A pounding headache was dialed up to eleven. Excruciating cramps twisted his guts. He coughed violently, the jarring convulsions just torturing him more. He fell back against his pillow, gasping.

"Take it easy there." Vanessa Calder hurried over to straighten out his blankets. She gently probed his distended abdomen with her fingers. "How does that feel?"

A pained wince was all the answer she needed. "The herbal treatments don't seem to be working," She fiddled with the IV. "I'm increasing the dosage on the painkillers. That should give you a little relief."

At least for a while. He appreciated her bedside manner, but he could tell from her worried expression that she was fighting a losing battle. He hadn't felt this bad since the time that Saracen scorpion thingie attached itself to his spine. That had nearly fried his entire nervous system before Myka figured out a way to get it off him. He could only hope she and the others were hot on the trail of another last-minute save.

"Crap!" His fist clenched in frustration. He hated being helpless like this, especially with so much at stake. He had always prided himself on being an active, take-charge kind of guy. Being stuck in bed, unable to fight for his own life, was killing him.

In more ways than one.

"Hey, look what I found." Myka entered the room, bearing an armload of comic books. She joined the doctor at his bedside. "Something to help you pass the time."

Grimacing, he pulled himself up to a sitting position. Vanessa helped by elevating the bed behind him, but the effort left him breathless and panting. Shaky hands accepted the comics, which turned out to be multiple back issues of *The Iron Shadow*.

His favorite.

"You've probably read most of them before," Myka said apologetically, "but I didn't know what else to get you."

"Don't matter," he croaked hoarsely. Despite the IV, his mouth felt as dry as the desert over Warehouse 2. He flipped through the brightly colored comics, getting a nostalgic charge from the familiar covers. There was even a copy of the classic summer annual featuring the return of the Iron Shadow's archnemesis, the Oxidizer. He remembered reading it at summer camp when he was a kid. "These are great. Thanks."

She bit her lip, visibly struggling to hold it together. "Who knew there was a comics shop just a few blocks away?" She nibbled on a piece of red licorice from a vending machine. Pete knew her sweet tooth acted up whenever she was stressed out. "Well, okay, Claudia knew. She found it on the Internet."

"That's our Claudia," he said, forcing a smile. "Have Google, will travel."

Myka looked anxiously at Vanessa. "How's he doing?"

"Let's talk outside," the doctor suggested, clearly reluctant to discuss his chances right in front of him. "So Pete can enjoy his new reading material in peace."

Taking Myka by the arm, she guided her out into the hall, where the two women conferred in hushed tones. Pete observed them discreetly. He couldn't make out everything they were saying, but he caught phrases like "already in stage two," "enlarged spleen," "high fever," and "distinct possibility of delirium." And what the heck were "bronchial rhonchi"?

Myka fretfully tied her licorice stick into knots. "But there must be something you can do."

"I've tried everything," Vanessa said. "All I can do is treat his symptoms now."

She placed a comforting hand on Myka's shoulder, then headed off to check on the latest test results. Myka took a moment to compose herself before rejoining Pete in the room. Her eyes were damp. "So, the Iron Shadow save the world yet?"

He knew she was just trying to keep his spirits up, but there was no reason she had to shoulder this burden alone. "You do remember that I can read lips, right?"

"Oh my God." Aghast, she looked back over her

shoulder at the hall where she and Vanessa had just been talking. "How much did you . . . ?"

"I got the gist of it."

His sister was deaf. He had learned to read lips ages ago, in support of her. It came in handy sometimes.

"It's okay," he assured Myka. "I'm a big boy. I can handle the truth."

She sat down beside him and took his hand. "I'm so sorry, Pete. We're working around the clock to find Nadia's glove, but Vanessa says your condition is progressing even faster than expected. We're running low on time."

He valued her honesty. "Thanks for being straight for me." He flipped through one of the comics. "And for actually setting foot in a comic-book shop again. I know that's not exactly your comfort zone."

"Hey, don't forget: I was a superhero myself once, for about ten minutes in Detroit that one time."

A vivid flashback, of Myka blasting energy bolts from a pair of high-tech gauntlets while wearing a skintight latex suit, drew a chuckle from his lips. "Trust me, that's burned into my memory forever."

"I'll bet." Her wry tone gave way to a more somber expression. "Pete," she said tentatively, as though uncomfortable with what she was about say. She twirled a lock of her hair, a nervous habit he often teased her about. "Speaking of reading lips, do you want me to call your sister? I'm sure Artie and Mrs. Frederic can arrange to bring her here. Just in case."

He shook his head. "I'm not ready to go there yet."

He and Myka lived dangerous lives, constantly placing themselves in jeopardy. He had already written his sister a letter, to be delivered to her someday when his luck finally ran out. That would have to be enough. "I'm not giving up. Just like we didn't give up on you when you were dying of old age thanks to that freaky camera."

"Don't remind me," she said. "I still cringe whenever I think I've found a gray hair."

Pete remembered Myka lying on her deathbed, just like he was now, Man Ray's camera having artificially aged her to the point of extinction. "The point is, we found a way to reverse the process. Just like you found a way to get that electro-scorpion off me way back when."

This wasn't the first time one or both of them had faced death. Hopefully, it wouldn't be the last.

He flipped through another comic. A two-page spread depicted the Iron Shadow breaking free from a supposedly escape-proof death trap. With a little help from his allies, of course.

"Artie and Claudia will figure something out. They always do, right?"

WAREHOUSE 13
"Got him!"

Artie leaned back in his office chair and crossed his arms over his chest. He contemplated the computer monitor in front of him with grim satisfaction. *Now we're making headway*, he thought. *Finally.*

"Him who?" Claudia scurried over from her own desk. She and Artie had pulled an all-nighter trying to track down one or both of Clara Barton's gloves. She peered over his shoulder.

"Who him?"

"Our mystery man, the one who infected Pete in Fairfield." He nodded at the screen, which displayed an enlarged driver's license photo of a gaunt, bald-headed fellow with sunken eyes and a sour expression. Ashen, waxy skin was stretched tight over a skull-like visage. He appeared much older than his birth date implied. "Meet Calvin Worrall, of the Palm Beach Worralls."

"Jeepers!" Claudia recoiled from the photo on the screen. Her face curdled in disgust. "Dude looks like Nosferatu's kid brother. On a bad day."

Artie couldn't disagree. Granted, DMV photos were seldom flattering, but Worrall's bloodless, haggard visage was enough to give small children nightmares. More important, he also matched Pete and Myka's description of the stranger who had assailed them outside the high school gymnasium. The one who was apparently in possession of Clara Barton's left glove.

"We'll need to transmit this photo to Myka for confirmation," he stated, "but I'm pretty sure Calvin's our guy. He fits the profile perfectly." Artie kicked himself for not thinking of Worrall earlier. "I should have realized it was him."

Claudia gave him a quizzical look. "You know this guy?"

"I know *of* him," Artie clarified. "He's a collector of rare curios, particularly those associated with healers and healing. I try to keep to keep tabs on various 'amateur' enthusiasts, just in case they stumble onto something dangerous. Worrall's been in the game for a few years now. He once nearly outbid me on Rasputin's prayer rope." The object in question currently resided on Level 5 of the Warehouse, after being re-neutralized several weeks ago. "But I'd always chalked him up as a dilettante, with more money than expertise. He seemed harmless enough. More of an occasional nuisance than anything else."

"Tell that to Pete," Claudia said.

"Indeed. It seems I underestimated Calvin. Looks like he's somehow managed to get his hands on a genuine artifact." Artie scratched his beard. "I wonder where he found it."

"Not sure that matters anymore," Claudia said. "We need to find this guy, pronto."

She had her priorities straight, Artie conceded. Myka's most recent update from the hospital suggested that Pete was declining fast. Tracing the provenance of the gloves could wait. Right now they needed to find them and neutralize them.

He forwarded Worrall's file over to Claudia's computer. "Do a complete search on Calvin. Credit cards, secondary residences, magazine subscriptions . . . anything that might tell us where he is now."

"You got it, chief!" She practically dived back into her seat at the other desk. Her nimble fingers danced over the keyboard. "I'm on this like wasabi on sushi."

Artie was tempted to supervise, but resisted the impulse. Claudia could handle this. After all, she had managed to track down Warehouse 13 by herself, with only a little covert assistance from MacPherson. If anything, her investigative skills had only grown sharper since then.

Don't be a backseat driver, he scolded himself. *Let her take the wheel.*

He glanced at his wrist watch. It was nearly six in the morning, which meant that it wasn't even eight a.m. in Connecticut. Probably too early to run Worrall's photo by Myka. She'd had a long night. He didn't want to wake her if she was actually managing to get some sleep. ID'ing the photo could wait another hour or so. Hopefully, they would have some solid leads for her by then.

He poured himself a cup of coffee. A plate of leftover donuts served as breakfast.

Where are you, Calvin? What are you up to?

While Claudia searched online, Artie stared at the photo on the screen, trying to get into their quarry's head. According to Myka, Worrall had been after Nadia's glove as well, but why? Simply to complete his collection, or was there more to it than that? Reviewing the man's file, he encountered a mother lode of old medical records and prescription refills. *That's right,* he recalled. Calvin had always been a veritable catalog of ailments and infirmities. No wonder he was so obsessed with healing talismans. Did he think Clara Barton's right glove could cure him for good?

Probably. But why was Worrall making people ill in the meantime?

He rested his chin on his knuckles, mulling it over. Artifacts had their own peculiar logic. You simply had to figure it out.

Fortunately, he'd had plenty of practice at that.

"Hold on," he muttered. "Didn't Pete and Myka say that they thought that healing people was making Nadia sick?"

Claudia looked up from her computer. "Yeah, I think so."

"Suppose the other glove does just the opposite? Healing Worrall by making other people ill?"

"You may be onto something there, Marcus Welby," she replied. "Sounds just twisted enough to be right." She rolled her eyes. "And the fact that it makes sense to me just proves that I've been working here too long."

"Just wait until you're my age." He ambled over to her desk. "Any progress?"

"Already?" She snorted. "Impatient much?"

"You have complete access to every database on the planet." He glanced again at his watch, wondering if he should wake Myka to debrief her. He wanted to know if Worrall had looked healthier after he infected Pete. "How hard can it be to find one walking epidemic?"

"Harder than it sounds, actually," she admitted, a trifle sheepishly. "He's gone off the grid in a major way. From what I can tell, he withdrew a large sum of money a while ago and dropped out of sight. He hasn't used his credit cards for months."

Artie frowned. "What about his cell phone?"

"No recent calls. To be honest, I get the impression this guy isn't much of a people person. He's not even on Facebook." She stubbornly bounced around the Internet, surfing from Web site to Web site. "He's probably relying on disposable phones, if he's talking to anyone at all."

"Sounds like he's being very careful," Artie deduced, "which means he's worried about being tracked or being linked to that chain of typhoid fever outbreaks." He gave Worrall points for paranoia. "Very clever, Calvin. I should have been paying more attention to you."

"Don't be too hard on yourself," Claudia said. "It's not like you haven't been distracted lately, first by MacPherson, then by H. G. Wells. Not to mention the usual Warehouse wackiness."

He refused to let himself off so lightly. "No excuses. Not when it might cost Pete his life."

In his stint at the Warehouse, Artie had outlived most every other agent. He had seen far too many good men and women killed, driven insane, petrified, bifurcated, lost in space/time, or worse, all in the line of duty. Their diversely tragic fates weighed on him. He was in no hurry to add Pete to the Warehouse's long list of casualties.

"You know," Claudia said, "I have to ask: Don't we have something on the shelves that might be able to fix Pete? Maybe Louis Pasteur's milk bottle or something?"

Artie shook his head. "Too dangerous. Using one artifact to counteract another is never a good idea. Mixing their energies can produce random, wildly unpredictable results, like that time the disco ball accidentally triggered Lewis Carroll's mirror. We could easily make Pete even worse."

"Really?" Claudia asked. "I hate to say it, but I'm not sure he's got a lot to lose."

Artie gave her his sternest look. He couldn't blame Claudia for grasping at straws, but this was something she needed to understand, especially if she was ever going take his or Mrs. Frederic's place running the Warehouse.

"There was an agent once," he said gravely, "who tried to keep his bones from dissolving by ingesting a rare vial of powdered ivory."

"And?" Claudia prompted.

"You've heard of the Elephant Man?"

She looked appropriately appalled. "Oh. Ick."

"Ick indeed." He trusted he'd made his point. "We have enough on our hands with Clara Barton's gloves, no pun intended. The last thing we—or Pete—needs is to throw another artifact at him."

"Okay," she said. "Message received, loud and clear. No shortcuts. It's the gloves or nothing."

She reapplied herself to the search, zipping through cyberspace almost faster than Artie could follow. Passport applications, tax returns, SAT scores, and library late notices flashed across the screen, one after another. Separate windows, each containing a different document or JPEG, fanned across the screen like playing cards dealt by a quick-fingered stage magician. She even called up a third-grade essay on how Worrall spent his summer vacation (getting his appendix removed, apparently). But all she found was dead ends.

"Frell!" she cursed in geek. She threw up her hands. "In the immortal words of the Shat, this guy needs to get a life. How am I supposed to find him unless he surfaces sometime soon? He's a ghost!"

He shared her frustration. Every minute that passed decreased Pete's odds of survival. "What about typhoid fever? When was the last outbreak?"

She had the answer at her fingertips—literally. "A football game in New Jersey, yesterday evening. A whole squadron of ambulances had to be dispatched."

"Who exactly was infected?" Artie asked. "The audience or the team?"

"Both. Everybody." She scanned the emergency dispatches and news bulletins. "Even the cheerleaders aren't so cheery anymore."

Artie was troubled by the reports, which he read over Claudia's shoulder. "This is not good. The infection rate is escalating, as is the list of fatalities. Hospitals all along Worrall's route are filling up with dying fever patients, none of whom are responding to treatment. Worrall could be approaching plague proportions soon."

"Plague?" She made a face. "I'm guessing we want to avoid that?"

"By all means," he stated. As much as they were all understandably worried about Pete, he couldn't lose sight of the bigger picture. Worrall and the left-hand glove were a menace, and exactly the kind of threat Warehouse 13 was meant to contain. "Any clue as to where he's heading next?"

"Nada," she replied. "Nobody even remembers seeing him there. I think they're all too busy groaning and puking their guts out."

Artie lost his appetite. "Thanks for that visual." He put away what was left of his donut before pacing back and forth behind Claudia. "Maybe we're going at this the wrong way."

"How do you mean?"

"We know the gloves are being drawn together, and that Worrall is after Nadia's glove. So perhaps we should focus our efforts on finding her?"

Claudia connected the dots. "Because where Nadia is, Worrall is sure to follow."

"With the glove that made Pete sick." Artie wasn't sure which glove they actually needed to cure Pete, but maybe it didn't matter. "Forget Worrall for now. Concentrate on finding Nadia."

"And then?" she asked.

"We'll cross that bridge when we come to it. Find me Nadia—and that glove."

"Sounds like a plan, Stan." She cleared her screen and started over. A blinking cursor awaited her direction. "Let's see, if I was mystical healer with delusions of grandeur, where would I be this weekend?"

"Don't forget," he coached her. "She may be using a new alias or stage name."

"Well, duh. Like I wasn't going to think of that?"

He backed off to give her a little space. Breathing down Claudia's neck was not going to find an answer any faster, or at least he didn't think so. He stretched his weary limbs. His creaking muscles and joints reminded him of just how long he had been at this. He envied Claudia's youth and enthusiasm. She was going to be a great agent someday—if she lasted that long.

"Okay, now. That's more like it!"

Her infectious grin boded well. New Age music

tinkled from her computer's speakers. He rushed back over to her desk.

"What is it? What did you find?"

"Take a gander at this, old man."

She gestured smugly at the monitor, which now displayed a Web site advertising a large psychic fair being held later today in New York's Central Park. OVER 150 PSYCHICS, MYSTICS, SEERS, HEALERS, AND VENDORS! the site proclaimed. AURA READINGS, CHANNELING WORKSHOPS, ANGEL GUIDES, CHAKRA IMAGING, DIVINATION, YOGA, MEDIUMS, AND PAST-LIFE REGRESSION. AN ENLIGHTENING AND SPIRITUALLY UPLIFTING EXPERIENCE FOR ALL OF MOTHER EARTH'S CHILDREN!

More like plenty of careless amateurs meddling in things that should be left alone, Artie thought crankily. He had cleaned up too many messes caused up by well-meaning people tampering with the preternatural. Not everybody knew how to handle their gifts like Leena.

"It says here that thousands of people are expected to attend," Claudia said. "Including a certain up-and-coming psychic healer?"

"Possibly." Artie was impressed by her discovery. This was a promising lead. He skimmed the Web site, perusing the fine print. "Any mention of Nadia or Princess Nefertiti?"

"Not by name," she conceded. "But c'mon, how can she resist a woo-woo-palooza like this? Think of all the people she could heal."

"Yes," he added soberly. "And all the people Calvin Worrall can infect."

The prospect of the gloves converging in Central Park of all places filled Artie with apprehension. This was bigger than just Pete and what might happen to him. This was a potential catastrophe in the making.

Artie's Farnsworth rested on a nearby bookshelf. He snatched it up.

To hell with what time it was on the East Coast. He needed to get hold of Myka.

Before New York City turned into a plague zone.

CHAPTER
14

WAREHOUSE 13

An electronic chirp awoke Claudia, jolting her from a freaky dream involving David Bowie, a computer virus, and the planet Mongo. "No, no, not the boreworms," she murmured groggily before lifting her head from her keyboard. An embarrassing puddle of drool provided forensic evidence that she had dozed off at her desk. She wiped off her cheek as she found herself back in Artie's office. Her computer beeped insistently, making her wish it came with a snooze button. A flashing red icon on the monitor announced that the motion detectors had registered a disturbance down on the Warehouse floor. WARNING: POSSIBLE ARTIFACT ACTIVITY! the message blinked, like a dashboard engine alert. IMMEDIATE ACTION RECOMMENDED.

"Okay, okay." She yawned and rubbed her eyes. Any lingering impressions of the dream receded back into her unconscious. She stuck her tongue out at the computer. "I hear you. Don't have a cow."

"What's the matter?" Artie asked from across the room. He looked up from his Farnsworth, where he seemed to be engaged in updating Myka on their recent discoveries. "Hold on a moment," he told Myka, annoyed by the interruption. His raised eyebrows interrogated Claudia. "Anything serious?"

"Doubtful." She stabbed a key to kill the alarm. Chances were, it was no big deal. The motion detectors were a relatively new addition to the Warehouse's security systems, and they were still working out the bugs. Random energy discharges triggered false alarms way too frequently as far as she was concerned. She didn't want to think about how much of her valuable time she had wasted checking on them. "Probably just another roving ball of static."

"You positive about that?" Artie glanced back and forth between his Farnsworth and the computers, his concentration pulled in two directions. He started to get up from his chair. "Maybe I should—"

"Don't worry about it," Claudia said, hurrying to beat him to the punch. Artie had more important things to worry about right now, like finding Clara Barton's gloves in time to save Pete. She could take care of any minor distractions. "I'm on it."

Her brain hadn't fully woken up yet, so she snagged a Red Bull from the fridge and took a long swig from the can before heading for the door. With any luck, the sugar and caffeine would give her enough of a buzz to check on whatever irritating glitch had given the sensors conniptions. *Talk about lousy timing,* she thought. *Like we don't have bigger fish to harpoon right now?*

"Don't forget your Farnsworth," Artie nagged her. "In case you need to check back with me."

She rolled her eyes. Did he really think she couldn't handle this on her own? She had only done this a zillion times before. "Yes, Mother."

Rummaging around, she located the device beneath a pile of old Civil War casualty reports. The polished black lozenge was not just any Farnsworth; it was Philo's original prototype, which Artie had gifted her with a while ago. It was her prized possession, so she tucked it carefully into the pocket of her denim jacket. Going back to her computer, she noted the coordinates of the disturbance. A roll-out map on one wall offered a row-by-row guide to the Warehouse, complete with handwritten corrections and annotations, and she looked up the address. Just her luck, it was way on the other side of the Warehouse.

One of these days she wanted to install a GPS unit in her Farnsworth, so she could navigate the Warehouse the twenty-first-century way, but Artie had practically blown a gasket the last time she had tinkered under the prototype's hood, so she was stuck relying on the map for now. *Just you wait,* she thought. *I'm gonna upgrade this gizmo eventually.*

Artie kept one eye on her as she got ready. "Let me know right away if there's a problem."

"You just concentrate on helping Myka and Pete." She gulped down the last of Red Bull and chucked the can into an overflowing wastebasket. "Leave this to me."

A door led out to a high gallery overlooking the Warehouse's main floor. Claudia closed it behind her before he could think of something else to kvetch about. It was bad enough that she had to bother with this right now. Artie needed to let it go—for Pete's sake.

She just hoped she wouldn't miss anything important.

The gallery offered a panoramic view of the Warehouse's vast interior, which stretched for miles above and below her. An oversize pair of binoculars, of the coin-operated sort found at scenic vantage points at the Grand Canyon or Mount Rushmore, were mounted on the railing, but she didn't bother using them to search for her destination. She already knew where she was going, more or less.

"Figures." The nuisance would have to be on the other side of anywhere, especially at a time like this. Why couldn't it be a short hop away from the office for once? It would take forever to get there by foot. Good thing there was a faster way across the Warehouse . . . assuming you weren't *too* afraid of heights.

A decrepit keyboard jutted from the brick wall behind her. Claudia entered her password, then keyed in the coordinates. An elaborate gear-and-pulley system responded, manipulating an inclined stainless steel cable that was stretched taut above the main storage area. The mechanism realigned the cable until it was pointed in the right direction. A pulley was suspended upon the cable at the top of the incline. Metal handlebars hung below the pulley.

"Oh, boy." She contemplated the zip line with little enthusiasm; this wasn't exactly her favorite way to get around the Warehouse. "Here we go again."

An upright metal locker rested against the wall. Rusty hinges squeaked as she tugged it open. Protective gear hung inside the locker, and she reluctantly helped herself to a crash helmet, a safety harness, thick leather work gloves, and knee and elbow pads. By the time she put it all on, she looked like she was ready to break up a soccer riot. She closed the locker and approached the zip line. A gap in the railing opened onto empty space. She peeked over the edge and instantly regretted it.

"Okay, that's a loooong way down."

She couldn't believe she was actually doing this while sleep deprived, but how else was she supposed to check on things without it taking all morning? Being careful not to skip a step in the procedure, she clipped the harness to the pulley, then took hold of the handlebars with both hands. She took a deep breath and backed up as much as she could to get a running start. Second, third, and fourth thoughts weighed down her feet, but she mentally consigned them to a garbage file. Pete and Myka were in trouble. She needed to get this over with and get back to the office ASAP, which meant taking a flying leap.

She dashed forward and launched herself off the gallery.

"Up in the air, junior birdman!"

The zip line carried her high above the floor of the Warehouse at a heart-stopping speed; she wished she hadn't been quite so conscientious about keeping the line well lubricated. Her legs dangled freely as she swung back and forth beneath the cable. The airborne descent was both terrifying and exhilarating. An adrenaline rush was more effective than any so-called energy drink. All at once, she wasn't drowsy at all.

Just scared out of her wits.

A bird's-eye view of the Warehouse rushed below her. She slid above towering shelves and elevated metal gantries and catwalks. A labyrinth of overstuffed aisles, vaults, and storage areas, intersecting at seemingly random angles, reminded her of just how ridiculously big and complicated the Warehouse was. Not even Myka could memorize its convoluted layout, although Claudia suspected that Myka had given it her best shot. Amidst the never-ending galleries and archives, Claudia glimpsed a squadron of Air Force bombers (salvaged with great difficulty from the Bermuda Triangle), a fully inflated zeppelin (floating over the postwar extension), a beached cruise liner, the *real* Rosetta stone, a larger-than-life-size fiberglass statue of Paul Bunyan, a Venetian gondola, and even a full-size replica of Leena's Bed-and-Breakfast, complete with turret and shuttered windows. Okay, to be exact, the one in the Warehouse was the original B&B and the one outside Univille was the reproduction, but why split hairs? A Claudia-size hole in the B&B's ceiling, left over from the last time she had (literally) dropped in, had yet to be repaired. One of these days, she really needed to take care of that. . . .

A shadow passed over her.

"What the frak?"

She glanced up quickly. For a split second she thought she glimpsed something out of the corner of her eye, soaring high above her; but when she swiveled her head to get a better look, it was gone . . . like it had never really been there at all.

Had she actually seen anything, or were her tired eyes just playing tricks on her? She was running on minimal sleep after all, and the crash helmet didn't exactly help her peripheral vision. She blinked and shook her head to clear it. Maybe she was just starting at shadows? The Warehouse was full of odd shapes and surprises.

Although they usually weren't quite so far up. . . .

The line slackened as she neared the desired coordinates, reminding her that she needed to concentrate on where she was going. She counted off the corridors and crossings as they zipped by underneath her. The cable sagged, dipping between a row of high shelves until it was only five or six feet above the floor.

Right, she thought. *This is where I get off.*

Grimacing in anticipation, she forced herself to let go of the handlebars, so that only the harness clips were holding her aloft. She grasped twin rip cords. This wasn't going to be fun.

"On second thought, maybe I should have walked. . . ."

She pulled hard on the cords, and the pulley released the harness. Gravity took over where the zip line left off and she plummeted toward the floor. *Roll into the fall,* she reminded herself, just as Myka had tried to teach her, but her gymnastic skills left something to be desired. Her shoulders banged against the floor and she somersaulted head over heels down the corridor before finally landing flat on her back on the hard concrete. The crash jarred a large stuffed swordfish on a shelf above her. It teetered precariously for a second, then toppled over the edge. Her eyes widened as she saw it falling toward her, sword first.

"Yoiks!"

Sheer self-preservation came to her rescue. Moving quickly, she rolled out of the way only seconds before the piscine pike could impale her between the eyes. The fish's freakishly sharp beak pierced the solid concrete floor instead, sending up a shower of luminous sparks, so that the trophy ended up posed upside down with its tail in the air. A handwritten tag stapled to the fish's scaly turquoise fin identified as it as "The One That Got Away."

That was one fish story too many as far as she was concerned.

"Suckity-suck-suck!" she cursed. "There has *got* to be a better way to get around this place!"

The rough landing, and near shish kebabing, left her bruised and breathless. She rolled onto her back, staring up at the distant ceiling while she waited for imaginary cartoon birds to stop circling her skull. Despite the helmet and padding, she felt like she had just been used for batting practice by the entire New York Yankees. Too bad the Warehouse had never heard of workmen's comp, let alone OSHA requirements.

Then again, she thought, falling back on the timeless wisdom of Super Chicken, *I knew the job was dangerous when I took it. . . .*

She clambered stiffly to her feet. Every square inch of her petite frame ached in protest. Forget black-and-blue, she was going to be positively ultraviolet tomorrow. Having no intention of riding the zip line again anytime soon, she took off the helmet and harness and hung them on the inverted swordfish, which made a convenient coatrack.

"Hang on to these for me, will you, Pointy? You don't look like you're going anywhere for a while."

She was more worried about her genuine-collector's-item Farnsworth. Rescuing it from her pocket, she was glad to find the prototype still in one piece; it had clearly been built to last. The burnished steel casing wasn't even scratched.

Let's hear it for old-time American craftsmanship, she thought. *Artie would ground me for life if I broke this.*

She considered checking in with him via the gizmo, but quickly rejected the notion. She had told him she would handle this herself, and that's what she intended to do.

Not that there was probably anything to handle.

Putting away the Farnsworth, she scoped out her surroundings. In theory, the zip line should have dropped her at the right address, give or take a bone-jarring tumble. She glanced around to see precisely where that was.

High shelves packed with boxes, bins, and artifacts could have been anywhere in the Warehouse, yet this particular aisle struck her as oddly familiar. It took her a second to place it, but then she spotted a stale piece of wedding cake under glass on a shelf to her right. The slice, she abruptly recalled, was all that was left of the cake served at the wedding of Queen Victoria and Prince Albert. It reportedly had the power to render almost anyone less than amused. Claudia had inspected the slice very, very recently. She realized at once where she was.

"Holy déjà vu, Batman."

This was the same aisle where she and Leena had been doing inventory a few days ago, right before that static ball nearly fried her. She probably should have recognized the address before, but lack of sleep, a dying friend, and the eminent threat of a killer typhoid epidemic must have distracted her somehow.

Imagine that.

That she was back here again couldn't be a coincidence. Had she accidentally disturbed something the other day, or was the area still kicking up plenty of static? The latter explanation let her off the hook, so she decided to go with it.

"Stupid fireworks. Messing with the motion sensors again."

Seriously, they had to figure out some way to deal with these random energy discharges. Maybe a network of grounded lightning rods, or counter-ionization generators? She had pitched various notions to Artie at least a dozen times, but he'd always blown her off. The way she saw it, he had been living and working in the Warehouse so long that he just accepted the occasional stray lightning ball as an occupational hazard, taking the danger and inconvenience for granted, just like he never wanted to change anything else around here. It was frustrating. She liked Artie, but he could be a real stick-in-the-mud sometimes. She had all sorts of good ideas on how to modernize the Warehouse and its systems, if only he would listen to her.

"What do I have to do around here? Go on strike?"

Grumbling to herself, she stumbled over something on the floor. She caught her balance and turned around to see what had tripped her. A fuzzy charred object, about the size of her fist, rested on the floor, where it obviously didn't belong. Playing it safe, she pulled on a pair of purple gloves before picking up it. She turned it over in her hands.

A blackened human face stared up at her.

"Jumping Jivaro!"

She almost dropped the shrunken head but managed to keep her cool. Holding it at a distance, she examined the out-of-place artifact. The shriveled eyelids were squeezed shut. It smelled like bacon and burnt hair. She shook it gently. "Hello? You awake, little guy?"

To her relief, the head did not react. It appeared to be inactive at the moment, but she bagged it just to be safe. But where had it come from and what had happened to it? Despite its extra-crispy condition, it was cool to the touch, which meant it hadn't been fried too recently. She hung the bag on the swordfish while she tried to figure out where the head belonged.

A tall metal vault was open nearby. She peered into the vacant cavity, which struck her as way too large for one little shrunken head. Glancing around, she spotted an empty space on a shelf across from the vault. A slick red puddle had formed atop the shelf and was now dripping over the edge. A draft carried a sickeningly salty aroma.

Claudia's nose wrinkled in disgust. Was that actually . . . blood?

That couldn't be good.

She cautiously approached the shelf. A crimson drop fell onto the gory puddle, and she traced its origin to an overflowing marble bathtub one level up, which was itself directly below . . . John Chapman's overturned pot-slash-hat. Apple cider dripped from the pot into the tub, which overflowed onto the empty shelf where the shrunken head must have been. A torn electrical cable had been gnawed apart.

"Jinkies."

Darting eyes reconstructed the entire, improbable Rube Goldberg scenario. This was what happened sometimes when you piled so many unpredictable artifacts in one place; in a way, it was a minor miracle that they didn't get more accidental chain reactions. Had this one been playing out ever since she and Leena had called it quits the other day? How long had it taken to fill up Elizabeth Báthory's bloody tub?

Long enough, apparently.

The rolling metal ladder was right where she'd left it. Anxious to put things right before another artifact got triggered, she shoved the ladder into place. A quick dash up the steps brought her to Johnny Appleseed's capsized pot, which was lying on its side. The cider dripping from the pot was a lot less gross than the blood spilling from the tub below. Hopefully, she could staunch one flow by fixing the other. All she needed to do was set the pot right side up again . . . just like so.

She made sure the pot was resting securely this time. The cider stopped dripping into the tub below. There would be no more trickling transubstantiation.

"Okay, that's better."

They'd have to drain the Blood Countess's tub later. Artie couldn't stand the sight of blood, so she was surely going to get stuck with the job, but she figured that could wait until she could put on a full hazmat suit sometime—or maybe talk Leena into helping her. The tub wasn't overflowing anymore. That was enough for now, right?

She surveyed the scene from the top of the ladder. Had she missed anything? She traced the disturbance from the pot to the tub to the shrunken head to the gnawed wires to . . . the empty metal vault? What was supposed to be in there, anyway? She squinted but couldn't make out the label from atop the steps. One thing was sure: the missing artifact had been *big*.

Maybe it was time to update Artie? She took out her Farnsworth, then hesitated. How exactly was she going to explain this to him? On second thought, perhaps she should go check out the vault first, just to find out how much trouble she might be in. The more information she had, the less upset Artie would be . . . hopefully.

"Please, let it not be anything *too* dangerous. Like maybe an arthritic old mummy or something?"

Another shadow fell over her. A bizarre caterwauling that sounded like a roar, a growl, and a squawk blended together nearly caused her to jump out of her skin. She looked up in time to see a huge winged creature swooping at her.

"Yikes!"

Her reflexes were on a roll today. She ducked in time to escape the sharpened claws or talons passing directly over her head. Another few inches and she would have been scalped by whatever had dived for her. But the surprise attack startled her enough that her Farnsworth slipped from her fingers. It crashed to the floor several feet below.

Exposed and vulnerable atop the ladder, she

scrambled down the steps and took cover beneath the rolling metal stairs. "What the pterodactyl was that?" She peered up through the metal slats at what appeared to be . . . a totem pole?

The carved Native American objet d'art circled above her like an immense timber bird of prey. Red-and-black paint colored the bestial heads and bodies of a thunderbird, a mountain lion, and a grizzly bear, stacked atop each other like some sort of weird surgical hybrid. Ten clawed limbs were extended below the tripartite beast. Its wingspan was at least ten feet across. Three pairs of feral eyes glared down at Claudia. The bear and the lion bared their respective fangs. A hooked beak snapped at the air.

Not a friendly relic, she was guessing.

The bird cawed loudly. Defying both aeronautics and gravity, the totem soared high above the shelves. Claudia glanced over at the open vault, which was just the right size. She figured there was a reason the vicious-looking totem was kept locked up.

"Okay," she asked herself. "Now what?"

There was no point in calling for help. The Warehouse was too big and Artie's office too far away. Even if he could hear her, which was highly unlikely, he'd need a telescope to see what was going on all the way out here. She might as well be on the far side of the moon.

Where was her Farnsworth? Peeking around the side of the ladder, she spotted it lying on the floor too many feet away. She kicked herself for dropping it before. Now how was she supposed to send out an SOS? The totem was still on the lookout overhead, its claws and talons ready to slash at her again. The Farnsworth taunted her, tantalizingly out of reach. Should she risk making a dash for it?

The totem didn't give her a chance. With an ear-piercing squawk and a couple of roars, it swooped down at her again. The bear on the bottom slammed into the top of the stairs and it spun away from Claudia, leaving her exposed. The ladder's wheels collided with the fallen Farnsworth and knocked it under a shelf, where it disappeared from sight. Her heart sank.

"Really? My karma's *that* bad?"

So much for calling for help. No way was the totem going to give her a chance to go digging around under the shelf, groping for the lost device. Running for her life took priority at the moment.

Hands over her head, she sprinted down the aisle. Adrenaline kicked her into gear. High above her, the totem executed a graceful turn and came gliding after her, the thunderbird's wooden talons extended ahead of its snapping beak. Claudia wondered which part of the totem was the hungriest: the bear, the puma, or the bird?

"No fair!" she protested. "Three against one . . . sort of!"

She tried not to panic. It was just an artifact, after all, albeit a particularly antisocial one. There were ways of handling it. What would Artie do at a time like this? She looked around frantically for the nearest emergency neutralizing station. There had to be one somewhere around here, just for unfortunate incidents like this. She remembered Artie pointing them out the first time he gave her the nickel tour.

"Searching, searching . . . there!"

What looked like a coiled fire hose hung upon a

support column, next to a circular metal handle. NEU-
TRALIZING STATION, a convenient label read. FOR EMERGENCY
USE ONLY.

Just what the doctor ordered! She made a beeline for
the hose and tugged on it with both hands. The dusty
hose refused to budge; it probably hadn't moved in years.
"C'mon," she pleaded with the stubborn mechanism.
"Don't be like that! Not now!" A hard yank finally got it
unspooling. Squeaky gears whined for oil as she pulled
the hose away from the pillar. "That's it, baby. Keep on
coming!"

The totem dived at her. Talons, claws, and fangs
raced each other to rend her tender flesh. The thunderbird's fearsome screech hurt her ears. The bear and the
mountain lion were eager for their turn. Their gaping
jaws slathered impossibly.

But Claudia was ready for them. She aimed the hose
at the oncoming creature, holding it up with one hand
while the other spun the metal handle next to it. The valve
stuck at first, but then it rotated freely, opening the tap. A
pump beneath the floor chugged to life. The hose stiffened
in her grip. Instead of water, a thick stream of purple goo
sprayed from its nozzle.

"That's more like it!" She directed the goo at the
totem. "Open wide!"

Easier said than done. The totem banked sharply
to the left, dodging the spray while still coming at her.
Claudia gulped, finding it harder than she expected to
control the spray and send it where it belonged. She was
a geek girl, darn it, not a firefighter! Claudia felt like she
was trying to shoot down an angry hornet with a squirt

gun. Why couldn't the stupid totem just stay still for a moment? Didn't it know she was trying to neutralize it?

The Indian arts-and-crafts project flew in descending circles above her. Claudia spun around, practically wrapping herself in the hose as she tried unsuccessfully to catch the totem in the purple spew. Cawing and snarling in harmony, the hostile artifact dived for her. She jumped out of the way and swung the hose around to defend herself. The totem veered away from the spray. The mountain lion's front paw slashed at a length of hose between her and the column. Sharp claws sliced through the hose. Unchecked goo gushed onto the floor.

"Uh-oh."

CHAPTER
15

WAREHOUSE 13

The severed end of the hose went limp in her grasp. The spray from the nozzle slowed to a trickle. Claudia shook it violently, but only a few drips fell out.

You know, she thought, *I don't remember this being covered in the manual.*

The totem came swooping back around. She hurled the now-useless hose at the creature like an old-time TV mobster flinging his empty gun at Superman—and with about as much effect. The nozzle bounced harmlessly off the thunderbird's crest, barely slowing it down.

"Feet, don't fail me now!"

She made tracks away from the totem. A spreading puddle of goo threatened to slip her up, but she bounded over it without missing a step. An intersection beckoned, and she ducked around a corner in hopes of losing the creature . . .

. . . only to run headfirst into a full-size New England lighthouse.

The whitewashed brick structure rose at least fifty feet above the floor, dwarfing the surrounding shelves.

A red steel cupola crowned the lighthouse, whose upper chamber was dark, its lamp long extinguished. The tower blocked the aisle completely. There was no way around it.

"Great," she muttered. "What genius left a lighthouse lying around?"

The totem was right behind her. A weathered wooden door faced her.

The only way out was up.

"Please don't be locked!"

She shoved the door, which swung open before her. She darted over the threshold and slammed the door shut behind her. The totem crashed into it a moment later, the impact rattling the heavy oak door. Frustrated growls and squawks penetrated the building. Claws scraped angrily at the wood.

The totem wasn't giving up. Claudia threw herself against the other side of the door, holding it shut with her body. The soles of her sneakers were braced against the rough cement floor of the lighthouse. The creature pounded against the door like a battering ram. Every blow jarred her spine. The solid oak bulged inward. The hinges started tearing loose.

She searched the murky interior of the building for something to bolt the door with. A spiral staircase led to the lamp room above. A few cobwebbed trunks and coils of rope offered little hope. By the time she could shove the jumbled jetsam against the door, the totem would already be inside.

"Go away!" she shouted through the door. "Find somebody else to harass! Shoo!"

Wood splintered. A lion's claw tore through the door, only a handsbreadth from her head. Another claw, this one belonging to the bear, broke through next to her hip.

Yelping, she jumped away from the door, which was knocked off its hinges. The shredded remains of the door crashed to the floor. The totem lunged forward, but its outstretched wings were too big for the opening. Screeching impatiently, it had to back up and fold its wings against its sides in order to squeeze through the narrow doorway.

Claudia took advantage of the delay to make for the staircase. She took the steps two at a time, the decrepit iron structure wobbling beneath her tread. The totem burst into the lighthouse right behind her. Three sets of carved wooden nostrils sniffed the air. Painted eyes turned upward, spotting its prey. The totem dropped onto its bear and lion legs, then charged up the stairs on all eights. The thunderbird led the way, its wooden feathers ruffling. The monster climbed the staircase with surprising speed. Bird, lion, and bear moved in sync with each other, much to Claudia's annoyance.

Did they *have* to work together so well?

She reached the top of the stairs only slightly ahead of the totem. A glass-walled chamber held the lamp and lenses. A complicated array of polished silver mirrors surrounded an old-fashioned kerosene lantern. She flung the door shut and bolted it securely.

Taking a second to catch her breath, she considered her options. Was there any way to use the lighthouse to signal Artie for help? She quickly inspected the lantern but couldn't figure out how she was supposed to light it. Claudia didn't smoke, but even if she did, smoking was strictly verboten in the Warehouse. She had no matches, no lighter, not even a pair of sticks to rub together. Why couldn't this stupid lighthouse have come with an electric lamp instead . . . ?

She searched her pockets anyway, hoping to find a miniature soldering iron or something, but time was not on her side. Triple growls announced that the totem had reached the top of the stairs. It rammed itself against the door once more. The hinges went flying off.

Drat!

A open metal gallery circled the lantern room. She rushed out onto the balcony and leaned over the safety rail, looking for an escape route. The top of a tall shelf was only a few yards below, but separated from the lighthouse by a gap of at least five feet. She scrambled over the railing and faced the gap. Could she make the jump? It was a long way down if she missed, and this time there was no zip line to hold her up. She peered over the edge.

I don't know about this. . . .

The relentless totem didn't give her any choice. Glass shattered as it crashed through the window behind her. She could feel the thunderbird's hot breath at her neck. It smelled of sawdust.

"Geronimo!"

Trusting her fate to the fickle whims of gravity, she leaped from the balcony. Her life flashed before her eyes as though dancing across a certain zoetrope several aisles over. She closed her eyes, afraid to look down, and didn't open them until her feet hit the shelf a long heartbeat later. She fell forward into a roll, then sprang to her feet, frankly amazed not to find herself spattered way down below. A dislodged birdcage hit the floor instead. It landed with a loud metallic clang. *Better it than me,* Claudia thought.

"And she sticks the landing!"

She would have an appreciated a moment to savor her death-defying feat, but the grumpy totem refused to oblige. The bear snarled at her from atop the lighthouse. The thunderbird spread its wings and took flight. The entire monster swooped down from the balcony.

"Ohmigod," she exclaimed. "Give it a rest!"

This routine system check was turning into a real workout. She ran along the top of the shelf, jumping over and around the topmost collection of artifacts as though the shelf were the world's most cluttered balance beam. She deftly evaded Bill Clinton's saxophone, only to step onto a loose waffle iron, which slid out from beneath her sneaker. Oops! She lost her balance and teetered along the brink. Her arms semaphored madly to keep her from falling. Both feet landed back on the shelf. She gasped out loud. That had been a close one.

A few more inches and she would have been a Claudia pancake.

She kicked the waffle iron out of the way. Glancing back over her shoulder, she saw the totem gliding toward her again. She looked around for something—anything—that might increase her odds of reaching drinking age.

A judge's gavel? A ventriloquist's dummy? A chunk of Halley's comet?

None of those struck her as very useful at the moment. To buy time, she snatched an artist's easel and hurled it at the totem. Growling at the top of his timber lungs, the mountain lion knocked it aside with a sweep of its paw. The lightweight wooden easel crashed to earth twenty feet below. Claudia winced at the clatter.

"Sorry, Artie," she blurted. "You, too, Renoir."

The totem was still coming. Was there anything else she could use? She was running out of shelf and hope until she spied a large wooden barrel stacked at the end of the shelf. Sturdy pine staves were held in place by rusty metal bands. A postcard of Niagara Falls was stapled to the side of the barrel. The faded souvenir showed a smiling daredevil in turn-of-the-century swimming trunks emerging from the very same barrel as Niagara cascaded majestically behind him. He had clearly just survived a reckless plunge over the fabled falls.

The things people do to make history . . .

A wild idea hit her. Wresting the lid off the top of the barrel, she dived inside just as the thunderbird's talons nearly grazed her again. Bear and lion claws barely missed her as well. Watching her fingers, she pulled the lid down and worked it back into place. The barrel was cramped and dark and smelled of pickles but was big enough for her to huddle inside. Peering out through a crack between the staves, she glimpsed the totem circling around for another go. Her northwestern nemesis obviously had no intention of abandoning the hunt.

She knew better than to expect the barrel to protect her for long. Memories of the totem clawing through the lighthouse doors were still disgustingly fresh in her mind. But maybe the barrel could provide a way out? After all, if it could survive going over the falls . . .

There was no time to think about it. Bracing her knees and shoulders against the inside of the barrel, she rocked back and forth while doing her best to ignore the squawk-growl-roars getting louder by the moment. The totem sounded like it was right on top of her.

Inertia held the barrel stubbornly in place. She threw her full weight, such as it was, against the left side of the barrel, finally producing the desired result. The barrel tilted to one side, then toppled over the edge of the shelf. It plunged toward the floor with Claudia inside. Her stomach climbed up her throat. Wincing in anticipation, she curled up into a tight little ball and braced for impact. If only there had been time to read the instructions . . . !

What if the barrel just magically pickled cucumbers or something?

It hit the floor with a resounding thud but, miraculously, not enough to flatten her. As she had hoped, the artifact had somehow shielded her from the full force of the crash landing, just as it had for that thrill seeker at Niagara back in the day. No bones appeared to be broken.

So far.

Landing on its side, the barrel rolled wildly down an unknown aisle. Claudia tumbled inside like a load of laundry in a spin dryer. "Ouch, ouch, triple ouch!" she yelped every time she smacked against the inside of the barrel. Thank goodness she was still wearing those knee and elbow pads from before, but she found herself longing for the discarded crash helmet. Her bruises were getting bruises. Not to mention splinters.

Just when she thought the thrill ride was never going to end, the barrel, well, barreled into something solid and unyielding, bringing it to a brutal stop. She caught her breath and took a moment to let her head stop spinning, then kicked the lid off the barrel. Woozy as a punch-drunk fighter, yet stoked to be alive, she crawled out of the barrel on her hands and knees. A quick look around revealed that the barrel had come to a stop against a tall obsidian obelisk engraved with arcane Celtic runes. The imposing monument reeked of antiquity and bygone pagan rites.

She didn't have a clue what it was.

Claudia climbed unsteadily to her feet. For a few minutes the entire Warehouse seemed to whirl around her like a vomit comet. She leaned against the obelisk to keep from falling.

"Wow," she gasped "What a rush!"

A sudden desire to do it again came over her. As her surroundings gradually stopped rotating, she gazed up at the surrounding shelves, wondering how she could get the barrel back up to the top again. Maybe if she rigged up some kind of block and tackle apparatus?

"Whoa!" she blurted, catching herself. *What the heck am I thinking?*

She cast a suspicious glance at the barrel, lying oh-so-innocently next to the obelisk. It had kept her safe going over the edge, sure, but what was the catch? Most artifacts came with a sting, and she had a sneaky feeling that she was experiencing the flip side of the barrel's special properties right now. Besides saving your life, did it also turn you into a danger junkie?

It sure felt like it. Even knowing better, it was all she could do to keep from climbing back inside the barrel for another spin. Maybe there were some basement stairs around here somewhere? She could ride the barrel all the way down. . . .

A blood-chilling growl snapped her out it. She slapped herself across the face, just to be sure, then looked around anxiously for the totem. The tripartite terror was nowhere in sight, but she could hear it snarling a short way back. It sounded way too close for comfort.

Escape was still the order of the day. The obelisk rested at the center of a four-way intersection, but which way to go. Left? Right? Straight ahead? Turning around was not an option, not with the totem right behind her.

"Eenie, meenie . . ."

Choosing at random, she dashed to the right, trying to put as much distance as possible between her and the barrel. This was her chance, she realized, to give the indefatigable totem the slip.

With any luck, the darn thing wouldn't know which way she went!

The totem pole hunted for its flame-haired prey. Gliding low down the halls of this strange, immense longhouse, it spied the wooden barrel lying out of place beside a spire of polished black rock. The hunter recognized the barrel as the one the girl had rode to elude it before. It snarled at the memory.

The creature touched down upon the floor. Lion and Bear took turns sniffing the barrel, while Bird peered inside. The man-made nest was empty now; their prey had fled the barrel, although her enticing scent lingered. Six nostrils flared. Three sets of jaws watered. It had been caged for too long. Three empty stomachs craved human meat. It licked its fangs.

Turning away from the barrel, the totem inspected the crossroad before it. All three heads sniffed the air, trying to catch the girl's scent, but the great longhouse was filled with too many confusing odors. Bear turned left. Lion looked right. Bird flapped its wings and tried to fly straight ahead, only to be held back by the other two. It cawed indignantly.

Conflicting intentions halted the totem, which found itself pulling in three directions at once. For a brief interval it appeared frozen in indecision, unable to reach a consensus. Then a harsh, wrenching sound, like creaking timbers, echoed off the crowded shelves. Joined for generations, the stacked creatures strained against each other. Determined growls and screeches added to the cacophony. Painted wood cracked and splintered like bones.

Bird broke free first. It tore loose from Lion's shoulders, taking flight on its own. It swooped and soared overhead, enjoying its newfound liberty. No longer encumbered by the upper carving, Lion and Bear fought and pulled in opposite directions before tearing noisily apart. Lion sprang from atop Bear, landing nimbly upon the floor. The beasts growled and roared in triumph. Not bothering to bid farewell to their former partners, they split away from each other.

Bear lumbered to the left.

Lion bounded to the right.

Bird circled above the intersection once more before soaring straight ahead.

It was a race now.

Winner take all.

CHAPTER 16

FAIRFIELD HOSPITAL

"Psychic Fair. Central Park. Got it." Myka peeked at her watch. "If I hurry, I can be there in a couple of hours. Maybe less if the traffic's not too bad."

"Good," Artie replied. His grizzled visage filled the screen of her Farnsworth. "But watch out for Worrall. I can't stress enough how dangerous he's becoming."

"You don't need to remind me of that."

She had been sitting at Pete's bedside all night. Vanessa had offered to give her a break, and Mrs. Frederic had even reserved a room for Myka at a nearby hotel, but she had been unable to tear herself away from the quarantined hospital room. He was her partner. It didn't feel right to leave him alone at a time like this. She knew he'd do the same for her.

"No, I suppose I don't." Artie tried to peer past Myka via the Farnsworth. He lowered his voice. "How is he doing?"

Her throat tightened. "Not good."

Pete stirred restlessly in the hospital bed. He had already sweated through several sets of sheets. A damp compress, laid across his brow, failed to ameliorate his fever, which was still well over a hundred degrees Fahrenheit. Frequent saline infusions fought a losing battle against dehydration. His pulse rate was erratic. There was no sign of internal hemorrhaging yet, but, according to Vanessa, that was only a matter of time. . . .

"I see." Artie didn't press her for details. "Then you had better get on your way. Claudia and I will be in touch if we find out anything more." He glanced around his office like he was looking for someone. "What's taking her, anyway?"

Myka wasn't sure where Claudia was supposed to be, but that was hardly her top concern at the moment. She'd let Artie wrangle his apparently wayward apprentice.

"Thanks for the lead," she told him. At least she finally had a name to go with Calvin Worrall's pallid face, and a new place to start looking for the gloves. That was something. "I knew I could count on you and Claudia."

"Just find those gloves." Artie looked as worried as she had ever seen him. "Before Worrall infects thousands of innocent people."

No pressure there, Myka thought. But she was up to the challenge. She had once been responsible for protecting the life of the president of the United States. High stakes had never daunted her.

Especially not when Pete's life was also on the line.

She had already lost one partner in her life. Sam Martino had been killed in a shoot-out in Denver a few years ago, while attempting to apprehend a would-be presidential assassin. Myka had blamed herself for

Sam's death for a long time. She'd be damned if she'd let another partner die on her watch.

"Sorry, Pete," she whispered as she rose to her feet. Her back was sore from sitting in the chair all night. She put the Farnsworth away. "I've got to go."

"Not without me," he said hoarsely.

His voice startled her. She had thought he was out cold. He had been murmuring deliriously just a few hours ago. Mostly about his ex-girlfriend Kelly . . . and cookies.

"Pete?"

His eyes fluttered open. They were sunken and bloodshot, reminding her far too much of Worrall's ghoulish orbs. Flinching, he pulled himself up to a sitting position. He clutched his stomach in pain. The blinking monitors reported an elevated heart rate. His lips were gray.

"You heard Artie," he grunted. "We've got a psychic fair to crash."

Had he been listening in on Artie's briefing? "How much did you hear?"

"Enough." He fumbled clumsily with the metal rail around his bed. Stubble carpeted his jaw. "Nadia's likely to make a surprise appearance at Central Park, which means that this Worrall dude's bound to be there too. Good. I owe that freak some serious payback."

Lowering the rail, he swung his legs over the edge of the bed. The effort exhausted him and he teetered precariously. Myka rushed forward to catch him before he fell.

"Pete?" She propped him up and looked urgently into

his eyes. "I don't think this is a good idea. You need to lie down and let me handle this."

"Not going to happen, Myka." He inhaled deeply, trying to rally whatever strength he had left. An outgoing breath wheezed from his lungs. "No way am I missing this shindig."

"But you're sick," she protested. "You have stage three typhoid fever. You want to do something, I understand that, but please, you've got to be reasonable."

"Says who?" He managed a pained smile. "This is me you're talking to, remember? Since when have I ever been reasonable?"

Granted, that was not a word one often used to describe Pete. She liked to think of herself as the reasonable one . . . which was why she had to talk some sense into him.

"Let me call Vanessa," she volunteered. "Maybe she can explain why you need to stay in the hospital."

She reached for the call button, but he grabbed her wrist. His hand was hot and clammy.

"Vanessa can't help me. We both know that. Only the gloves can."

"I can get the gloves," she pleaded. "I promise."

"They won't do me any good if you're hundreds of miles away and can't get back to me in time. I need to be there when you find them. Otherwise, it might be too late."

He had a point. Pete was running out of time and Central Park was hours away. What if she couldn't get back to Fairfield fast enough?

"But you're in no shape to take on Worrall or Nadia, let alone both of them. It's too dangerous."

He shrugged. "Beats lying around waiting to die." He tugged the IV from his arm. A thin stream of saline sprayed onto the sheets before he clipped off the flow. "C'mon, Myka. Give me a fighting chance."

Was that just his pride talking, or did he deserve a chance to go out swinging? It was true that he didn't have much to lose.

"I'm not sure," she admitted.

"Look," he said, "you know me. If you don't take me with you, I'm going to find a way to get there on my own. So what's it going to be, Mykes? You going to force a sick man to hitchhike to NYC on his lonesome?"

The scary thing was, she could actually see him trying.

She wavered. "Are you sure you're up to it?"

"Just try to keep up."

Myka realized that his mind was made up. She gave in reluctantly. "Okay, but I'm driving. No arguments."

"Deal." He looked down at his flimsy hospital gown. "So, I got a change of clothes around here anywhere? I don't exactly feel like saving the world with my butt hanging out."

She smiled despite herself. That was Pete all right.

"I think Central Park would just as soon avoid that too." She headed over to the closet, where his suit was hanging. "Let me see what I can do."

There was a hesitant knock at the door. It didn't sound like Vanessa returning. Myka went to the door and opened it. "Hello?"

A male orderly stood outside, holding a long rectangular box. A surgical mask covered his face. Goggles protected his eyes. The rest of his body was tucked inside some hermetically sealed blue scrubs, the better to brave the quarantine zone. He fidgeted nervously, like he was anxious to move on, and declined to actually step into the room. The paper mask muffled his voice.

"Package for Agent Lattimer."

A puzzled expression furrowed her brow. She eyed the box curiously. It was postmarked South Dakota.

Funny, she thought. *Artie didn't say anything about a package.*

"That's for me," Pete called from the bed. A coughing jag momentarily delayed his explanation. "Something I ordered from the Warehouse. Just in case."

WAREHOUSE 13

"Claudia?"

Artie stuck his head out the back door of his office. He peered impatiently at his watch. What on earth was taking so long? She should have taken care of that alert and gotten back to the office at least half an hour ago. Myka and Pete were already en route to Central Park. Now was no time for Claudia to go wandering off. Didn't she realize how serious the situation was?

Exasperated, he shut the door and retrieved his Farnsworth from his desk. Had she remembered to take hers as instructed? A quick rummage around her work area didn't turn it up, but that was less than conclusive. Their efforts to track down Clara Barton's gloves and their current owners had left the office even more littered with notes and documents than usual. Claudia's Farnsworth—the original, he reminded himself—could well be buried beneath the clutter. And the girl herself could hardly be counted on to follow his directions, no matter how sensible they were.

"She never listens to me," he muttered irritably.

He switched on his own Farnsworth and tuned it to her frequency. The screen remained blank, and after about a dozen buzzes he gave up. If she did have Philo's prototype on her person, she wasn't answering. Who knew why. He had no idea what went through her head sometimes.

All right, then. There was always the PA system. He didn't often resort to it, but it had been installed for a reason. In theory, she should be within earshot of one of the mounted loudspeakers, which were mostly used for recorded announcements in the event of emergencies. Like a possible meltdown, for instance.

An open Yellow Book was lying on top of the intercom. He nudged it aside and leaned over the mike. His index finger jabbed the SPEAK button.

"Paging Claudia Donovan." His impatient voice boomed throughout the Warehouse. "Please check in immediately—if you're not too busy, that is!"

Staying up all night, searching for leads, had left him cranky and irritable. Yawning, he wished he had time for a quick nap. Was that what had happened to Claudia? Had she dozed off somewhere? He frowned.

She had better not be catching forty winks in the Procrustean Bed. . . .

"Claudia?" He turned up the volume on the PA system. "Yoo-hoo, Claudia? This is your boss speaking!"

There was no response, by Farnsworth, phone, or any other means.

"Oh, for heaven's sakes," he grumbled. "Of all times for her to pull a vanishing act . . ."

Apparently there was nothing to be done but to go looking for her, as if he didn't have better things to do. He slogged over to her computer and checked on the alert himself. To his dismay, multiple red icons flashed upon the screen, which meant that the motion detectors were going crazy all over Sector Delta 373. Claudia had placed the security program on mute, probably to keep it from bothering him in her absence, but when he restarted it, a chorus of agitated beeps assaulted his ears. The Warehouse was unhappy.

Maybe this was more serious than he thought?

A worried look displaced his irritated scowl. Claudia could be surprisingly resourceful for her age, but what if she had run into something she couldn't handle? The Warehouse was not without hazards, as he knew better than anyone else. Or at least, anyone still in one piece.

Silencing the alarms once more, he rushed out onto the gallery. At first glance, there didn't appear to be any commotion on the main floor of the Warehouse, but who knew what might be transpiring in its innumerable nooks and crannies. He noticed at once that the zip line had been deployed, presumably by Claudia on her way out to investigate the disturbance. He briefly considered retracting the pulley and using it himself, but decided against it. It had been a long night and he didn't feel like emulating Tarzan on zero sleep. *Which reminds me,* he thought, *I need to follow up on Johnny Weissmuller's original loincloth when this is all over.* Rumor was, it was going to auction soon.

Choosing an alternative means of transportation, he scurried down several flights of stairs to where a one-of-a-kind vehicle was parked. Thomas Edison's electric automobile resembled an antique luggage cart with seating for four. A pair of padded benches rested atop a stripped-down, rudimentary chassis minus any sort of exterior body. Brass handrails faced the seats. One of the original architects of the current Warehouse, Edison had built the prototype for Henry Ford but had donated it to the Warehouse after Ford decided to stick with the internal combustion engine. Not for the first time, Artie regretted Ford's lack of foresight. The polar ice caps would be in much better shape today if the auto tycoon had only listened to the Wizard of Menlo Park.

Artie climbed into the backseat behind the steering wheel. Ideally, the old-time flivver could be powered by the bioelectric energy of at least two passengers, whose vital spark was channeled into the auto's transmission by gripping the front handrail. One person alone, however, did not provide enough juice to get the wheels turning. For solo excursions, a regular car battery was required. Conveniently, one was already hooked up.

Yellow hard hats hung on pegs near the auto. Artie put one on for safety's sake.

Considering its age, the electric cart warmed up with admirable ease. He steered it in the direction indicated by the alerts. He had barely needed to consult the map before. After forty years, he knew the basic layout of the Warehouse like the back of his hand, although, like his hand, the Warehouse kept developing new and unexpected wrinkles.

Driving at top speed—which, alas, was only about fifty miles an hour—he headed across the Warehouse. As he did so, he instinctively scanned the shelves to see if anything was awry. He was relieved to see that the Red Velvet Swing was not swinging at the moment, and that Keats's Grecian urn was right where it belonged, ensuring the safety of grandmothers everywhere. Sealed crates and banker's boxes appeared undisturbed. A pencil sharpener, an iron trivet, and a souvenir ashtray were reassuringly inert, as was a rocking chair that had once belonged to Whistler's mother. The Oaxaca Piñata remained unbroken. The final square on a turn-of-the-century, Currier & Ives Advent calender had not been opened.

Thank heavens!

He started to relax, easing his grip on the wheel. Maybe nothing was seriously wrong and Claudia was simply taking her own sweet time. He had thought she appreciated the urgency of the situation, but not everyone could be as focused as he had to be. Even Pete and Myka were relatively inexperienced by his standards. "Kids these days," he muttered. "If you want something done right . . ."

He neared the sector in question. The missing apprentice was nowhere to be seen.

"Claudia!" He cupped a hand around his mouth to form a megaphone. "Answer me if you can. I'm not getting any younger!"

A low growl responded. It did not sound remotely like Claudia.

"Oh, no," Artie murmured. A menagerie of dreadful

possibilities stampeded through his imagination before a large ursine shape lumbered into view. The creature reared up on hind legs carved from the base of a massive log. Red eyes and jaws painted a bestial portrait. Jagged fore claws slashed the air. Artie swallowed hard. "How did you . . . ?"

He recognized the beast at once, naturally. It was the infamous Nisqually Totem Pole, or at least its bottom third. The artifact's gruesome history came back to him. The sacred pole, enraged at the slaughter of its tribe by white prospectors, had massacred an entire frontier settlement back in 1848. . . .

But what was it doing on the loose in the Warehouse in this day and age? It was supposed to be locked up safely in its vault.

Only a few rows away from here.

"Of course." He slapped his forehead. "I should have seen this coming."

Claudia's inexplicable absence suddenly made sense, but he had only a moment to fear for her safety before self-preservation moved to the top of his agenda. The wooden grizzly dropped onto all fours and charged at him with alarming speed. A full-throated roar made clear its intentions, as if its documented body count were not unnerving enough. This was no cuddly teddy bear, like the one in the Roosevelt collection; it was pure animal fury.

Time for evasive action, Artie realized.

Yanking hard on the wheel, Artie spun the cart around. The narrow corridor made a U-turn difficult, and he accidentally knocked over a stack of wooden packing crates. The boxes made a huge racket as they avalanched to the floor. He hoped there was nothing particularly fragile and/or lethal inside the crates, but there was no time to check. Squealing tires laid down rubber as he peeled away from the bear, which chased after him with bloodthirsty fervor.

Artie shifted the flivver into high gear, pushing the battery-powered auto to its limits. He glanced back over his shoulder to see the grizzly gaining on him. The bear was trouble enough, but he couldn't help wondering where the rest of the totem pole—the puma and the thunderbird—were lurking. His gaze darted from side to side, then turned upward, keeping an eye out for the bear's savage accomplices. He had to assume they were on the prowl as well.

The more the merrier, he groused. *Like I really have time for this!*

The auto reached the end of a corridor. He took a tight left turn, trying to shake the bear, but the creature had his scent now and was not about to abandon the hunt. Keeping one hand on the wheel, Artie reached beneath his jacket for his Tesla, only to discover that he had left it in his office. He mentally chastised himself for not thinking to bring it along. Was lack of sleep to blame, or had he simply had what Claudia insisted on calling a senior moment?

"Hardly," he grumbled. "It just slipped my mind."

Regardless, he was going to have to improvise.

He mentally mapped out the area in his head. The canned food aisle was right around the corner and he accelerated through it, hoping that perhaps the various preternatural delicacies on display might distract the hungry grizzly . . . and maybe even give it a serious belly-ache. The assorted tin cans, bottled preserves, and freeze-dried treats lined up on the shelves looked deceptively harmless and maybe even tempting, but most of these edible artifacts were more than enough to make the carved bear wish that it had never awoken from hibernation. Just wait, Artie thought, until the grizzly took a bite of those sardines from the Shackleton Expedition, or gulped down the original can of worms. . . .

Either foodstuff, or any number of their shelf mates, would have settled the bear's hash nicely, but no such luck. Intent on devouring Artie, the grizzly thundered past the dangerous goodies without even giving the crammed shelves a sideways glance. Apparently, it had its timber heart set on human prey.

On the bright side, the bear's voracious appetite gave Artie reason to hope that it hadn't snacked on Claudia yet. Not that there was much meat on the teen to begin with. Especially split three ways.

Don't even think like that, he scolded himself. Claudia had survived the Warehouse's more temperamental side before. She could do it again. *I haven't wasted all this time babysitting just to let her get eaten by a peckish totem pole!*

The pantry aisle came to an end. Artie racked his mind for another stratagem. There had to be a way out of this primeval predicament. The Warehouse held many hazards, but its spacious confines also hid the occasional much-needed miracle.

You just needed to know where to look.

Shrewd eyes scanned the shelves as he sped the

flivver down another corridor. Familiar landmarks, like the zeppelin on the horizon, helped keep him oriented. His brain ran through the inventory, searching for something that would serve as a grizzly deterrent. What else was there in this vicinity?

Reagan's jelly beans? Van Gogh's ear? The seventy-six trombones?

None of those were going to do him any good right now, but what about . . .

"That's it!"

The ideal solution was right up ahead. He just needed to get there before he became bear chow.

Unfortunately, the rampaging beast was practically breathing down his neck. If the flivver had possessed an exhaust pipe, which it didn't, the grizzly would have been choking on the fumes. The artifact in question was still several yards away. Artie realized he wasn't going to make it there unless he did something drastic.

And extremely uncomfortable.

I'm going to regret this tomorrow.

Shifting gears, he slammed the cart into reverse. The auto sped backward on a collision course with the bear. Flinching, Artie hurled himself from the driver's seat. He hit the floor hard, rolling across the rough concrete. The hard hat protected his skull, but his glasses went flying. He could only hope they wouldn't break.

Less than ten feet behind him, the flivver crashed into the bear. Its rear bumper crumpled against the grizzly's burly forequarters. Unfazed by the impact, the bear swiped the auto with its paw, flipping the cart onto its side. The crunching of abused metal made Artie cringe;

he hated seeing any artifact damaged. Repairing the antique vehicle was not going to be cheap. There went next month's maintenance budget.

Provided he lived to worry about it.

He groped for his glasses but couldn't find them. Lifting his head from the floor, he looked around. The shelves and their contents blurred myopically. Now he knew how Mr. Magoo felt, assuming that cartoon character had ever been pursued by a man-eating wooden grizzly bear.

Heavy paws pounded behind him. Artie didn't waste time looking back to see how close the bear was. Ignoring his battered bones, he sprinted to the desired shelf and felt around for the artifact he was looking for. Without his glasses, he had to rely more on his memory than his vision, and he fumbled hastily with a ball of yarn, a pencil sharpener, a ceramic teapot, a set of Russian nesting dolls, and a vinyl LP in its original sleeve. None of which were precisely what he needed at the moment. He dug around at the back of the shelf.

"Stop hiding," he muttered. "I know you're around here somewhere."

His fingers closed around a single dusty brick.

Right where it belonged . . . thank goodness!

Snatching the brick from the shelf, he turned to see the grizzly bearing down on him, no pun intended. Sap drooled from its slobbering jaws. Artie knew he would have only one try at this. It would have to count.

He hurled the brick at the bear.

It bounced harmlessly off the grizzly's snout, landing directly in its path. Artie didn't falter; he hadn't expected to knock the bear out with the brick. He was staking his life on the artifact's history, not its mass.

"Ich bin ein Berliner," he whispered.

The impact activated the brick, which suddenly replicated itself with preternatural speed. One brick became two became four became sixteen, multiplying until they formed an impenetrable brick wall around the bear. Barbed wire sprouted atop the wall. Phantom searchlights strobed the bricks. The echoes of bygone sirens wailed briefly in the background. Graffiti, spray-painted across the bricks in German, hinted at the brick's former location.

The Berlin Wall.

"Welcome to the Cold War," Artie said. "No freedom for you."

The trapped bear roared from the other side of the Wall. Wooden claws clawed impotently at the unyielding bricks. The beast threw its ponderous weight against the barrier, again and again.

Artie wasn't worried. The Berlin Wall had stood for nearly thirty years. It would hold the frustrated grizzly until he had time to properly neutralize it. If only the rest of the totem pole was also accounted for.

"One down, two to go."

Winded, he slumped against the shelf for a few moments before proceeding to search for his glasses. He stepped cautiously, dreading a sudden crunch beneath the soles of his sneakers. A glint of light caught his eye, and he spotted the lenses lying on the floor outside the Wall. He bent over to retrieve them, then held them up to the light. He had lucked out: they were unbroken. He wiped the lenses with his sleeve prior to putting them back on. The Warehouse came back into focus.

"That's better."

At last, he could afford to worry about Claudia. The bear might be caged, but that still left the mountain lion and the thunderbird on the loose. He couldn't relax until he knew Claudia was safe, no matter how much she got on his nerves sometimes.

He looked around, wondering which way to go.

The unmistakable roar of a lion, coming from somewhere to the east, answered that question.

"All right. I'm coming."

He wished to God that he had remembered his Tesla gun.

CHAPTER
17

WAREHOUSE 13

So much for losing the totem.

Claudia had hoped to ditch the feral carving at the obelisk, but a vicious growl tore that bit of wishful thinking to shreds. She spun around to see the mountain lion bounding after her, at the far end of yet another interminable corridor. Racing paws propelled the beast with feline grace and power.

Wait a second, Claudia thought. Blinking in surprise, it took her a heartbeat to register that *only* the lion was in evidence. Where was the rest of the pole?

That mystery would have to wait until she wasn't in immediate danger of being mauled. Running for her life, she started to wish that she had stayed inside the Niagara barrel. Now she needed another helpful artifact to save her skin. Her eyes scanned the shelves as she skedaddled past them as expeditiously as almost anyone being chased by a painted wooden puma would. Her arms churned at her sides. Her sneakers slapped against the pavement.

"C'mon, Warehouse, old pal. Don't let me down!"

Random artifacts flickered past her peripheral vision. A pygmy blowpipe. An electron microscope. A complete set of the *Encyclopaedia Britannica*, circa 1966. A bag of industrial-strength catnip would come in really handy right now, but the pet toy collection was way on the other side of the Warehouse, next to the aquarium section. Her odds of getting there before the lion brought her down like a wounded antelope were only slightly smaller than those of Mrs. Frederic letting her hair down and dancing the Macarena. In other words, zilch.

She would have to make do with whatever was immediately at hand.

So where exactly was she, anyway? What with jumping off a lighthouse, scampering atop a shelf, and taking a ride in a pickle barrel—not to mention fleeing madly from a homicidal totem pole—she had understandably lost her bearings. She struggled to place herself, while keeping one eye on the lion chasing after her.

A large jade Buddha rang a bell, as did fragments of a crystal chandelier from the Paris Opera House. It seemed to her that she had been this way not too long ago, like maybe in the last few weeks. What had she been doing around here? Putting something away?

A metaphorical lightbulb ignited above her head. All at once it hit her, along with a possible way to declaw the psycho pussycat. She knew exactly which artifact she needed.

The trick was going to be getting to it before the lion got to her.

Was there any way to get the creature to back off for a few minutes? She briefly considered going on the offensive. After much wheedling on Claudia's part, Myka had been trying to teach the younger woman some nifty martial arts moves, albeit with mixed results. Claudia flirted with trying to discourage the lion with a spinning roundhouse kick or an openhanded strike to the snout, but quickly decided against it. She was no black belt. Odds were, she'd just end up breaking a toe, which really would put her in the position of an injured gazelle.

Not where she wanted to end up.

Forget the kung fu moves. She needed to get out ahead of the lion, Warehouse-style. Her darting gaze fell upon a cratered gray rock held down by overlapping strips of Velcro. Plucked from the Sea of Tranquillity by *Apollo 11* decades before she was born, the moon rock was on permanent loan from NASA, due to certain extraordinary qualities it had manifested upon splashing down to Earth. Qualities that just might keep her out of the lion's claws for a few minutes more.

"Come to Momma, you beautiful chunk of lunar lava!"

She yanked the rock free from its Velcro restraints. Gripping it in her fist, she instantly experienced its effect. Gravity slackened its pull on her by roughly five-sixths, leaving her oddly light-headed and only about eighteen pounds. Her soles lifted slightly, so that she felt like she was walking on air. Her mouth tasted like Tang.

And just in time.

The lion pounced. Claudia jumped—and went bounding into the air as though her sneakers were made of Flubber. The hard concrete floor turned into a trampoline, at least as far as she was concerned, and she leaped away from the startled lion like a redheaded grasshopper.

"One small step for me, one giant step for geek-kind!"

As thrilling as these microgravity maneuvers were, she knew she couldn't hang on to the moon rock too long. Artie had briefed her on its dangers when she had first started working here. Unless she let go of it soon, she would quickly achieve escape velocity and wind up the first woman on the moon, minus a space suit. Explosive decompression would make being torn apart by a timber lion seem neat and tidy by comparison.

In short, the moon rock was just a temporary fix, but hopefully it would keep her out of the lion's reach long enough to get to the artifact that might actually save her bacon. If she remembered right, that particular item was only a lunar hop, skip, and jump away. She made like an astronaut down the hall, with the snarling lion in hot pursuit.

It growled unhappily every time Claudia jumped away from its claws.

The designated shelf came into view. As it happened, the artifact was on one of the upper shelves, making it harder to get at. A pile of wooden crates spilled into the hall, waiting to be unpacked. A large medieval tapestry hung like a curtain over a neighboring stretch of shelves. Bouncing up and down, she tried to catch a glimpse of the artifact, but it was hard to focus while taking her very first moon walk. Was that it there? She couldn't tell, what with all the jumping around. *It had better be,* she thought. *Or I may have to choose between being eaten or going into orbit.*

Neither prospect was particularly appealing.

Rather than trying to grab the artifact in mid-bound, she leaped to the top of the piled boxes, which wobbled scarily beneath her. "Please tell me somebody stacked these things carefully." The markings on the crates provided little indication of their contents, but the top box felt surprisingly hot to her feet, almost like there was a miniature volcano inside it. A scorching gust of overheated air shot up through a crack in the crate. The blast rustled her hair and lifted the corners of her jacket. Bizarrely, it smelled like pineapples.

A roar revealed that the lion was still hot on her trail. Determined to sink its chiseled fangs into its prey, the beast started scrambling up the boxes after her. Just her luck, it had to be a *mountain* lion and thus quite adept at climbing. It was going to reach the top in no time at all.

Her feet began to lift off from the crates, losing contact with the solid wood. She grabbed a shelf to keep from floating all the way up to the ceiling. Realizing that the moon rock was getting too strong, she hurled it away from her before she could say good-bye to gravity altogether. The lunar fragment ricocheted off a gilded Egyptian sarcophagus before drifting up toward the ceiling like a lost helium balloon. Recovering it was going to be a bitch. . . .

She dropped back onto the crate, suddenly feeling a whole lot heavier than she had just instants before. The stack teetered precipitously, but that was the least of her worries right now. The lion was only a few crates beneath her, nearly nipping at her heels. A furious claw slashed at her ankle. She yanked it back just in time, nearly tumbling off the crate. White knuckles clung to the shelf for dear life. What was it with her and dangerous heights today?

"Eyes on the prize," she reminded herself. "Don't forget what you came for."

Her free hand groped across the shelf above her head, searching for the right artifact.

It has to be here, she thought. *I just put it away a few days ago!*

Her fingers closed on a metal hilt.

"Yes!" she exclaimed. "Got you!"

Anne Bonny's cutlass was just what she was looking for. She rescued it from the shelf and spun around to face the berserk lion, who lunged at her, going in for the kill. Claudia swung the cutlass with all her strength.

"Yo ho ho!"

The blade flashed brightly, times fifty. Multiplied two score and ten by the sword's grisly résumé, the single swing instantly reduced the wooden lion to kindling. Painted wooden shavings flew in all directions. A roar like a buzz saw drowned out the creature's final growl before trailing off into silence. Sawdust and splinters wafted down the hall.

"Hah!" Claudia laughed. She posed triumphantly atop the wobbly crates. "Take that, puddy-tat!"

The cutlass fit her grip perfectly. A savage exhilaration made her blood sing. A briny smell filled her lungs. A lilting sea chantey echoed inside her head, growing louder and louder, until she couldn't help singing along:

"Oh, where is the trader of London town? His gold's on the capstan, his blood's on his gown . . ."

She slashed at the empty air with her cutlass.

Just as Artie showed up looking for her. Bushy eyebrows lifted warily.

"Claudia?"

Artie was relieved to find Claudia intact and unbloodied. He was less pleased to spot Anne Bonny's cutlass in her grip. A manic gleam in her eyes that varied significantly from her usual exhausting impishness sent warning bells ringing at the back of his mind. She held the sword at the ready. Sawdust clung to her rumpled outfit. Artie got the distinct impression that he had arrived a few minutes late. He really needed to work on his timing. . . .

"Er, Claudia?" He nodded at the cutlass. "I think you can put that down now."

A fifteenth-century French tapestry depicting a unicorn frolicking with a griffin hung from a top shelf a few feet away from where Claudia was perched. With swashbuckling élan, she leaped from atop a rickety pile of boxes and drove the point of the cutlass into the heavy tapestry, which slowed her descent as she rode the sword down the torn fabric. The stunt was an old pirate trick, once known as "sail sliding." But how had Claudia learned it?

Artie thought he had a pretty good idea.. He kept his eye on the cutlass.

This could complicate matters. . . .

She landed nimbly on the floor at the bottom of the tapestry, which magically reknit itself behind her. The curator in Artie was glad that artifact had not been permanently harmed by the cutlass. Within seconds, it was as good as new.

Too bad he lacked the same ability. He suspected he was going to need it.

Claudia sauntered toward him, cutlass in hand.

"Strike your colors, Cap'n Bligh! This be a mutiny!"

I was afraid of this, Artie thought. He gave her the benefit of the doubt. "I don't suppose you're just kidding around?"

A sneer twisted her lip. She brandished the cutlass menacingly. "You've dragooned your last luckless galley slave, you dried-up piece of driftwood!"

Nope, not joking. The cutlass had ignited Claudia's rebellious streak, fanning it into a potentially lethal conflagration. Hackers . . . pirates . . . too much of a convergence there.

He attempted to talk her down.

"Listen to me, kiddo! This isn't you. It's the cutlass." He held up his hands and backed away. "Just put the sword away, all right?"

Out of the corner of his eye, he noted an old golf club resting on a shelf to his right. He eased toward it, while trying not to provoke her. This required delicate handling.

"You want cookies?"

"Belay that! I'm done with taking orders from a worm-eaten old tyrant like you." A lunatic rage twisted her features. Raising the cursed sword high above her head, she charged at him with murder in her eyes. "There's a new captain at the helm!"

Artie grabbed the golf club, a sturdy nine iron, from the shelf. Holding it upright like a sword, he parried the cutlass before it could relieve him of his head. Sparks flashed where the blade glanced off the long metal shaft. He shouted over the ringing steel.

"Stop this! You're not Anne Bonny. You're Claudia Donovan, junior agent and first-class pain in my butt. You have a brother, Joshua. You gave me a T-shirt and a coat for Christmas. Neither of them fit!" He blocked another thrust with the nine iron, almost losing his fingers. Sadly, golf clubs did not come equipped with hand guards, only rubber grips. And the club's special properties only extended to guaranteeing holes in one. "I know you, Claudia. You don't want to do this!"

"Don't ye dare tell me what I want, you high-and-mighty muckrake!" She drove him back, slashing wildly with the sword. Her voice held a southern lilt that had never been there before, almost as though she had been born and raised in Charleston. "I'll have you keelhauled and fed to the fishes!"

"What fishes?" he protested. "We're in the middle of the Badlands!"

"Don't try to confuse me!"

Cutlass clanged against club. She feinted, then thrust at his heart. The solid iron foot of the golf club weighed it down, but he managed to block the attack in time. She stabbed at him again, keeping him on defensive. The club was longer than the short sword, which helped to keep her at a distance, but his arm was already getting tired. Nine irons weren't meant for fencing!

Claudia showed no sign of letting up.

"I'm sticking to my course," she declared, "come fair weather or foul!"

She said so, but did she really mean it? Despite her

colorful invective, she hadn't actually run him through yet. Did that mean that, deep down inside, she was resisting the sword's piratical influence?

Artie wanted to think so.

"Fight it, kid! Don't let that cutlass do your thinking for you. You're smarter and more independent than that! And don't I know it!"

The gleaming blade sparked off the club's shaft, jolting his arm fifty times a blow. His muscles ached; the club felt like it weighed a ton. Its foot drooped for a second, and she lunged at him again, but he deflected the thrust to the side. This wasn't his first duel; he knew what he was doing. The trick was to always remain aware of your surroundings and take advantage of the terrain. Between parries, he glanced around for a way to defuse the situation bloodlessly. Wasn't there an emergency rinse around here somewhere?

Yes! There it was.

An industrial-looking showerhead, of the sort installed in nuclear reactors and college chemistry labs, was mounted on a metal track running across the top of a tiled alcove. A glass pane guarded a bright red metal lever, labeled IN CASE OF CONTAMINATION. He looked away from the label to avoid betraying his intentions. Giving ground, he let himself be backed into the alcove, trying to lure her in. "What are you waiting for?" he baited her. "It's not a mutiny unless you dispose of the old skipper!"

"That's what I'm trying to do, you grumpy, bushy-eyed old walrus!" She pouted as she slashed at him repeatedly. "Stand still so I can gut you proper!"

He found himself cornered in the alcove, his back

against the wall. He risked a peek overhead. Claudia wasn't quite under the showerhead yet.

Her sword whipped in and out, sneaking past the golf club. A button went flying from his vest. He flung himself sideways to avoid being skewered. Gulping, he wished he had another brick from Berlin.

Instead he took another tack.

"We don't have time for this!" he barked. "Pete and Myka need us!"

"Pete?" She wavered. The tip of the cutlass sank toward the floor. "Myka?"

"That's right. You remember, don't you?" He lowered the golf club slightly, ready to take up arms again at the first hint of another attack. He tried once more to get through to her. "Pete is sick. He's going to die . . . unless we help find Clara Barton's gloves!"

For a second he thought that might be enough to snap her out of it, but the cutlass was too strong. The defiant bloodlust that had made Anne Bonny a legend gripped her again.

"Hold your tongue, you lying sack of bilge! I'll swab these decks with your blood!"

She came at him, rushing directly under the shower-head. Her blade scraped against the foot of the golf club, sending up a shower of sparks. Artie felt the blow all the way down his arm. At the same time, he shattered the glass pane with his elbow. Broken fragments rained down onto the tiles, exposing the emergency lever. He seized it with his free hand and yanked it all the way down. He threw himself back against the wall.

"Sorry about this. You'll thank me later."

A huge shower of purple goo poured down on Claudia, sliming her. The blinding flash forced Artie to avert his eyes. Golden sparks, as bright as any pirate booty, flared along the length of the cutlass before blinking out. Liberally bedecked in purple, she sputtered and wiped the gunk from confused, brown eyes that no longer looked quite so intent on tossing him overboard. She spat out a mouthful of goo.

"Artie?"

The neutralizer bath had done the trick, snapping her out of the trance like a bucket of cold water to the face. The last vestiges of Anne Bonny's seductive fury washed down the drain at her feet. Claudia stared aghast at the gooey cutlass in her hand, then dropped it like the proverbial hot potato (which, Artie recalled, was actually located four annexes away). Purple goo dripped from her hair and ran down her face.

"Careful," he warned. "You don't want to swallow any of that."

Neutralizer was not to be taken internally. Ingesting it made you see . . . things, the nature of which was better left unspoken.

"Holy smokes, Artie!" Guilt showed through the goo. "I nearly . . ." She couldn't bring herself to finish. "I swear, I didn't mean it!"

Overcome with emotion and drenched to the skin, she rushed forward and gave him a very messy hug. Fresh neutralizer squished between them. He felt it soak through his clothes.

"You know, this probably could have waited until *after* you toweled off."

"Shush." She squeezed him tighter. "Don't make me rethink not eviscerating you."

He awkwardly extricated himself from the hug, being careful not to slip on the puddle forming beneath them. He stared down at himself and sighed wearily. Second-hand goo dripped down the front of him, pooling at his feet. He shook it from his fingers. The purple castoff fell on the discarded cutlass, which waited to be bagged. He cautiously nudged it with his toe.

"On second thought, maybe Leena was right: that cutlass might belong in the Dark Vault."

Claudia gave him a look. "You think?"

A fierce squawk announced that the thunderbird was still flying free. A winged shadow fell over them as the avian artifact circled high above them, cawing angrily. Artie clutched the golf club with both hands, but the creature kept its distance. Had it sensed the destruction of its leonine brother? Probably, he speculated. They had both been carved from the same log after all.

"Careful!" Claudia ducked under the dripping shower head. She tugged on Artie's arm, pulling him to safety. "There's a grisly grizzly around here somewhere too."

"All walled up," he updated her. "But the bird is going to be a challenge. It's the most dangerous of the three." Eyewitness reports of the 1848 massacre, based on the testimony of a single half-mad survivor, made chilling reading even after more than a century. He knew precisely what they were dealing with. "A vicious man-made creature, driven only by an unquenchable appetite for vengeance."

"As opposed to its more cuddly playmates?" Claudia shuddered but made no move to retrieve the cutlass, not even in self-defense. She peered up at the bird. "You got any ideas on how to bag that canary?"

"I'm thinking!"

The thunderbird chose the better part of valor. Perhaps hoping to avoid the lion's fate, it soared toward the ceiling, where an old skylight offered a fuzzy glimpse of morning. The bird's timber wings flapped strenuously, carrying it higher and higher.

"Watch out!" Artie took shelter beneath the shower. He plopped his hard hat onto Claudia's skull instead. "It's making a break for it!"

The bird monster smashed through the skylight on its way out. Cubes of safety glass rained down on them. Artie raised an arm to protect his eyes. The glass cubes pelted him like hail. They bounced off Claudia's hard hat.

"Whoa!" she said. "That's what I call an exit."

Alarms sounded all over the Warehouse. Spinning red lights imitated the tops of cop cars. A stentorian voice, immediately recognizable as belonging to Mrs. Frederic, boomed from the PA system.

"Red alert! Warehouse security breach in progress. Repeat: security breach in progress."

"Tell me about it." Artie silenced the alarms by clicking a remote device in his pocket. He glowered at the shattered skylight. "That glass was supposed to be unbreakable. Do you know how much it cost?"

"Never mind that." Claudia took off the hard hat. Her hair was still plastered with goo. "Big Bird has flown the coop." She sounded like she didn't know whether to be relieved or concerned. "Where do you think it's winging to now?"

Artie already knew.

"The thunderbird is a bird of prey. Its predatory instincts will surely drive it to attack the nearest populated settlement, just as it did over one hundred and fifty years ago."

"Populated?" Claudia didn't need to consult a map. "Ohmigod. You don't mean . . . ?"

Artie completed the thought for her.

"Univille."

CHAPTER 18

"UNIVILLE"

It wasn't even noon yet, but the UnFounders Day celebration was already under way. The town had lucked
out, weatherwise, with a clear blue sky and tempera-
tures climbing toward the eighties. Not a single cloud
threatened to dampen the annual festivities. A bustling
street fair extended the length of Main Street, which
had been closed off for the duration. Temporary booths
hawked lemonade, cotton candy, and roasted corn on
the cob. Local businesses offered special UnFounders
Day bargains. A high school band performed in the town
square, their bombastic renditions of the latest Top 40
hits benefitting more from enthusiasm than execution.
Clubs and charities raised funds by selling homemade
birdhouses, ceramics, bonsai plants, and other crafts.
Bake sales competed with the snack stands. An inflatable
moon bounce had been set up for the kids. A papier-
mâché replica of Mount Rushmore gazed from atop the
bandstand. The street and sidewalks were packed with
locals. Getting into the spirit of things, various townsfolk
had dressed up in frontier garb. Sitting Bull and Buffalo

Bill mingled with Laura Ingalls Wilder. Leena counted at least three Crazy Horses.

Most everybody looked like they were having a good time. Shining auras commingled, creating a dazzling prismatic effect. At least, for those with eyes to see.

Leena wished she could enjoy it more. As a local business owner and card-carrying member of the Univille Chamber of Commerce, she'd felt obliged to make an appearance, but her heart wasn't in it. How could it be, with Pete dying of typhoid fever thousands of miles away?

Her throat tightened as she remembered the first time she had met Pete, the day he and Myka had moved into the B&B. They had both been very frazzled and disoriented, but she had done her best to make them feel at home. To be honest, she'd found Pete attractive at the start and had flirted with him shamelessly that first afternoon. There had been a definite vibe between them, although she had known better than to let it go any further than that; getting involved with a Warehouse agent would have been much too complicated. Besides, she no longer thought of Pete that way. He was family now.

Which made his terminal condition all the more frightening.

"Are you all right, dear?"

Mrs. Lozenko eyed Leena with concern. Her bulldog tugged at its leash. The old woman's aura was looking much healthier today. She must have remembered her vitamins.

"I'm fine, thanks for asking." Leena discreetly dabbed

a tear away. "I just got something in my eye." She petted the dog, who was sniffing at her ankles. "Is Lola enjoying the festivities?"

"Too much so. I have to make sure she doesn't eat too much junk food off the ground." She dragged the dog away from Leena. "Come along, baby." She waved at Leena. "You have a nice day, dear."

"I'll try."

She watched them depart, then let her friendly smile fade. She'd hoped that the street fair might take her mind off Pete's impending demise, but it wasn't working. Trying to put on a happy front for her neighbors while Pete lay dying was just too hard. *I've been here long enough.* Turning around, she decided to retreat back to the B&B.

Not that she expected to feel any better there.

When a Warehouse agent died or disappeared in the line of duty, his or her personal quarters and effects were carted up and transported to the Warehouse, where they were stored indefinitely. Tucked out of sight, and accessible only via an elaborate conveyor belt mechanism, were the private rooms of every lost agent, preserved exactly as they had left them, right down to the last detail. Leena had helped Artie pack up such lodgings before. She was in no hurry to do the same for Pete's room.

Or Myka's, for that matter.

She offered up a silent prayer that Artie and Claudia had a line on Clara Barton's gloves by now. Forget stewing at the B&B. Maybe the others could use a hand back at the Warehouse? Her car was parked at home, just a few blocks away. If she hurried, she could be in Artie's office by lunchtime. She could throw together a salad and some healthy snacks too. Artie and Claudia could probably use a decent meal at this point.

Her cell phone buzzed. She plucked it from her purse. Caller ID informed her that the caller was not listed anywhere.

The Warehouse, in other words.

Maybe there was good news about Pete?

She answered the call. "Hello?"

Artie didn't waste exchanging greetings. "Where are you?"

"Downtown. At the festival." His urgent tone frightened her. "What is it? What's wrong?"

"The festival?" She could practically hear him process that data. It was odd not to see his face on a screen, but a Farnsworth might have attracted unwanted attention. Better to stick to an ordinary cell phone for now. "UnFounders Day, right. Is that today?"

The occasion had clearly slipped his mind. No surprise, given all that was going on.

"Yes," she informed him. "Everybody is here."

"Of course they would be," he said mordantly. "This would have to happen on UnFounders Day. . . ."

"*What* would happen?" she pressed him.

"The Nisqually Totem Pole. It got loose."

A horrified gasp escaped her. She was well acquainted with the totem's savage history.

"How?"

"No time to explain." He sounded stressed and impatient, even by Artie standards. "The thunderbird is heading your way."

She instantly grasped the danger. "But . . . the festival. The streets are packed."

"Easy pickings for the thunderbird." His dour expression was easy to imagine. "You need to get everybody off the street. There's no time to lose."

She glanced around at the bustling commotion. Pretty much the entire population of the town had turned out for the event. Hundreds of unsuspecting people enjoyed themselves, completely unaware of the danger they were in. An entire Boy Scout troop swept past her on the sidewalk, jostling her as she spoke. Mrs. Lozenko and her dog hadn't gotten far. The high school band was still going strong. Applause greeted their off-key interpretation of Lady Gaga.

"Easier said than done, Artie. The festival is in full swing."

She was tempted to take out her Farnsworth so he could see for himself, but he seemed to get the idea.

"Which just makes it all the more important that you get everyone indoors, pronto," he stated, "or we're going to have a full-scale massacre on our hands."

Leena remembered what had happened in 1848. She had personally scanned the original newspaper bulletins and U.S. Cavalry reports into the new computers. The totem's attack had been a feeding frenzy. The thought of the same thing happening here, in her home, filled her with dread—and resolve.

"All right, Artie. I know what to do." She marched briskly toward the park. "But what about the thunderbird?"

"Leave that to Claudia and me. We're on our way."

Leena peered up at the sky, looking anxiously for a pair of ominous red and black wings. There was no sign of them yet, but that was small comfort. Univille was only about seven miles away from the Warehouse, maybe less as the crow flew. The voracious bird could be here any minute.

"Hurry, Artie!"

Hanging up, she broke into a full run, dashing to the park as fast as her limber legs could carry her. A dawdling crowd impeded her, but she pushed past them. "Excuse me! Coming through."

Her frantic dash drew curious stares. "Hey, Leena!" Bert the grocer called out. "Where's the fire?"

She couldn't have explained even if she'd had the time, which she didn't. "No fire!" she shot back. "Just in a bit of a hurry!"

If only they'd had nothing more serious than a raging fire to deal with!

The park was just as packed as Main Street. A barbershop quartet, dressed in striped suits and straw boaters, performed in the gazebo. A kite-flying competition filled the clear blue sky with colorful paper boxes, dragons, and streamers. Squealing kids clambered over the playground equipment while their parents, older siblings, and nannies looked on. A vendor dispensed soft-serve ice cream cones from a refrigerated cart. A local politician handed out campaign flyers and pins. Leena curtly declined both. She wasn't planning to vote for him anyway.

Amidst all the activity, a certain abstract sculpture went ignored. A half-dozen metal tubes pointed at the sky almost like an antiaircraft emplacement. A hose connected the array of cylinders to the reflecting pool at the base of the sculpture. A handful of toddlers was wading in the pool. A paper boat, constructed from a folded pizza menu, drifted across the shallow pool, which reflected the cloudless azure sky overhead. Rippling water sparkled in the sunlight.

But not for much longer. Leena dropped to her knees beside the pool. She glanced around furtively to see if anyone was watching, but thankfully the distracted townspeople were more interested in their own varied pursuits and diversions. The only person paying attention to her was a pint-sized moppet wearing a baggy *Dora the Explorer* T-shirt. The little girl gazed at Leena with wide blue eyes while her mother chatted with some neighbors a few yards away. She sucked on her thumb.

Leena raised a finger to her lips. "Sssh!" she whispered before reaching beneath the surface of the pool. Graceful fingers located a submerged knob hidden in the pool's mosaic design. She turned it hard to the right. A metallic click was muffled by the water.

A low hum emanated from the "sculpture," which was actually far more than that. A tingling sensation tickled Leena's skin. Static frizzed out her hair. Ozone teased her nose. She withdrew her hand from the pool.

Here goes nothing, she thought. *Let's hope this thing still works.*

The sky darkened abruptly. Thick black clouds accumulated as if from nowhere, throwing the entire park into shadow. Confused citizens turned their faces upward.

"What in the world . . . ?" the little girl's mom blurted. "What happened to the weather?"

The toddler eyed Leena suspiciously. She shook a pudgy finger at the grown-up.

"Sorry," Leena said.

The sky went from sunny to stormy in a matter of minutes. Lightning flashed ominously. Thunder boomed directly overhead. A solitary raindrop fell upon Leena's upturned face. She wiped it away. All around her, people started scurrying for shelter.

That first drop was just a warning. The clouds burst like water balloons. A torrential downpour came on strong, driving the crowd from the park. Pounding sheets of rain drenched the fleeing people. Hail pelted the town with icy pebbles that bounced off the streets and sidewalks, setting off car alarms and crying children. The toddler's mother snatched up her daughter and bolted from the park, ignoring the high-pitched babbling of the child, who pointed accusingly at Leena. Kites blew away or else crashed to earth. The folded paper boat took on water and sank beneath the reflecting pool. Swirling winds chased after the dismayed townspeople. Startled shouts and curses came from Main Street as well.

UnFounders Day had been rained out—with a vengeance.

Within moments Leena found herself standing alone in the park, soaked to the skin. She sincerely doubted that anyone else would be foolhardy enough to stay outside in this deluge. Noah would have felt very much at home. She gave the humming sculpture an affectionate pat. "Mission accomplished."

Thanks to Wilhelm Reich's cloudbuster. The device, invented by the famed Austrian psychoanalyst, channeled "orgone energy" to act as a highly potent rainmaker. It had been hiding in plain sight all these years, in anticipation of emergencies just like this one. After all, you never knew when it might be a good idea to get the people of Univille off the streets.

Like when a bloodthirsty wooden thunderbird was on the prowl.

She hurried back toward Main Street, finding it abandoned as well, every booth and ride deserted. Plastic tarps had been hastily thrown over the various stands. Unable to cope with the deluge, the sewers were already backing up, flooding the street. Leena splashed through puddles as she walked the length of the empty fair, making sure everyone was indoors. She had the entire street to herself. The cloudbuster had done its job.

And none too soon.

Hail peppered her face as she peered upward into the storm. Worried brown eyes searched the sky. A white-hot flash of lightning broke through the gloom, and the thunderbird came swooping out of the clouds, gliding on chiseled wooden wings. A lost kite blew across its path, and the bird ripped it to shreds. Vicious talons made short work of the kite.

Leena gasped. She had only read about the thunderbird before. She had never seen it in action. Watching it tear into the kite, she could only imagine what its sharp beaks and talons could do to a human being, what they *had* done back in 1848. . . .

She dived for cover beneath the bandstand.

Rain-swept litter washed against her, but that was the least of her worries. She cautiously poked her head out to see what was happening. "Come on, Artie," she entreated. "Where are you?"

The thunderbird descended toward Univille.

Followed closely by a vintage World War I triplane. . . .

CHAPTER
19

"UNIVILLE"

"Hold on tight!"

The Fokker DR-1 triplane dove through the storm. Its wings and fuselage were a brilliant shade of red, except where an Iron Cross was painted black against a field of white. A contraption of wood and canvas held together by wire, the primitive flying machine felt uncomfortably flimsy compared to more modern aircraft. Yet this particular plane, Artie recalled, had survived some of the most deadly aerial dogfights of the First World War.

He hoped it had one more victory in it.

The spinning propeller sliced up the air. He clutched the control stick with both hands. Tinted goggles and a leather aviator's cap protected him from the elements. A thick wool scarf was knotted around his neck. Twin Spandau machine guns were mounted directly in front of him, their sights lined up with the nose of the plane. Its powerful nine-cylinder engine was nearly drowned out by the crashing thunder.

"I'm holding, I'm holding!" Claudia shrieked over the roar of the plane, her arms wrapped tightly around him.

She was squeezed into the cockpit behind Artie, acting as spotter. A red, white, and blue USAF flight helmet was clamped over her skull. A brown leather bomber jacket covered her goo-splattered clothing, which there had been no time to change out of. She batted the tail of Artie's scarf away from her face. "What am I doing here anyway? I thought the Red Baron always flew solo!"

"I'm not the Red Baron, okay?" He thought that was obvious. "I can use the backup!"

Manfred von Richthofen, the infamous Red Baron, had been the most lethal flying ace of World War I, with a record-setting eighty kills to his name. He had died in this very plane, shot down by ground fire while flying too low beyond enemy lines, but he had never lost a dogfight. And he had even managed to land the Fokker safely before expiring. Warehouse agents had acquired the plane decades ago, after its more unusual properties caught their attention. It had been gathering dust for as long as Artie remembered. He had been tinkering with it for years.

The Fokker broke out of the clouds. It leveled off above the town.

"There it is!" Claudia let go of Artie's waist long enough to point below them. "T-bird at twelve o'clock!"

The totem soared low over Univille, hundreds of feet below the triplane. Hot on its tail, Artie was relieved to see that the flooded streets were empty, thanks to Reich's cloudbuster. *Good job, Leena,* he thought approvingly. *I always knew that "art installation" was going to come in handy someday.*

Deprived of human prey, the bird screeched in

frustration. It flew low over the deserted streets and sidewalks, hunting for a hapless victim. Rain sluiced off its chiseled feathers, but it appeared quite at home in the torrential downpour. The storm did not deter it.

No surprise there. According to North American Indian mythology, the thunderbird was the harbinger of both war and fierce weather. Lightning was said to be the flashing of its eyes; thunder the flapping of its wings.

"What are you waiting for?" Claudia hollered. "Shoot it!"

"Not yet!" Artie held his fire. The old plane had a limited quantity of ammo. He didn't want to waste it. "We need to get closer."

"Says you!" Claudia objected. "Me, I'd rather keep my distance."

Not an option, Artie knew. The Fokker's ancient guns were not very accurate at long range. The Red Baron himself never opened fire until he was within three hundred feet of his target. Firing too early just gave your location away. Those tactics had been passed along to his plane, which had done this many times before. Artie was not about to second-guess them now.

Working the stick, he tried to get the wooden raptor in his sights. The bird's painted tail feathers came into range, and he let loose with a short burst of machine-gun fire. An ingenious mechanism, designed by the famed Dutch aeronautical engineer Anthony Fokker, synchronized the guns' fire with the motion of the propeller so that the bullets shot through the spinning blades without damaging them. The twin muzzles flared a brilliant purple. The guns rattled over the storm.

A round of handcrafted 8mm ammo chipped away at the flying totem but failed to kill it. A neutralizing compound had been mixed with the alloy to give it more punch against renegade artifacts and their effects. Sap, not blood, dripped from the gouged wood. Did the unnatural creature even have any vital organs to hit? The Red Baron had died from a single shot to his heart, but the thunderbird was made of wood, not flesh and blood. Even with the glowing purple bullets, how was one supposed to kill it?

He tried targeting its head, but the bird banked hard to the left. Artie wasted a round on empty air. The DR-1 had been faster and more maneuverable than its peers back in the Great War, but the thunderbird had it beat by a long shot. The monster zigged and zagged before him, making it all but impossible to get a bead on. Not that he even knew where to shoot.

"Tracer rounds!" he shouted back at Claudia. "Give me the tracer rounds."

Fumbling awkwardly, she reloaded the right-hand gun. This was a difficult operation to perform in midair, but her agile fingers were used to handling intricate mechanisms under pressure. She had once defused a doomsday bomb with seconds to spare.

"Locked and loaded!" she reported. "Light her up!"

Artie opened up the throttle to catch up with the bird. An elevated water tower suddenly loomed in front of the thunderbird, which smashed right through it, emerging intact from the other side. Twin cataracts of water poured down onto the already flooded street fair, washing away booths and bandstands, even as the punctured tower loomed directly in the triplane's path.

"Artie, watch out!"

"I see it!" he shouted back. "I'm not blind, you know!"

"Could've fooled me."

Artie pulled back on the stick, and the Fokker climbed steeply. He held his breath. History recorded that the DR-1 sometimes lost power climbing at high altitudes, but he hoped that wouldn't be a problem here. The tower filled the view before him, so close that he could read the graffiti spray-painted on its tank. The Class of 2010 "ruled," apparently.

"Artie?" Claudia asked nervously.

"We're going to make it. Probably."

Climbing at top speed, the triplane barely cleared the towers. Its landing gear scraped the top of the empty tank, sending a bump up his spine. He wondered if Vanessa knew a good chiropractor.

"Ouch!" Claudia got bounced as well. "You have flown this thing before, right?"

"I never said that." He switched into lecture mode. "But this plane is an extension of the Red Baron. His tactical genius and flying skill passed into it upon his death." The controls felt alive in his hands, guiding him in their use. "It practically flies itself!"

"'Practically'?" Her eyes searched the cockpit. "And the parachutes are . . . ?"

"There aren't any," he explained. "No room."

"Now he tells me."

"Never mind the parachutes." He eased up on the

stick, leveling off at about five hundred feet above the town. Fortunately, Univille was not known for its skyscrapers. Few buildings were more than three stories high. "Just keep your eye out for that bird!"

He had lost track of their avian adversary. Where had it gotten to?

"Incoming!" Claudia shrieked in his ears. "Dead ahead!"

The thunderbird brought the battle to them. It dived at the Fokker head-on, its talons extended. The triplane rose to meet it, playing a deadly game of aerial chicken. Artie got the wooden monster in his sights. "Let's see just how flammable you are."

He opened fire with the tracers. The incendiary rounds, which contained phosphorus as well as neutralizer, burned brightly, blazing through the rain, before strafing the thunderbird's chest. Flames ignited, causing spilled sap to bubble and blacken. Burnt paint chipped off. The bird broke away, screeching in rage. Smoke trailed behind it. Golden sparks flashed amidst the fumes.

"We did it!" Claudia cheered. "Burn, baby, burn!"

Artie appreciated her team spirit but held off from celebrating until he knew for sure that the threat was over. Years of experience had taught him never to underestimate an angry artifact. That wary attitude had kept him alive and sane longer than any other Warehouse agent in recent memory. He wasn't ready to fly a victory lap just yet.

"Not so fast," he cautioned Claudia. "Keep watching!"'

His reservations proved sadly apposite. Setting the totem ablaze had been a good idea in theory, but the inclement weather worked against them. Soaked timber refused to ignite. Sheets of rain doused the sputtering flames as the thunderbird flapped into the storm, disappearing into a churning black cloud. Wailing winds carried the smoke away.

"Blast it!" Artie pounded the dashboard in frustration. "We lost it again!"

He climbed after the bird, heading straight into the storm. The Fokker balked; the Red Baron had always refused to fly during thunderstorms, except when directly ordered to. His plane shared his reluctance. The stick twisted in Artie's grip, fighting to change course, but he kept a firm grip on the controls and didn't let the plane veer away from the clouds. A jagged bolt of lightning, frying the airspace before them, tried to warn them off. Thunder yelled at the plane to keep away.

Artie didn't take the hint.

Claudia blanched behind him. "You sure you know where you're going?"

"No choice."

They couldn't let the thunderbird get away. It was too dangerous. There were other towns in South Dakota besides Univille, and many more potential victims.

"Brace yourself. This could get bumpy."

The Fokker flew into the clouds. A cold, wet fog enveloped them. Wind and rain buffeted the fragile aircraft, which rocked from side to side. Artie wiped his goggles with his sleeve. A windshield and wipers would have been useful, but those were hardly standard issue back in the days of the Red Baron, who had known better than to wage a dogfight in these sort of conditions. Artie started to wish he had listened to the plane and followed von Richthofen's example.

Visibility was practically nonexistent. He craned his neck, searching for the enemy.

"Do you see it?"

"Are you kidding?" Claudia asked. "It's like the frigging Mutara Nebula in here!"

He didn't get the reference. "The what?"

"Dude, you've never seen *The Wrath of Khan?*" Utter disbelief infused her voice. "We have *got* to do something about your video literacy!"

"Some other time, maybe." He had been kind of busy for the last forty years, protecting the world and all that. "Just keep an eye out for that bird!"

Lightning flashed on the right, close enough to leave spots before his eyes. *That was a close one,* he thought, thinking the bolt had missed them. Then he smelled the smoke. He turned his head in alarm. Bright orange flames danced across the plane's right middle wing. The crimson canvas crackled and burned, despite the rain.

"Leaping lizards!" Claudia yelped. "We're hit!"

"I know!" He doubted the Fokker could fly without all three wings. "Put it out!"

"I'm trying!"

She dug around for the fire extinguisher, the cramped cockpit slowing her down. Artie scooted forward to give her a little more room, but there wasn't much to spare. "Hurry!" he nagged her. "The wing's on fire!"

"You think I don't know that?" She wrestled the extinguisher from the floor of the cockpit. "Got it!"

She had to stand up behind Artie to target the blaze.

Foam sprayed from the extinguisher as he tried to keep the plane level in the storm, which was no easy task. "Keep her steady, okay?" She shook her head as she fought to maintain her balance. "Seriously, who takes up an old crate like this without parachutes? That's all I'm saying. . . ."

"Less griping, more spraying!"

At least the fire extinguisher did its job without complaining. Vaporous bursts snuffed out the flames eating away at the wing. A gust of wind blew some of the foam into Artie's face. He sputtered and wiped it away . . . just in time to glimpse a winged silhouette through the fog.

He let loose with a round of conventional ammo mixed with tracers. The Spandau machine guns rattled loudly. Muzzle flashes lit up the murky interior of the cloud.

"Whoa there!" Claudia dropped back into her seat. The empty extinguisher clunked against the floor of the cockpit. "A little warning next time, hotshot!"

Artie lifted his splattered goggles but didn't see a flaming thunderbird crashing to earth. No indignant squawks had greeted his latest salvo.

"Missed it!"

"Uh-oh." Claudia twisted around. "Don't look now, but we've got a T-bird on our tail!"

The vengeful totem swooped down on them from behind. Talons raked across the triplane's upper wings. Canvas tore noisily.

Not good, Artie thought. He needed to save the wings before they were shredded beyond repair. He threw the Fokker into a barrel roll, spinning the wings away from the bird. Claudia shrieked and held on to Artie hard enough to crush his ribs. The fire extinguisher spilled from the cockpit. It fell like a missile toward the deserted park below. Good thing Leena had already cleared everybody out!

The plane turned upside down. The landing gear smacked the thunderbird in the side, knocking it away with a thunk that shook the cockpit. The creature fell back into the swirling cloud cover. The landing wheels spun in the air.

Take that, Artie thought. *Next time, leave our wings alone.*

The impact jolted the triplane, sending it into an uncontrolled spin. They fell out of clouds, corkscrewing headfirst toward the earth. Downtown Univille came rushing up at them. A cold wind whipped past Artie's face, drowning out Claudia's screams. He was screaming too.

Pulling out of a spin was a challenge even for an experienced pilot, which he most certainly was not. He had no idea what to do next.

Maybe the plane did?

He let go of the controls. "Over to you," he ordered the plane. "Do your thing!"

The DR-1 took immediate action to save itself, the controls moving on their own. The throttle shifted into idle, cutting the power. The ailerons flattened into neutral, and the opposite rudder was applied to halt the plane's rotation. The Fokker waited until the spinning stopped before pulling out of the dive at the last minute. The landing gear clipped the top of a kid's Moon Bounce. Air hissed as the torn ride deflated.

"Mother Fokker!" Claudia blurted. "Not so close next time!"

"We're not done yet." He took the controls again. "Get ready for another go-round."

"Again?"

Glancing back over his shoulder, he spotted the thunderbird chasing after them. "That's it," he encouraged the creature. "Keep on coming."

He needed to think like the Red Baron if he wanted to down the bird. A strategy occurred to him, one that should come naturally to the crimson Fokker.

"Hold on," he warned Claudia. "We're going up."

Testing the ancient plane's limits, he climbed sharply at nearly one thousand feet per minute. The Fokker shot through the gathering storm, dodging thunder and lightning, then broke through the cloud cover into the bright blue sunlight above the tempest.

Seconds later the thunderbird flapped out of the clouds as well.

"It still on our tail?" Artie asked urgently.

"That's a big 10-4," the reluctant spotter reported. "We have a plan?"

"Working on one."

The Red Baron had always preferred to stay between the sun and his foe, so that he could strike undetected. Taking a page from his playbook, Artie guided the Fokker into a loop. The world turned upside down again, the sky below them, the earth above, before they rolled out of the top of the loop and came diving out of the sun at the confused thunderbird, which was now right in front of them. Artie held his fire, waiting until he was within range. Scorch marks and burnt paint mottled the bird's chiseled feathers. Traces of purple goo streaked the wood. The wood had been chipped away and gouged by his previous rounds, but the bird was still flying.

Not for much longer. He had figured out what to shoot at. "Got you right where I want you!"

The artifact was less than a hundred feet away. Ignoring its tempting head and torso, Artie targeted a wing instead. His finger tightened on the trigger. The machine guns blared.

Four hundred rounds a minute tore into the totem's wing. Wood chips trailed from the wing, bouncing off the Fokker's spinning propeller. Sparks ignited where the neutralizer clashed with the artifact's energies. High-caliber surgery amputated the thunderbird's right wing, which went flying off into the sky. Squawking in pain or fury, the mutilated totem went into a death spiral. It plunged out of control into the storm below.

"Yes!" Claudia hugged Artie. "You really got it this time!"

"Maybe." He still wasn't going to count his chickens— or a thunderbird—until it was cooked for sure. "We need to verify the kill."

The Fokker dived through the clouds after its victim. Sizzling lightning bolts threatened to set the triplane ablaze again, but for once luck was with them and they managed to get through the tempest relatively unsinged. The plane emerged from the clouds into the rain and hail.

"Where?" he asked anxiously. "Where is it?"

"Going down." Claudia pointed below. "Next stop: Univille Park!"

Sure enough, the crippled thunderbird crashed into the park—right on top of Wilhelm Reich's cloudbuster. In a perverse twist of fate, the totem smashed the rainmaker to smithereens. A blinding flash of light consumed both artifacts as their arcane energies were discharged in a spectacular display. A pillar of golden fire shot into the sky.

"Artie!"

"I know!" This wasn't the first time he'd seen an artifact or two go pyrotechnic. "You don't need to shout!"

He banked hard to the left, evading the towering fountain of flame. The pillar glittered brightly for a moment, then dissolved into drifting sparks. All at once, the rain stopped and the hail ceased falling. The sun broke through the clouds as the storm came apart.

So much for the cloudbuster, Artie thought ruefully. *Sorry, Wilhelm.*

Still, the artifact had served its purpose. Univille was safe.

He circled over the park once more to be certain. Nothing but a smoking crater remained where the totem had bombed the so-called sculpture. Charred pieces of wood were impaled on lengths of twisted metal. All the water in the reflecting pool had steamed away. Bits of cracked mosaic tile had been fused together by the heat of the explosion. The bottom of the crater had a glassy sheen, like the aftermath of a nuclear blast.

"Talk about a waste of time," Artie grumped. He mourned the loss of the artifacts. It was a shame they'd had to destroy two-thirds of the totem pole, but at least the bear was still intact. He'd have to make sure it was put back in stasis . . . eventually.

First things first, he thought. They still needed to get Clara Barton's gloves—and cure Pete before it was too late. "You up for a trip to New York?"

Claudia contemplated the snazzy red plane. "How fast can this bird go anyway?"

"Funny you should ask."

He turned the throttle all the way up.

CHAPTER
20

CENTRAL PARK, NEW YORK CITY

A taxi dropped them off at Sixty-fifth and Central Park West. The nearest available parking spot had been several blocks away, so they'd been forced to take a cab the rest of the way, since Pete was in no shape to navigate the subways, let alone several hectic city blocks. Heavy uptown traffic crawled past them. Horns honked at every intersection. Myka tried to help Pete out of the cab, but he stubbornly rejected her assistance.

"I can manage, okay?" A strained expression belied his words. He thrust a handful of bills at the driver. "You don't need to baby me."

"Then don't act like one." She didn't take his grumpy attitude personally. She could only guess how hard this was on him, both physically and mentally. Frankly, she was amazed that he was even standing. He had to be getting by on sheer cussedness, as her dad would have put it. "At least let me take your cane."

"Okay, okay. Whatever."

The walking stick in question was a polished hickory cane topped by a miniature silver elephant. A steel tip shod the bottom of the cane. Claudia had shipped it to the hospital at Pete's request yesterday, before they found out about the fair.

Probably not a bad idea. He looked like he needed it.

She held on to the cane while he painfully hauled himself out of the cab. The effort left him breathless and sweating, despite the cool autumn weather. The sun was still high in the sky and the sidewalk was filled with both locals walking at a brisk New York pace and wide-eyed tourists slowing them down. A horse-drawn carriage trotted by, offering a leisurely tour of the park. Myka admired the old-fashioned hansom cab as she handed the cane back to Pete. He leaned heavily on it as he caught his breath.

A park bench beckoned several yards away, beneath some shady trees. The leaves were already turning colors. "Maybe you should wait here," she suggested, "while I scope out the park."

She still wasn't convinced that bringing Pete along was a good idea. He belonged in a hospital, not traipsing through Central Park in search of two renegade artifacts. Vanessa Calder had objected strenuously to his departure, but had finally relented in the face of his pigheaded refusal to listen to the doctor. Only the fact that he was already dying anyway, despite all of Vanessa's best efforts, had allowed him to get his way in the end.

Myka did not find that terribly reassuring.

"Forget it." He hobbled past her into the park. "You coming or what?"

She briefly considered knocking him out with the

Tesla, but wasn't sure he would survive the shock. Leaving the sidewalk behind, she caught up with him.

Central Park was a king-size oasis in the middle of a concrete jungle. Skyscrapers, visible even through the trees, enclosed the park, which stretched for blocks above and below them. Myka took a moment to orient herself. According to Artie, the psychic fair was being held in the Sheep Meadow, slightly northwest of here. At least Pete wouldn't have to walk too far.

In an eerie coincidence, a Civil War monument was installed on a grassy rise a few yards away. A solitary Union soldier posed atop a tall pedestal, his bronzed hands resting vigilantly upon his rifle. An inscription on the pedestal dedicated the statue to the honored dead of the Seventh Regiment, who had given their lives to defend the Union. The memorial reminded Myka of the death and carnage that Clara Barton had witnessed over a hundred years ago. A chill ran down her spine.

She caught Pete eyeing the statue as well. They exchanged a wordless look. He didn't say anything. He didn't have to. They both had to be thinking the same thing.

The Civil War was over. Clara Barton's gloves needed to be retired.

No more reenactments, she thought. *No more fever.*

"Come on," Pete said. He turned his back on the monument. "We can play tourist later."

They headed west along a paved walkway. Bare branches testified to the changing of the season. Fallen leaves littered the grounds. Myka resisted an urge to take Pete by the arm. She knew he wouldn't appreciate it. However, that didn't stop her from casting frequent, anxious glances in his direction.

He was looking worse than ever. His face was drawn. His hands were shaking. His lips were cracked and dry. Although he tried not to show it, he grimaced with every step. He bit down on his lip to keep from making a sound, but didn't always succeed. His hollow cheeks, in need of a shave, hinted at how much weight he had lost just in the last forty-eight hours. A jacket and sweatshirt hung loosely on his shrunken frame, like they no longer fit him. Purple shadows haunted his eyes. The haggard, halting figure bore little resemblance to the gung ho, hyperactive Pete she was used to. The contrast was so heartbreaking Myka had to look away. She couldn't bear seeing him like this.

I can't lose another partner, she thought. *I can't.*

As it turned out, locating the fair was not an issue. Throngs of people were converging on the meadow, carrying the two agents along with them. Myka let the crowd herd them in the right direction, even as she fretted at the size of the turnout. If what Artie surmised was true, and Worrall was growing more and more infectious every day, all of these people could be in danger. Typhoid fever had killed at least thirty thousand soldiers in the Civil War. For all they knew, Worrall was just getting warmed up.

Her eyes searched the people around them, but didn't see their target anywhere. Nadia was nowhere in sight, either. Myka hoped this wasn't a wild-goose chase.

They have to be here, she agonized. *Pete can't last much longer.*

An irresistible current of humanity swept them to their destination. An open, fifteen-acre lawn near the center of the park, the Sheep Meadow had a long history of hosting large public gatherings. Over the years, it had attracted numerous outdoor concerts and shows, political demonstrations of every stripe and persuasion, love-ins, bed-ins, fireworks displays, dog shows, "star parties,"and even the world's biggest water-pistol fight back in 2008. Myka remembered visiting the meadow as a child during a vacation to Manhattan. She had been disappointed to discover that sheep no longer grazed there.

The 2011 Psychic Exposition had taken over the meadow in a big way. Row after row of tents and booths and stages filled the lawn to capacity, while hordes of people crowded between them. Flapping banners advertised everything from tarot readings to ancient Atlantean spirit guides. New Age music blared from loudspeakers, competing with the hubbub of thousands of excited conversations, lectures, and sales pitches. Wind chimes tinkled in the breeze.

The crowd was a diverse one, typical of NYC. Along with the hippieish New Age sorts Myka had expected, sporting ponytails, tie-dye, and beads, there were also well-groomed yuppies, college kids, senior citizens, Goths, punks, wannabe rappers, and families pushing strollers. People sat on park benches, tapping on their laptops, or meeting up with friends. Trash bins overflowed with discarded coffee cups, newspapers, and fast-food wrappers. Every other person seemed to have a cell phone or Bluetooth surgically melded to their ears, and was stubbornly attempting to conduct a conversation amidst the buzzing chatter. It was an eavesdropper's paradise.

"Oh my God." Myka was overwhelmed by the enormity of the crowd. She had thought that carnival back in West Haven was packed, but that was nothing compared to the vast extravaganza enveloping them. There had to be at least fifteen thousand people squeezed into the meadow, if not more. "It's like Woodstock."

"But without the sex, drugs, or rock 'n' roll." Pete gaped at the mob. "So why bother?"

They wandered randomly through booths hawking crystals, massages, and Native American dream catchers. The fair expanded across the length and breadth of the entire meadow, spilling over into adjacent fields and clearings. Crowd control was a lost cause. Innumerable strangers bumped against them. Myka closed ranks with Pete to avoid losing him in the crush.

"It's so huge," she said "I don't even know where to begin."

"You and me both." Pete paused to observe a Reiki exhibition, where a small troupe of enthusiastic practitioners, wearing matching yellow kimonos, were laying their hands on volunteers from the audience. A painted backdrop illustrated the placement of various key chakras. "Trying to find a specific psychic healer at this place is like looking for a Klingon at a *Star Trek* convention. They're everywhere."

He wasn't wrong. Myka tried to figure out some way to narrow the search. How were they supposed to find Nadia—or Calvin Worrall—in a mob this size? "Even if they're here, we could roam all day without spotting either of them."

Pete leaned on his cane. He sucked in air. "Not really sure I'm up to that, Mykes."

"I know."

That Pete was even willing to admit that he was nearing the end of his rope meant that he was in seriously bad shape. The end couldn't be far away. Myka discreetly took hold of his arm and started looking around for someplace he could sit down. Perhaps inside one of the tent shows? "Do you need to rest for a moment? Maybe a drink of water?"

He licked his cracked lips. "I don't suppose I can get a corn dog?"

She didn't know whether to laugh or cry. "Not that kind of fair, I'm afraid. This looks more like a green tea and macrobiotic tofu kind of place."

"In that case, I'll pass." Pete's face twisted and he clutched his stomach. "Probably couldn't keep it down anyway."

A sudden cramp struck him. He doubled over, gasping in pain. A racking cough shook his body. He placed a hand over his mouth. A crimson mist sprayed between his fingers.

"Oh, God, Pete! You're coughing up blood!"

"I'll be okay," he moaned unconvincingly. His white knuckles gripped the cane, which, along with Myka's arm, seemed to be the only things holding him up. "Just need a sec. . . ."

He needed a lot more than that, she realized. And time was running short.

"That's it," she insisted. "We're getting you to a hospital now." Her photographic memory called up a map of upper Manhattan. Where was the nearest emergency room? St. Luke's? New York Presbyterian?

"N-no!" Pete struggled to straighten up. It killed her not to help him up. "Not until we find those gloves—and the bastard that did this to me."

Myka appreciated the sentiment, but had to face facts. "You're too sick. It's not possible."

"Then forget about me." He shoved her away. "Find Worrall. Don't let him do this to anyone else."

She knew he was right—that her top priority had to be stopping Worrall from unleashing a plague on New York City. "But I can't just leave you here!"

"You have to! This is bigger than just me. We both know that." He hunched over the cane. His voice, although shaky, was just as obstinate as ever. "Let me take a bullet for the team. That's what we were trained to do."

She didn't know what to do. Duty called, but every part of her rebelled at the thought of abandoning Pete. Hell, she didn't even know for sure that Worrall was here, or how to find him if he was. What if Pete died alone while she was running around in circles?

I'm not sure I could live with myself if that happened. . . .

Another spasm did him in. His face twisted and his knees buckled. She grabbed on to his sagging body before he could hit the pavement. His head lolled backward and his eyes lost focus. For a second she thought he was going to pass out. He mumbled deliriously, or at least semi-so. "I think I need a cookie. . . ."

"Whoa, man!" a young black man wearing an NYU sweatshirt and glasses noticed Pete's distress. "You look like you're in pretty bad shape." He hurried over to them. "You folks need any help?"

She was grateful for his assistance. Placing her arm around Pete's shoulders, she tried to steer him away from the fair. "We need to get him to a hospital."

"No." Pete shook his head. "Won't do any good anyway."

"He's right, you know." Their Good Samaritan gestured around them. "Screw the modern medical establishment. You want a healer, you've come to the right place."

Myka was in no mood for a lecture on alternative medicine. "I don't think any crystals or copper bracelets are going to do him any good."

"I'm not talking trinkets," the student insisted. "You wouldn't believe the healer they've got here today. She's the real deal. Everyone's talking about her."

That got Myka's attention. "'She'?"

"Yeah. Some young chick, calls herself Sister Clara." His bright eyes glowed with enthusiasm, like they'd just seen the light of a genuine miracle. He was a true believer. "She's astounding. Trust me, if anybody can fix your boyfriend, she can."

"Not her boyfriend," Pete murmured. "Although I was inside her body once . . . ."

"TMI, dude," the young man said. "Not cool."

Myka ignored Pete's rambling. Hope flared inside her, brighter than an artifact being neutralized. He had to be talking about Nadia. Who else could it be?

"Where?" she demanded. "Where is she?"

The boy tilted his head toward the northern end of the field. "Just follow the crowd. You can't miss her."

She saw what he meant. Distracted by Pete's near collapse, she had failed to notice a sudden surge of traffic in the direction her new friend had indicated. Excited voices spread the word about the phenomenal new healing sensation. "You have to see her!" somebody exclaimed. "I've never seen anything like it!"

I'll bet I have, Myka thought. *At a sideshow in Connecticut.*

But if Nadia was here, where was Worrall?

"You haven't heard about anybody getting sick, have you?" she interrogated the helpful college kid. "Like my friend?"

"No." He seemed puzzled by the questions. "Why do you ask?"

She took his confusion as a good sign. Maybe Worrall wasn't here yet. In which case, she could get to Nadia and her glove before Worrall did, which had to be easier than dealing with both halves of the artifact at once. *First things first,* she thought. Perhaps the right glove would be enough to heal Pete on its own. Once Pete was cured, they could concentrate on stopping Worrall before he hurt anyone else.

Maybe it wasn't too late to turn things around.

She debated leaving Pete behind with the student while she went after Nadia, but decided against it. She was in the market for a healer right now, and the sooner she got Pete to her, the better. He looked like he already had one foot in the grave. Every minute mattered.

"What's your name?" she asked their anonymous helper.

"Robbie," the boy supplied.

"Okay, Robbie. I"m going to need your help getting my friend to this astounding healer." She looked him over. "You up to it?"

"Sure." He helped her hoist Pete to his feet. "Just wait until you see her. You're not going to regret this."

I hope not, she thought. But at least they seemed to be one step ahead of the epidemic at the moment. That was something. "Hang on, Pete. It's almost over."

Or so she thought.

Frantic screams erupted from the other end of the fair. The sky darkened abruptly, just as it had outside that gym in Fairfield. Violent gusts whipped through the fair, causing banners and pennants to flap wildly before tearing loose from their moorings. Wind chimes pealed in alarm. The temperature dropped like Myka's hopes. She had seen this before.

Damnit, she realized. *We're too late.*

The crowd, which had been funneling toward Nadia, suddenly reversed direction. Panicked people, fleeing the screams, rushed from the park. Myka and Robbie scrambled out of the way, dragging Pete with them, to avoid getting trampled. They flattened themselves against the back of a fair trade coffee stand as a human tsunami flooded past them, stomping over everything in their path. Tents and booths were knocked over in the chaos. Myka drew her Tesla. Pete clung to the elephant-headed cane. Robbie stared at the madness in shock.

"What is it?" he asked. "What's happening?"

He was better off not knowing. "Go!" she ordered. He had done enough already. He didn't need to risk getting infected by Worrall too. "Get out of here, while you still can!"

The boy hesitated, until he saw the antique ray gun in Myka's grip. That was enough to convince him that he was in way over his head. He wisely bolted from the scene, joining the fear-crazed exodus around them. Myka watched for a second, to make sure he got away safely, but quickly lost sight of him in the crowd. She hoped he'd be okay.

Even though nobody was really safe as long as Clara Barton's gloves were causing havoc.

I need to do something about that.

The commotion roused Pete from his delirium. He sagged against her, gripping his cane.

"Hey," he wheezed "Remember that time a job went easier than we expected?"

"No," Myka replied.

"Yeah, me neither."

CHAPTER
21

EN ROUTE

Ten thousand feet above the eastern half of the United States, the scarlet triplane flew toward New York at speeds unimaginable to the flying aces of the First World War. In theory, a Fokker DR-1 could achieve only 115 miles per hour tops, but the Red Baron's fabled fighter wasn't any ordinary triplane, at least not anymore. Fierce winds buffeted Claudia's face and goggles, forcing her to bury her face against Artie's back. Her scarf came loose and went flying off into the sky.

She considered stealing Artie's.

The Fokker's flimsy wood-and-canvas construction rattled alarmingly. Its whirring propeller spun too fast to be seen. Scorched and shredded wings still bore the scars of the plane's heated dogfight with the predatory thunderbird. Artifacts tended to be supernaturally durable, Claudia reminded herself, but she couldn't help wondering if they were pushing the old warbird too hard. What if the primitive aircraft came apart under the strain?

"Maybe you should ease up on the throttle?"

"Huh?" Artie's hands clutched the stick, working

it like a pro. Or, more likely, the stick was working him. "What did you say?"

She shouted above the wind and engine. Her teeth chattered. "You think you should slow down?"

"No time," he barked. "The psychic fair has started, Pete's sick, the gloves are in play, and Myka needs backup, ASAP. We may already be too late!"

"Well, when you put it that way. . . ." She resigned herself to a bumpy ride. "Explain to me again: How exactly are we getting this old bird to go jet speed?"

"I've souped up its engine over the years," he divulged, "using parts salvaged from one of Robert Goddard's experimental rockets." Goddard, a pioneering inventor, had been the father of modern rocketry. Flames shot from the Fokker's exhaust pipe. A sudden burst of acceleration pressed Claudia against the back of the cockpit. "I always thought it might come in handy someday!"

"And that's safe?"

"In theory," Artie said, less authoritatively than she would have liked. "This is the Red Baron's triplane. It's never crashed before!"

There's always a first time, Claudia mused, but kept the thought to herself. "Tell that to Snoopy."

The New York skyline appeared on the horizon. Claudia glimpsed the shamelessly phallic outline of the Empire State Building. No giant gorillas were in evidence, thank goodness. Triplane or not, she didn't feel like re-enacting the last act of *King Kong.* That bloodthirsty totem pole had been enough for one day. Plus, they still had those darn gloves to deal with.

"Look for someplace to land," Artie shouted. "Preferably out of the way. . . ."

She scanned the terrain below, searching for an empty field, a deserted parking lot, or the grounds of an abandoned factory. The view gave her vertigo. It was a long way down. "You do know how to land this thing, right?"

"No," he admitted. "But hopefully the plane does."

A sonic boom rattled New Jersey.

CENTRAL PARK

"Gather round, everyone. Sister Clara will be ready again in a moment."

Jim addressed the crowd while Nadia gathered her strength. Their "stage" consisted of a used Persian carpet they had rolled out atop the lawn. A red velvet sheet was draped over an aluminum lawn chair at the center of the rug, giving her someplace to rest between shows. *Sessions,* she corrected herself. A sturdy red box was set up in front of a microphone facing the audience. Twin poles, driven into the ground, supported a hand-painted white backdrop bearing a large red cross in honor of Clara Barton. Nadia had been reading up on the legendary nurse ever since those Secret Service agents had mentioned her back in Fairfield. She had felt an immediate kinship, a sense of connection, to Clara Barton, who had been everything Nadia wanted to become. She didn't understand how it was possible, but she felt convinced now that her healing gifts came from Clara. Had the miraculous glove once belonged to the real Clara Barton? In her heart, Nadia knew it had to be so.

I need to live up to her example, she thought. *Even if it kills me.*

A starched white nurse's uniform, several decades out of fashion, served as her latest costume. A blond wig helped to disguise her identity, or so she hoped. Jim had wanted her to lay low for a while, after that close call outside the gymnasium, but she had found her calling; she couldn't turn away from it if she tried. There were too many sick and injured people in the world, waiting to be healed. The moment she'd heard about this fair, she'd known it was where she belonged, no matter what. Where else could so many needy souls be able to find her, especially now that she was afraid to advertise online? It hadn't been easy, but grateful supporters and benefactors had worked their connections to get her booked into the fair at the last minute, albeit under an assumed name.

She couldn't disappoint them.

Despite their rudimentary setup, which had been thrown together on the run, a growing crowd surrounded the carpet, waiting for her to begin again. Hushed voices murmured excitedly about the miracles they had already seen "Sister Clara" perform. Curious skeptics waited to be convinced. After initially drawing only a handful of spectators, the throng had grown until it stretched across a large portion of the busy meadow, cannibalizing the audiences outside neighboring booths and stages. There were hundreds of people, maybe even a thousand, waiting for her now. The most eager and hopeful jostled to get to the front of the crowd, but no fights had broken out, she was glad to see. Everybody seemed to be behaving so far, although, in the future, she would probably have to think seriously about arranging for crowd control. The sheer size of the mob was more than a little intimidating. Could she really heal so many people in one day? Was it even safe to try?

Jim seemed to read her mind.

"You're already looking wasted," he whispered. "Maybe you should call it a day?"

She shook her head. "No way."

To be honest, she was seriously exhausted, but Jim didn't need to know that. Clara Barton had risked her life to help wounded soldiers on the battlefield. She had spent her entire life doing good.

How can I do less?

She sipped an energy drink to keep going. Maybe it would help.

"Don't be crazy." Jim kept his voice low, but there was no mistaking how worried he was. "You've done enough for today."

He was wasting his breath. She hated to put him through this, but it wasn't his decision.

"We've talked about this before. I *have* to do this. The glove chose me." She scratched at her right palm, which was starting to itch again. "If you really love me, you'll accept that."

"You know I love you. That's why I don't want to lose you."

She didn't doubt it. "I love you too. But this is what I was born to do." She finished off the energy drink and handed him the empty aluminum can. "I wish you could understand that."

"All right," he grumbled. His fist crushed the can with more force than was necessary. Scowling, he scanned the hopeful horde awaiting her. "But if I catch even a glimpse of those Feds, or that creepy bald dude, we're out of here, okay?"

"We'll see."

Nervous fingers checked to make sure her wig was still in place. She didn't want to get ambushed again, either, but that had been hundreds of miles from here, in a whole other state. There was no way those Secret Service types could find them here, was there? Amidst all these thousands of people? *I didn't even know I was going to be here until a few days ago.*

"'We'll see'?" Jim echoed unhappily. "What's that supposed to mean?"

She searched the crowd herself, but didn't spot either the agents or the sinister intruder who had accosted them. All she saw was a legion of pilgrims longing to be healed by her gift. Hundreds of expectant faces and fragile, fallible bodies called out to the glove, called out to her. She couldn't keep them waiting any longer.

"Shush," she told Jim, raising a gloved finger to her lips. Before he could object once more, she rose to her feet. A wave of dizziness washed over her, and her legs threatened to give out, but she closed her eyes, took a deep breath, and the moment passed. She still felt feverish and light-headed, yet she thought she could manage, at least for a little while longer. After that . . . well, maybe Jim had a point.

Just one more healing session, she promised herself, *then I'll get some rest.*

Maybe.

Stepping away from the chair, she walked slowly toward the audience. Jim helped her up onto the box so that the people in the back could see her. She took the mike from its stand and, with her left hand, held it to her lips. Her amplified voice rang out over the meadow.

"Thank you for your patience," she began, "and for joining us at this wonderful celebration of spirituality and the healing arts." Her voice was a little shaky at first, but grew stronger as she felt a familiar compulsion grip her. "I look forward to sharing my gift with all who need it."

The susurrus of hundreds of individual conversations fell silent. The crowd surged forward in anticipation, and for a terrifying moment she feared that she might be swept away by a tidal wave of suffering humanity, but she held up her hand like a traffic cop and the tsunami receded. The crowd halted at the edge of the carpet, hanging on her every word. Anxious parents thrust their children forward. Senior citizens were supported by younger, more able-bodied relatives. A young woman in a wheelchair waved her arm, desperate to be heard. A chorus of voices competed for her attention.

"Help me, please!"

"Are you for real? This isn't just an act?"

"Me first! Me first!"

She couldn't begin to count them all. Healing each of them individually would take forever.

Thankfully, that wasn't necessary anymore.

"Don't worry," she assured them. "There's no need to push ahead. No one is going to miss out, not even those of you way in the back." She perched on her tiptoes in hopes that all could see her. A sea of heads bobbed before her. "Just a word of warning before we begin. Some of you, those most in need of healing, with the most dire afflictions, may experience a momentary shock. You might even faint. So be prepared and look out for each other. I promise, it's just a temporary side effect. You'll all feel amazingly better afterwards."

She waited a moment or so to see if anyone wanted to change their mind about experiencing her gift, but nobody looked like they wanted to leave. If anything, the crowd seemed to be expanding by the minute. Nadia was deeply moved by their trust. She couldn't wait to get started again.

"All right," she declared. "Brace yourselves."

Without any further preliminaries, she raised her right hand in benediction. The audience gasped as a phosphorescent blue glow emanated from the glove. Nadia's stomach turned over queasily, but she couldn't stop now if she wanted to. Her gift was growing stronger. She didn't need to touch people one by one anymore. She just had to let the healing power of the glove flow out of her.

"Fear not! Let the light bathe you—and banish all your afflictions!"

Sparking azure beams radiated outward, spreading over the crowd like a laser light display. The audience oohed and aahed before succumbing to its restorative effect. People swooned throughout the crowd, often sagging into the arms of friends and loved ones. Not everyone collapsed, however. Others merely moaned or sighed as minor aches and pains were washed away by the unearthly effulgence. Mere spectators, drawn only by curiosity or ailing companions, gaped in wonder. There was a smattering of applause. A few overwhelmed people sobbed in joy.

Don't thank me, Nadia thought. *Thank Clara's glove!*

She basked in the moment. An overpowering sense of exhilaration allowed her to ignore the nausea churning in her belly. She swayed atop her makeshift podium, a dreamy expression on her face, as she held her right hand aloft. The azure light grew brighter and brighter, outshining the sun. All her doubts dissolved into the light. Forget the glove's occasionally unpleasant side effects: this was the greatest moment in her life. She could die happy now . . . if she had to.

Jim came up beside her, ready to catch her if she slipped.

"New York City, babe," he whispered proudly. She could tell he was making an effort to overcome his fears long enough to share this moment with her. "You've hit the big time."

Spoken like a born showman. She smiled indulgently. *You can take the boy out of the sideshow, but you can't take—*

A disturbance in the distance cut off her thought. There seemed to be something going on at the rear of the crowd, several yards away from the stage. Agitated shouts and exclamations reached her ears, contrasting sharply with the grateful sighs of the people nearer the front. People started racing madly away on the outskirts of the mob. They looked scared.

I don't understand, Nadia thought. *What's happening?*

She peered over the heads of the swooning pilgrims,

but there were too many people in the way. She couldn't make out what the problem was. Had somebody had a scary reaction to the light? People often collapsed after being healed, but they had always recovered quickly before, and without any lingering effects. Maybe someone was just panicking prematurely?

"It will be all right," she called out in a calming tone. "If anybody's feeling faint, just give them air. There's nothing to be afraid of, I promise."

But the cries grew louder and more frightened, like something was seriously wrong. The commotion was impossible to ignore. The rest of the audience started looking around anxiously. Jim tugged on her arm.

"Screw it!" he blurted. "I knew this was a bad idea. We need to get out of here!"

"I can't!" Nadia resisted his pull. "These people trusted me. I can't just leave them!"

The glowing glove flickered, then flared up even more brightly than before. Her palm itched like crazy. She fought an urge to scratch it. Her heart was pounding and her legs felt like rubber. She wiped her brow with her free hand.

Had this ever happened to Clara?

The crowd parted before her, starting at the outer fringes but working its way toward the front. People started collapsing down the middle of the audience while the folks at the sides ran away in fear, forming a wedge-shaped gap pointed at the stage. Terrified men and women trampled over each other in their haste to escape. A wheelchair was knocked over, spilling a young paraplegic woman onto the grass. Newly healed, she sprang to her feet and joined the frantic exodus. A desperate father clutched a crying toddler to his chest as he shoved and shouted his way past the panicked people blocking his path. Right behind him, a family of four dropped to the ground in unison. They hadn't gotten away quickly enough.

Is this my fault? Nadia wondered. *Am I doing this?*

Her audience fell away, revealing the source of the tumult. A solitary figure wearing a tan trench coat strode down the center of the wedge. A swirling gray fog accompanied him, wafting about him like a misty aura. Oily tendrils spread outward from his presence, rolling across the meadow, close to the ground. Nadia recognized his gaunt face and baleful gray eyes at once.

So did Jim.

"Crap! It's that freak from before!"

You could literally see the sickness fuming off him. The noisome vapors reeked of rot and disease. The contaminated air rippled around him as though burning up with fever. A familiar-looking white leather glove resided on his left hand. It pulled on her like a magnet.

He's come for me, she realized. *For my glove.*

The stranger cut a swath through what was left of her audience, infecting people left and right. He swept his left arm before him to clear a path to the stage. Like her, he didn't need to touch anyone to get to them. Fog billowed from his glove, throwing off infection with every wave of his hand. The plague felled all it touched. People dropped like flies, convulsing upon the ground. They coughed and moaned. Some even vomited.

"This is effed-up!" Jim tried to drag her away. "Come on! We can still get away!"

"No!" She yanked her arm free. "You go! I can help them!"

She had to undo whatever the stranger was doing. Her face wrinkled in concentration as she called upon the full power of the glove. *Help me, Clara!*

The spectral nimbus enveloping her hand intensified. Blazing blue light shone through the noxious gray mist, driving it back. The stranger was slowed as well. He staggered backward, as though repelled by the light, but quickly regained his footing.

"Very well." A sardonic smile played upon his thin lips. He threw out his left hand. "Let's see what you've got!"

A battle of wills ensued. Left versus right. Sickness versus health. Blue against gray. Caught in the middle, hundreds of innocent victims thrashed in agony upon the grass, their bodies and souls pummeled by conflicting waves of infection and relief. Nadia tried to heal them all, over and over again, even as the stranger spread his disease like wildfire. The luckiest souls, farther away from the conflict and as yet untouched by the fog, ran screaming from the meadow. Their headlong flight threw the entire fair into an uproar. Thousands of confused and frightened people, most not even knowing what had started the panic, started running as well. Pandemonium emptied the park, except for those who were already too ill to escape. They flailed about in torture.

This is a nightmare, Nadia thought, her heart breaking. *It wasn't supposed to be like this. I only wanted to help people!*

The weather was going wrong too. Angry black clouds came charging in from nowhere, hiding the sun. They clotted thickly overhead. Howling winds tore through the abandoned fair, blowing over deserted tents and booths. New Age pamphlets and trinkets flew about wildly. Fallen leaves swirled like red, yellow, and brown dust devils. The temperature dropped to freezing. What had been a beautiful fall afternoon turned bleak and wintry.

Just like in Fairfield.

Clara Barton's gloves, separated by time and fate, yearned for each other. Nadia felt the other glove pulling on her. Her palm itched like an entire colony of ants had burrowed beneath the glove and were chewing voraciously on her flesh. His arm outstretched, the stranger marched toward her, callously stepping over and around the convulsing bodies strewn in his path. Despite herself, Nadia stepped off the box. She lurched toward him.

"Wait! Where are you going?" Jim grabbed her around the waist, holding on to her like a lifeline. The irresistible force surprised him. "Son of a bitch! It's sucking on you!"

"Run!" she urged him. "Don't let him get you!"

"Not a chance!" He strained against the pull until they were leaning at nearly a forty-five-degree angle. Veins and tendons bulged on his neck. He grunted through clenched teeth. "I'm not going to let you go!"

"You have to!" She tilted forward, dragging him behind her. Both of his arms were wrapped around her. Callused fingers, strengthened by years of knife practice, dug into her side. "Please, Jim. Save yourself!"

"Not without you!"

They were fighting a losing battle, but she couldn't give up. While Jim pulled with all his might, she kept trying to dispel the contagion spreading from the other glove. It was getting harder, though. She had never before healed so many people, so horribly sickened, and she had already felt wasted *before* the dreadful stranger had crashed her party. Now the strain was killing her. Perspiration beaded on her forehead and dripped into her eyes. Her head felt like it was going to explode. She was sick to her stomach. This was worse than ever before. Despite the cold, she felt like she was burning up.

But she couldn't surrender. Too many innocent pilgrims were depending on her.

I can do this, she thought, even as she shivered uncontrollably. *My glove is just as strong as his.*

But was she?

The stranger moved toward her decisively. His once ashen face was pink with health. A triumphant grin mocked her efforts. "What's the matter?" he heckled her. "Feeling a little under the weather, are we?"

It wasn't fair. He seemed to be getting stronger even as she got weaker. The blue light began to dim. A fetid gray fog bank rolled toward her.

Ferocious winds assailed the stage from all directions. The painted backdrop tore loose from one post and flapped noisily behind her. It cracked like a gunshot. The red fabric draped over her seat blew away, exposing the folding aluminum lawn chair underneath. The chair tumbled across the carpet. The air was full of flying debris. Dry leaves and litter smacked against her face.

"Holy crap!" Jim yelled over the wailing winds. He shifted his grip around her waist, struggling to hold on. "Watch out!"

The overturned chair took flight. It came zooming at her head like a missile and he spun her around, shielding her with his own body. The chair clipped him in the side of the head. Airborne metal collided with flesh and bone, yielding a nauseating *thunk*. He grunted in pain. "Aaagh!"

"Jim?"

The chair bounced away. Nadia twisted her head to look behind her.

"Jim! Ohmigod, Jim!"

Blood dripped from his scalp. His arms slipped away from her waist. He reeled backward, clutching his head. His fingers came away stained with red.

"I'm sorry, babe," he said weakly. "I promised to take care of you. . . ."

He collapsed onto the carpet.

"Jim!"

She wanted to go to him, heal him, but the gloves chose otherwise. Without Jim to anchor her, she was yanked off her feet in the opposite direction. She stumbled helplessly toward the stranger. The Fever Man.

"At last we meet." His bony face held an arrogant smirk. "You may not know it, but I've been following your career for some time now."

They came together at the edge of the stage. He seized her throat with his right hand while his gloved left hand grabbed onto her right. Thunder boomed overhead as the two gloves met. A sudden shock jolted Nadia. The ghastly fog swirled about their ankles. Her palm stopped itching.

"Let go of me!" She struggled to get away, but he was stronger, healthier. She was too sick to fight back. Her limbs felt like lead weights; she could barely lift them. The world spun dizzily around her. She couldn't catch her breath. "Who . . . who are you?"

He tightened his grip on her throat. "Under the circumstances, I hardly think introductions are required." Busy fingers unbuttoned her glove at the wrist. He tugged on the precious relic. "I'm not interested in you, only this miraculous glove."

"No, don't!" Her heart sank as she felt the cozy leather slide off her fingers. "It's mine!"

"Not anymore." Spittle sprayed from his lips. His sour breath made her gorge rise. "You have no idea how long I've been searching for this particular item. My whole life, really."

The glove came away from her fingers, leaving her. He shoved her away and she tumbled to the ground, where she joined the hundreds of other quaking bodies strewn across the meadow. The fog surrounded her, seeping into her bones and invading her lungs. Too weak to get up again, she choked on the fumes. Chills and fever ravaged her prostrate form. She clawed feebly at the ground, trying to get away. The nausea was overpowering. She threw up in her mouth.

"Clara Barton's gloves," the Fever Man gloated. He stood amidst a field of agonized victims, like a scene out of Dante's *Inferno*. He caressed the stolen glove reverently. "You never deserved this. You could never appreciate how much I needed it. It always belonged with me."

The gloves were a perfect match.

"They belong together."

He stepped away from the false healer. She didn't matter anymore.

Even before he put it on, he could feel the power of the glove. It called to him like a drug. Fumbling with excitement, barely able to contain himself, he slipped it onto his naked right hand. White kid leather magically stretched to accommodate him. Eager fingers wiggled into the glove. He couldn't don it fast enough.

Finally!

For the first time in generations, the gloves were reunited. Worrall stiffened in shock as their power met and merged within him. He stretched out his arms. Silver lightning arced between the matching gloves before blinking out of sight. His bloodshot eyes cleared. Constricting veins receded beneath his skin. A ruddy pink glow tinted his cheeks. Every last trace of fatigue and illness vanished from his body. He had never felt so alive, so powerful. He flexed his fingers.

At long last, he held both life and death in his hands.

Surging clouds circled above him, heralding his long-delayed apotheosis. An icy wind lifted the corners of his coat. No longer caught in the crossfire of his duel with the girl, the anonymous masses littering the meadow stopped convulsing. Devastated by their ordeal, they sprawled comatose upon the ground. Their still and silent forms surrounded him like a garden of cadavers. *Let them sleep,* he thought coldly. *They were just getting in my way before.*

He sneered at the girl on the carpet. "You have no idea how long I've waited for this."

"Who are you?" she whimpered, too weak to lift herself. Her bare right hand reached futilely for the stolen glove. Anguished eyes filled with tears. "What are you going to do with them?"

"Whatever I feel like, I suppose." To be honest, he hadn't given it much thought. He had always been too intent on finding the glove—and healing himself—to worry much about what came next. But now that he felt the power of both gloves coursing through his veins and sinews, all sorts of intoxicating possibilities flooded his imagination. "I've wasted too much of my life being sick and miserable. It's about time I enjoyed myself and lived life to the fullest." He held up his hands, admiring the gloves. They fit perfectly, as though custom-made. "These treasures are the key to my success."

"No," she moaned. "You don't understand. The glove is a gift. You need to use it to help people, like I did. . . ."

"And look where that brought you." Her pathetic state was an unwelcome reminder of all the hours he'd spent sick in bed, too wretched to go anywhere or do anything. Years of envy and resentment demanded expression and he kicked her in the ribs, punishing her for hoarding *his* glove for so long. She rolled away from him, clutching her side. Worrall relished her misery. "You're the one who doesn't understand. With these gloves, I alone will choose who will live and who will die." He gazed out over the stricken rabble spilled across the meadow. The sight of so many helpless victims, all lying pitifully at his feet, only fueled his fantasies. His voice rose in exultation. "Heads of state and titans of industry will plead for my favor and fear my wrath. I'll sicken entire nations if I feel like it, and bestow my blessings only on those who pledge allegiance to me. . . ."

"Yeah, right," a female voice intruded. "Like we're going to let that happen."

CHAPTER
22

CENTRAL PARK

Myka faced Worrall across a field of sick and dying people. The grassy meadow resembled a battlefield after the shooting was over. The Civil War had finally come to Central Park, only a century or so late. She advanced carefully to avoid stepping on any of Worrall's unconscious victims. They moaned and whimpered all around her, dazed and thoroughly out of it. Nobody appeared to be dead yet, but Myka couldn't be sure of that. There were far too many casualties to check on right away. She couldn't remember the last time she'd seen this many innocent bystanders affected by a single artifact at the same time. Maybe that night with Lucrezia Borgia's comb, or the riot at the prison?

But this was no time for a trip down memory lane. Her keen eyes instantly took in the scene. Calvin Worrall, now in possession of *both* gloves and looking much stronger and spryer than she remembered. Nadia down on the ground, her right hand bare. Her boyfriend out cold several feet away, bleeding from what looked like a nasty head wound. Hundreds of plague victims strewn about the meadow. The weather freaking out like it was the end of the world.

Close enough, she thought. *If only I'd gotten here a few minutes earlier!*

But maybe there was still a chance to save all these innocent people.

And Pete.

"Give me those gloves, Worrall." She had the human epidemic in the sights of her Tesla. Its glass chamber glowed threateningly. Its batteries were fully charged. "Both of them."

"You know me?" He was taken aback by her use of his name, but quickly recovered. His patrician tones dripped with sarcasm. "Sorry. Can't oblige." He glared at her with undisguised contempt. "I have other plans."

"Tough." Myka wasn't taking no for an answer. According to Artie, Worrall had been sick his whole life and perhaps worthy of their pity, but right now she wasn't feeling particularly sympathetic to his plight. He had already hurt too many people. And the fact that he also appeared to be a smug, pompous son of a bitch only made her trigger finger that much itchier. "Last chance, Calvin. Hand them over before I prescribe a hefty dose of shock treatment."

He clasped his gloved hands together. Tangential energy crackled between his intertwined digits. He didn't look worried.

"Give me your best shot."

"If you insist."

She squeezed the trigger, unleashing a devastating bolt of electrical kick-ass. The blast should have been enough to knock Worrall flat on his butt, but he merely staggered backward a few steps, like he'd been thunked in the chest by a large swinging pillow. Traceries of purple energy crackled across his body before dissipating harmlessly into the stormy atmosphere. Worrall laughed out loud.

"Is that all you've got?" He straightened up, shrugging off the blast. "I've lived with pain my entire life. You think a little tickle like that is going to stop me?"

It should have been more than a tickle, she thought. Clearly, she had underestimated the effect of bringing the two gloves back together. Worrall was supercharged now, and more than a little out of his mind. So what was it going to take to stop him?

She tried to reason with him. "Listen to me, Calvin. What you're doing is dangerous. We have no idea how those gloves might be affecting you. They might even be messing with your mind." She adopted a concerned tone. "Trust me. I've seen it before."

"You have no idea what you're talking about." He cracked his knuckles inside the white kid gloves. "This is the answer to my prayers. I've never felt better in my life!"

"And what about all these innocent people?" She nodded at the comatose civilians while keeping the Tesla aimed at Worrall. The meadow looked like the site of a nerve gas attack. "They look like they're feeling better now?"

"Not my problem," he said coldly. "I've paid my dues. It's their turn to suffer."

Okay, that cinched it. Unlike Nadia, Calvin Worrall was *not* a nice person. Myka just wished she had a better idea of how to wipe the smirk from his face. To think that those same gloves had once tended gently to the sick, wounded, and dying. *Clara Barton must be rolling over in her grave.*

"You do not want to mess with the Secret Service," she warned, switching from good cop to bad cop all on her own. She used the same steely gaze and manner she had once employed to disarm presidential assassins. "Hand over the gloves. That's an order."

"Your badge doesn't impress me, Agent." He snickered. "As your partner found out back in Fairfield." A cruel grin taunted Myka. He shaded his eyes with one hand and made a show of looking for someone. "So where is he anyway?"

"Right behind you, buster!"

Pete could barely stand, let alone walk. Sneaking up on Worrall from behind had taken pretty much the last of his willpower. His head was spinning and he could hardly breathe. Every time he coughed, his mouth tasted of blood. Darkness encroached on his field of vision. His gut felt like a ferret was trying to dig its way out of his stomach. His legs wobbled like those licorice sticks Myka was always nibbling on. Sweat bathed his face and soaked through his clothes. Alternating hot and cold flashes washed over him, so that he was burning up one moment and chilled to the marrow the next. A metal pole was thrust into the ground nearby, next to a flapping canvas backdrop. He held on to the pole to support himself. His right fist gripped the hickory cane.

"Yeah, you heard me, bub. Ready for a rematch?"

Startled, Worrall spun around to face Pete. The creep was looking distinctly less cadaverous than he had the last time around, but there was no mistaking his ugly mug. Pete had been seeing it in his fever dreams ever since Worrall had blindsided him outside the gym. More than once, he had fantasized about blasting the scumbag's head off his shoulders, then using P. T. Barnum's top to grow Calvin a new head so he could do it all over again.

Hey, it beat counting sheep. . . .

"You!" Worrall snarled, recognizing Pete as well. He looked shocked to see Pete up and about, not to mention alive. His eyes bulged. "You shouldn't be here. I already disposed of you."

"Sorry to disappoint you, Infectious Lad." Pete doubted that the other guy would get the comic-book reference, but what the hey. He needed to use up all his good material before he kicked the bucket—which felt like it could be any minute now. "I don't dispose easily."

"And yet you came back for a second dose?" Worrall got over his surprise. His snotty attitude reasserted itself. "Perhaps you should have your head examined, Secret Service Man? Sounds to me like there's something seriously wrong with you."

Pete shrugged. "Says the guy wearing ladies' gloves."

Worrall scowled; he didn't like being the butt of a joke. "You think that's funny?" He started to raise his left hand. Clara's Barton's glove glowed ominously. An icky gray miasma seeped from his fingers. "Let me remind you what this 'ladies's glove' can do."

Uh-uh, Pete thought. *Two can play at that game.*

Digging deep, he stomped the cane upon the ground. An incandescent pulse of energy radiated from the cane's steel-shod tip before vanishing beneath the surface of the lawn, which rippled unexpectedly like a carpet being shaken. A seismic tremor shook the earth. Clouds of sediment puffed upward where the cane had struck. Nearby booths and stands toppled over, crashing onto the grass. Trembling trees shook loose their last leaves, leaving their branches completely denuded. The strewn bodies of Worrall's victims bounced atop the shaking earth.

"Take that, Creepy Cal," Pete crowed. "Bet you didn't see that coming."

The elephant-head walking stick had once belonged to an eccentric British military man named Brigadier General Laverlong. An inveterate world traveler, he had constructed the cane using rare elements from the four corners of the earth. It had resided in a museum in Lakefield, Illinois, before Pete and Myka had retrieved it for the Warehouse a while back, and with good reason. Funny thing about the cane: it caused earthquakes. . . .

The tremor knocked Worrall off his feet, breaking his concentration. The toxic miasma around his glove faded and he landed upon the grass not far from Nadia. Myka lost her balance as well. She toppled backward into a tangle of groaning bodies. The quake jolted many of Worrall's victims from their stupor and they scrambled to their feet. Confused and disoriented, they stampeded from the park. Dazed by the dueling gloves and shaken by the earthquake, they'd probably have only foggy memories of what had happened to them.

"Wha—? What's going on?" a tattooed teen called out to his buddy. A skateboard was tucked beneath his arm. "Is this, like, a terrorist thing?"

"I don't know, man! Just run!"

Pete lost sight of Myka in the chaos. Had she managed to get to her feet in time, or had she been trampled by the maddened crowd? Standing at the epicenter of the quake, Pete was unaffected, but the stunt exhausted the last of his reserves. He crumpled onto the lawn, gasping for breath. The elephant-head cane slipped from his fingers, which were too weak to hold on to it anymore. It felt like an elephant was stepping on his chest, actually, and jabbing his skull with its tusks. His heart was racing out of control. He couldn't stop coughing.

Damn, he thought. *I could really use a drink right now. . . .*

Trembling fingers groped feebly for the cane but couldn't reach it. The seismological stick was only inches away, but it might as well have been back in South Dakota. A handgun was holstered beneath his jacket, but he'd be afraid to use it even if he still had oomph enough to draw it. The way his hands were shaking, he'd hit Myka or one of the bystanders instead. He didn't want to die with an accidental shooting on his conscience. Not stopping Worrall was hard enough.

I did my part, he thought. *It's up to Myka now.*

He hoped he'd live long enough to see her kick Worrall's ass.

The ground stopped shaking. Through blurry eyes, Pete watched helplessly as Worrall scrambled to his feet, looking distinctly worse for wear. Blood dripped from a split lip. His trench coat was rumpled and dirty. He spit red onto the lawn.

But his injuries were nothing the gloves couldn't fix. He ran his right index finger over his lip, which healed beneath its touch. A self-satisfied smirk tested the repaired mouth. He brushed the leaves and grass from his soiled attire before turning back toward Pete, whom he regarded warily. You could practically see the wheels turning behind his wrinkled brow.

"How did you . . . ?" Worrall's gray eyes zeroed in on the cane. "Ah, I see. Another interesting toy, much like my gloves." He chuckled. "You are full of surprises, I'll give you that." He cast a covetous look at the artifact and started toward it, his greedy fingers curling in anticipation. The cane lay unguarded upon the lawn. "You don't mind if I help myself to that quite remarkable walking stick, do you? From the looks of things, you won't be needing it much longer."

The thought of Worrall getting his germy gloves on the cane terrified Pete, but there was nothing he could do to stop him. He tried to drag himself across the grass, hoping to shield the cane with his own body, but his useless limbs refused to cooperate. The pain in his gut was almost unbearable. Pete wasn't quite sure what peritonitis was, but he guessed this was it.

"Hands off, Calvin," Pete rasped. "You've caused enough damage."

Worrall found the dying agent's defiance amusing. "I don't think you're in any position to issue orders, my moribund friend." He strolled past Pete's prone body, whistling a classical melody. Myka would have known what it was. "Perhaps I should test my new cane on your thick, impenetrable skull. Put you out of your misery once and for all."

The horrible thing was, that almost sounded like a good idea, except for the part about Worrall gaining the power to create earthquakes at will. Like being the king of sickness and health wasn't enough for the slimy bastard. . . .

Where was Myka? Pete lifted his head enough to see his partner sprawled unconscious on the grass along with the remainder of Worrall's victims, who were still slowly coming to. The quake, or maybe getting trampled by the fleeing populace, had taken her out of the game at the worst possible moment. He silently urged her to snap out of it and stop Worrall before it was too late.

Get up, Myka! Don't let this jerk get the cane too!

He suddenly wished he had left the cane in the Warehouse where it belonged.

"So wherever did you find this singular item?" Worrall asked out loud. "I can't imagine it's standard government issue."

Pete was not about to satisfy the bad guy's curiosity. "You'd be surprised. . . ."

"Fine," Worrall answered, sounding slightly peeved. "Take your classified secrets to the grave. I'll soon have influence enough to find out whatever I want."

He bent to pick up the cane.

Pete got ready to be turned into a fault zone. He wondered if they'd be able to feel the tremor all the way in South Dakota.

Bye, Artie. Bye, Claudia, he thought. *Sorry I let you down.*

At least he was dying sober. That had to count for something.

But before Worrall could grasp the cane, a pounding vibration startled both men. For a moment Pete thought it was some sort of aftershock, but then he recognized the sound, which was probably the last thing he had ever expected to hear in the middle of Manhattan.

The thunder of racing hooves.

CHAPTER
23

CENTRAL PARK

"Giddy-yap!" Claudia yelped.

A horse-drawn carriage, commandeered by her and Artie, came galloping across the meadow like the cavalry. Perched in the driver's seat behind a wild-eyed brown horse, Artie worked the reins while Claudia rode shotgun—literally: a Super Soaker squirt gun, roughly the size of a bazooka, was clutched to her chest. Purple neutralizer goo sloshed inside the squirt gun's ample reservoir. A spare tank of goo rested in the open passenger compartment behind her, alongside the carriage's actual driver, who was snoring off the effect of Artie's Tesla next to a trio of unconscious Japanese tourists. After some debate, she and Artie had decided to cart the whole party along, rather than leave them defenseless on a New York City sidewalk, where they would have likely been trampled by the panicked mob fleeing the park. The frantic crowd had been their first indication that Pete and Myka were in trouble. Claudia glanced back at the sleeping driver. She hoped they weren't taking the poor driver and tourists straight from the frying pan into the fire.

And the horse too.

The situation sure looked craptastic enough. Myka and Pete were both down for the count, surrounded by oodles of wiped-out civilians. The Psychic Fair was a shambles, with overturned tents and booths catering to absolutely no one. Discarded pamphlets, crystals, and candles had been ground into the lawn by thousands of racing shoes, boots, and sandals. A homemade Red Cross had fallen over. Loose tarot cards blew about in the wind.

Yikes, Claudia thought. *Talk about bad karma. . . .*

She spotted Worrall at once. His driver's license portrait hardly did him justice. The contagious culprit looked even more malevolent in real life. Claudia shuddered at the sight of him—and cried out when she spotted Worrall going for the earthshaking elephant-head cane, only a few paces away from Pete. A mental image, of a freak tremor flipping the speeding carriage over with bone-shattering results, played before her mind's eye with Blu-ray clarity.

"Artie! There he is! He's after the cane!"

"I know, I know! I'm not blind!" Artie cracked a whip above the horse's head, spurring it on. The driver's seat bounced uncomfortably beneath Claudia, adding to the bruises she had sustained while evading the angry totem pole. Her teeth rattled and she struggled to hold on to the goo-filled squirt gun, which, let it be noted, had been her brilliant idea, just in case anyone was wondering. The horse's hooves tore up the lawn, sending clumps of sod flying up behind it. Steam shot from its nostrils. Artie tugged on the reins, steering the runaway carriage right toward Worrall. "Not so fast, Calvin!" he shouted. "Those gloves and that cane are property of the U.S. government!"

Worrall's jaw dropped. He froze, momentarily transfixed by the unexpected sight of an old-fashioned hansom cab charging toward him. "What the devil?"

Abandoning the cane, he dived out of the way just in time to avoid being run over. "Whoa!" Artie hollered, pulling up on the reins. Overexcited, the horse kept on going, galloping between Worrall and Pete, effectively cutting the felon off from both Pete and the cane. "Whoa, whoa!" Artie repeated, and not in the Keanu sense. "Slow down, you deranged nag, before I have you stuffed alongside Trigger!" He fought to bring the crazed equine under control while also circling Worrall, who had clambered to his feet and was now looking like he wanted to make a break for it.

"This is insane," he protested. "Who are you people?"

"Who are you calling crazy, Looney Tunes?" Claudia shot back. "There's a blackened pot back at home base that would like to have a word with you."

Artie nudged her with his elbow. "What are you waiting for?" he groused impatiently. "Take the shot!"

"Slow down first!" The way the carriage was careening across the lawn, she could barely hold on to the squirt rifle. Artie expected her to take aim and fire too? "Who do you think I am, Annie Oakley?"

"Actually, the real Annie Oakley, a.k.a. Phoebe Ann Mosley, visited the Warehouse back in 1915," Artie said pedantically. "She and Buffalo Bill were close friends of Thomas Edison, who featured them in some of his early kinetoscopes. . . ."

"That was a rhetorical question!" she exclaimed, cutting off a typically Artie-ish digression. The seat rocked beneath her and she had to grab onto a rail to keep from tumbling off the carriage. That hair-raising dogfight in the Fokker was starting to seem like a leisurely sightseeing tour by comparison. She wished she'd thought to hang on to her crash helmet. "Not really a good time for a history lesson!"

"I suppose not," Artie conceded. He glanced at the squirt gun. "So are you going to fire that thing or not?"

"Okay, okay!" She rolled her eyes. "Don't be such a noodge."

Down on the ground, Worrall darted from side to side, searching for some way to evade the carriage and its drivers. Finding himself trapped without a horse of his own, he threw out his left hand. A hazy gray mist began to manifest from his fingers.

"You asked for this!" he snarled. "You have no idea who—or what—you're dealing with!"

"*Au contraire,* fever freak," Claudia replied. "This is what we do."

Exhausted, the horse began to slow to a trot. *That's more like it,* Claudia thought. Taking aim, she let loose with the Super Soaker. A thick purple spray shot from its muzzle, reminding her of the emergency hose back at the Warehouse. The spray arced through the air before dousing Worrall in a grape-colored cascade. Both gloves briefly lit up like all ten fingers were wearing Benjamin Franklin's electric ring (which Claudia sometimes used to explore murky conduits back at the Warehouse). A blinding flash brought tears to Claudia's eyes. Worrall's own eyes were protected by a heavy layer of goo.

"Bull's-eye!" She pumped the squirt gun and gave him a second blast for luck. This time she hit him square in the chest. "You've been slimed, dude!"

Artie nodded approvingly. The carriage slowed to a stop in front of her target. "Nice shot."

"I'll say!" she agreed. "Did you see that? Do I get a gold star or what?"

"How many times do I have tell you? We don't do stars."

"Maybe it's time to reconsider that policy?" Claudia suggested. "Personally, I'm feeling very starworthy right now."

The Super Soaker had lived up to its name—and then some. Worrall looked like he'd been dipped in a vat of purple sludge. Neutralizer dripped from his hair, face, and clothing. Claudia knew the feeling. Her own clothes were still sticky. She couldn't wait to change into some clean duds if and when they saved the day.

"What—" Worrall sputtered, spitting goo from his lips. He was smart enough not to swallow any of it. Wiping the gunk from his eyes, he gazed down in bewilderment at the slimy, drippy mess he had become. He glowered at Claudia and her squirt gun. "Are you serious?" He sounded seriously pissed off. "Do you think this is some sort of silly slapstick comedy?"

Clearly, he had no idea what the neutralizer was for.

"I don't who you are," he fumed, "but that's the last imbecilic prank you're ever going to play." He shook his left fist at Claudia and Artie. "Prepare to choke to death on your own phlegm and bile!"

Ick, Claudia thought. Despite her surprisingly expert marksmanship, she experienced a moment of anxiety. The neutralizer was *mucho* effective, most of the time, but it didn't *always* work. Defanging artifacts was not an exact science. What if the gloves still had a little mojo left? She tried squirting Worrall again, just to be safe, but only a few last drops dribbled from the muzzle. That last mega-blast had emptied the gun. *Remind me to bring a backup soaker next time,* she thought. If *there's a next time.*

Worrall's gaunt face grimaced in concentration. He clenched his left fist. Claudia nervously felt her forehead to see if she was running a fever, but her brow seemed to be just normal body temperature, at least as far as she could tell. A sideways glance at Artie didn't find him keeling over, either.

She crossed her fingers. "Looking good so far."

"Damnit!" Worrall stared in anger and confusion at his gooey glove. Whatever he was trying to do wasn't happening. The gloves sparked briefly before fizzling out entirely. A tiny wisp of gray mist issued from the left glove, then dissipated. The right glove couldn't even muster a glow. He smacked the gloves together, trying to get them to work. "What's wrong? Why isn't it working?"

Claudia grinned at Artie. "Looks to me like the fever has broken."

"My diagnosis as well, Nurse Donovan."

"'Nurse'?" She feigned indignation. "Sexist much?"

"Well, I'm not going to be the nurse," Artie replied. "I can't even stand the sight of blood."

"Wimpazoid."

Their banter was wasted on Worrall. His angry expression was overwritten by panic as he realized that the gloves were out of commission. Abandoning the cane as well, he bolted from the stalled carriage. A stand of elm trees at the west end of the meadow offered cover, and he made for it on foot. No doubt he hoped to escape the park altogether and lose himself in the teeming streets of Manhattan.

He didn't get far.

Myka blocked his escape. A bit rumpled and battered-looking, she didn't look disposed to go easy on him.

"Let's try this again," she said.

Unlike Worrall, her Tesla still had plenty of juice left. Artificial lightning leaped from the gun to Worrall, who could no longer heal himself or shrug off the powerful electrical jolt. Scorched goo sizzled and he toppled backward onto the lawn. In the distance, the bronze Union soldier looked on from atop his granite pedestal. The sun came out, forming a halo around the Civil War monument. A trick of the light made it seem like the statue was smiling.

Myka threw the solder a salute before hurrying to check on Worrall. She approached the supine figure cautiously, just in case he was playing possum, and nudged him sharply with the toe of her boot. He didn't stir. It appeared that he was out cold for real. His eyes were shut. His body was limp. The smell of singed neutralizer rose from his motionless form.

"About time," she muttered.

Taking no chances, she cuffed his wrists before peeling the gloves from his hands. They were covered with goo, but she didn't care. Purple gloves protected her own hands from whatever power might still be lurking in Clara Barton's corrupted hand wear. Worrall whimpered in his sleep, and tried to yank his hands away from her, but Myka didn't let that slow her down. Every minute counted.

"Hang on, Pete. I'm coming."

Claiming both gloves, she left Worrall sprawled on the grass and sprinted back to where Pete lay dying. Claudia and Artie were already attending to him while the carriage horse grazed on the lawn a few yards away. The animal's flanks were drenched with sweat. Myka didn't give the horse a second glance.

"How is he doing?" she asked anxiously. *Please, don't let it be too late!*

Artie crouched beside Pete, checking his pulse. He shook his head dolefully. Claudia swallowed a sob as she clutched Pete's hand. His face was gray. His whole body was shaking. A thin stream of blood trickled from the corner of his mouth. Myka had seen enough old movies to know that almost always meant somebody was a goner. An almost-physical pain walloped her. She stared at him in horror.

"We're losing him," Artie confirmed.

"No! Just . . . no." She had hoped that simply neutralizing the gloves would be enough to cure Pete, but apparently it didn't work that way. More active measures were called for. She fought back against despair. Pete needed her now. "I'm not going to let that happen."

The gloves were still dripping with goo, but she wiped them off on the grass as best she could. She removed her own latex gloves and tossed them aside. Ignoring the left glove for the moment, she started to put on Nadia's glove. The right glove, in more ways than one.

"Hold on," Artie said. His bushy eyebrows shot upward in alarm. "What are you doing?"

"What do you think?" Myka replied. The glove felt too big at first, but it shrunk to fit her. She took that as a sign that she had wiped off enough neutralizer—and that maybe she was meant to do this. It was only her hope. "I'm going to try to heal him."

Claudia gave her worried look. "You sure about that? I thought curing people with that glove made the healer sick. What if bringing Pete back from the brink . . . isn't good for you?"

"She's right," Artie said bluntly. "It's too dangerous. You might die instead."

"I don't care." Myka flexed her fingers. The glove fit her snugly. "He's my partner. I can't just stand by and watch him die."

Even though Pete was the one who was dying, their times together flashed before her eyes. She remembered hanging out with him at the Warehouse and Leena's place, sharing jokes and meals on the road, and comforting each other through hard times, like when her dad was sick and after Pete's girlfriend left him. Snowball fights, birthday parties, and movie nights competed with narrow escapes and unforgettable moments of mutual wonder in her mental photo album. She and Pete had traveled through time together and even shared the same body on occasion. His reckless attitude had driven her nuts back at the Secret Service, but now she couldn't imagine a life without him. If he died, part of her would too. Forever.

Unless the glove could save him.

A photographic memory of Nadia laying hands on the afflicted in that stuffy tent in West Haven came back to Myka. She reached out for Pete.

His hand shot up to stop her.

"N-no, Myka! Don't!" Pete croaked. Palsied fingers gripped her wrist. He somehow found the strength to try to hold her hand back. "I'm not . . ." A wrenching cough broke up his words. ". . . not going to let you do this. . . ."

"Please, Pete!" She gently wrested her hand from his grip. He was too weak to really stop her, but she didn't want to heal him against his will—not unless she absolutely had to. Her voice cracked. "You don't understand. I can't lose you like this. I *have* to save you."

For a second she was back in Denver, cradling Sam in her arms as his life slipped away before her eyes. A madman's bullet had claimed his life, just like this goddamn fever was killing Pete. *Not again,* she thought desperately. *I can't go through this again.*

"Forget it!" He scooted back across the grass, trying to get away from her. "Not going to . . . let you trade your life . . . for mine." He fought to get the words out. Every halting syllable seemed to tear itself painfully from his chest. "Couldn't live with that. . . ."

Artie tried to pull her away. "Myka, you don't want to do this. Believe me."

He was hoarse with emotion. She knew he had to

be thinking of the Phoenix, a mystical artifact that had once brought him back from the ashes—at the expense of another's life. He never spoke of it, but she could only imagine what that knowledge must feel like. One more guilty burden to add to those he was already carrying. A lifetime of survivor's guilt.

Would Pete be able to shoulder that sort of load? Was it fair to ask him to?

"But I have to do something!" She pulled away from Artie. Her eyes brimmed with tears as she wrestled with her conscience. What was the right thing to do? And did she even care about doing right if it meant losing Pete like she had lost Sam? The glove taunted her, tempted her. She understood now why Nadia had clung to it so fiercely. "What's the point of chasing miracles for a living if I can't use one when it matters most?"

"That's the hell of it," he said sadly. "Miracles break the rules. It's why we have to lock them away."

She knew he was right, in theory. All her life she had tried to go by the book, play by the rules. Just this once, couldn't she make an exception?

Even if it meant sacrificing her life?

"Let me do it," Nadia volunteered. She came up behind Myka, so quietly that the distraught agent had not even heard the younger woman approach. Her bare hand fell softly on Myka's shoulder. "I chose this. It's my responsibility."

"Uh-uh." Claudia let go of Pete's hand and jumped to her feet. She hurried around to grab hold of Nadia and tug her away from Myka. Still weakened from her ordeal, the healer was in no shape to fight back. "Not so fast, medicine woman." Claudia glanced anxiously at Artie. "There's gotta be another way!"

But was there?

Pete was slipping away. His arm dropped limply to his side. His head lolled against the ground. His bloodshot eyes rolled up until only the pinkish whites could be seen. Tremors shook his body. His chest rose and fell shallowly. "Dad?" he murmured deliriously. "Is that you?"

Pete's father, a fireman, had died when he was just a child.

"Please," Nadia begged. She reached in vain for the glove even as Claudia held her back. "Let me heal him. I know I can do it."

Just for second, Myka considered taking her up on her offer. But no, she couldn't let anyone else risk themselves. Pete was her partner . . . and her friend. He had been infected while defending her. *This one's on me.*

"C'mon, Pete," she pleaded with him. "Stay with me."

He didn't seem to hear her. This was Denver all over again. . . .

"Oh, crap," Claudia said behind her. "This can't be happening."

"It's not." Myka made up her mind. Pete had risked his life for her more times than she could count. Now it was her turn. She raised her gloved hand and looked at Nadia. "So how does this work, anyway? Do I just think about healing him? Is there a trick to it?"

Artie looked aghast. "Myka, wait!"

She shot him a warning look. "Don't try and stop me, Artie."

"But I have an idea," he said urgently. "Let me try something else!"

Myka hesitated. Pete only had moments left. What if she missed her chance?

If he dies because I made the wrong call, I'm through. I'll never trust myself again.

"Trust me, Myka." Artie looked her squarely in the eyes. "I just want to save you both."

She searched his weathered face for certainty. Artie knew more about artifacts, she reminded herself, than anybody else except maybe Mrs. Frederic. If she couldn't trust him, what was she even doing here?

"All right," she said. "What do you want to do?"

"Let's put both gloves on him. Quickly!"

He snatched Worrall's glove from the ground and starting pulling it onto Pete's limp left hand. Following his lead, Myka yanked off the right glove and tried to put it on Pete's hand instead. His trembling fingers didn't exactly cooperate, but the glove itself seemed to mold itself to Pete's hand. He gasped weakly. His breathing slowed.

"Hurry, guys!" Claudia urged them from the sidelines. "I think the clock is running out."

Myka tried to ignore Pete's final groans. Wearing both gloves had made Worrall almost invincible. She could only hope that Pete would benefit from them as well. Frantic fingers buttoned the glove around his wrist, then reluctantly let go of his hand. "Done!" she reported to Artie. "You?"

"Almost." He checked to make sure the left glove was properly fitted. "There!" He scrambled backward, as though anticipating some variety of pyrotechnic reaction. He tugged Myka away as well. "With any luck, the healing and the horror will cancel each other out...."

Something happened right away, that was for sure. Violent convulsions rocked Pete's body, which practically lifted off the ground. A thick gray mist oozed from his pores even as a brilliant blue radiance spread across his body. The light combated the fog, but it was impossible to tell which was winning. Was the glow dispelling the haze, or was the fog extinguishing the light? And could Pete's debilitated body even survive the eldritch forces battling within him? Myka prayed that Artie had calculated correctly, and that she hadn't missed her last chance to save Pete.

What if they had only made his final moments all the more excruciating?

"What's happening?" she asked, wringing her hands. The suspense was almost more than she could take. She *had* to know what was happening. "Is it working?"

"Maybe," Artie said. "I don't know."

The grayness swirled furiously around Pete, briefly hiding him from view. Scintillating blue flashes shone through the haze like lightning strobing deep within a storm cloud. Myka could feel the raw energy against her face. Tiny hairs rose up at the back of her neck. Her anxious gaze strove to penetrate the tumult, but the blinding flashes forced her to look way. Huddled beside her, Artie shielded his eyes with his arms.

"It'll be over soon," he predicted. "One way or another."

There was nothing more they could do, Myka

realized. Pete was in Clara Barton's hands now, so to speak.

"Um, guys?" Claudia called out. "Maybe you should back up a bit more?"

Probably not a bad idea, but just a second too late. The blue light merged with the gray fog like matter colliding with antimatter. A burst of pristine white energy knocked Myka and Artie backward, sending them tumbling across the lawn. The shock wave radiated outward, uprooting Claudia and Nadia as well. The carriage horse whinnied in fright. Rising up on its hind legs, it pawed the air with its front hooves. Pete himself was lost at the center of the eruption.

And then, in a heartbeat, it was over.

The intense white glare blinked out of existence. The shock wave exhausted itself. Myka found herself sprawled upon the grass at least three yards from where she had been crouching before. Fallen leaves cushioned her body. Artie moaned a few feet away. He rescued his glasses from the leaf litter. Miraculously, they appeared to be unbroken.

"Are you okay?" he asked.

"Forget me." She jumped to her feet. "What about Pete?"

Thankfully, the blast had not scattered him all over Central Park. She saw him lying on his back, still in one piece. The grass was flattened around him like a crop circle. But was he alive or not? Had the gloves saved him or killed him?

Myka ran toward him, holding her breath. She couldn't tell if he was moving or not.

Please, Pete. Don't let this be the end. I don't want to do another job without you.

He sat up abruptly, coughing. His eyes blinked in confusion and he shook his head. He still looked thinner than usual, but his color was already looking better. His skin no longer had that awful grayish cast. He licked his lips.

"Wow," he mumbled. "My whole mouth tastes like fudge."

Myka gasped in relief. Joyful tears streamed down her face. Dropping to his side, she hugged him as hard as she could. "Ohmigod, Pete . . ."

"Hey, not so tight!" he griped. "I'm trying to breathe here."

She let go and punched him in the shoulder instead.

"Don't you ever do that to me again, you jerk!"

CHAPTER 24

CENTRAL PARK

"How's he doing?" Pete asked.

Nadia cradled Jim's head in her lap as her battered boyfriend came to. A fresh bandage, courtesy of Artie's satchel, had been applied to his brow. Nadia pressed gently on the compress. "His head's stopped bleeding. I think he's going to be okay."

"Nadia?" Jim looked up at her. "What . . . what happened?"

"It's all right," she shushed him. "I'll tell you all about it later."

"But that man?" He shuddered, remembering Worrall's attack. He clutched Nadia's hand. "Are you all right?"

"It's okay, man," Pete said. "Everything's under control. Just take it easy." He gave Nadia a reassuring nod. "Head wounds can be tricky," he told her. "Lots of time they look a lot worse than they are." From what he'd seen, he doubted if Jim would even need stitches. "You probably ought to have him checked out for a concussion, though."

Nadia contemplated her naked right hand. "I don't suppose . . . ," she asked him tentatively. "Just once more?"

Pete shook his head. The gloves remained on his hands, just in case they needed a little more time to fix him, but he wasn't tempted to use them. They had caused enough trouble already. "Let's not push our luck, okay?"

Calm had finally descended on the Sheep Meadow, which they had all to themselves for the time being. Worrall's panicked victims had all fled the scene. Chances were, they would have only foggy memories of what had happened to them. The local authorities were staying away as well. Pete wouldn't be surprised to find out that Mrs. Frederic had quietly pulled strings to arrange for a temporary quarantine, just to give the agents a chance to take care of any loose ends. She was good at that kind of thing. After all, she had been doing it since who knew when.

One of these days, Pete thought, *I really want to find out what her story is.*

For the moment, however, he was just happy to be alive. The storm clouds had all dispersed, leaving behind a beautiful fall afternoon. Pete took a deep breath, filling his lungs. He was still a little wobbly, but he was definitely starting to feel like his old self again.

Thanks to Myka and Artie and Claudia.

"Hey, partner." Myka strolled over to join him, after returning Artie's first-aid kit to his bag. She looked Pete over. "How are you feeling?"

"Honestly, I'm starving for something beside hospital

food." He patted his stomach. "I feel like I could eat a horse."

The brown nag lifted its head over by the carriage. Pete shrugged apologetically.

"Present company excluded, of course."

The horse whinnied indignantly. Its passengers were still out cold. Pete figured the tourists and the carriage driver would be pretty confused when they finally woke up. Not that they'd actually remember anything. The Tesla blast would have done a number on their memories.

And speaking of loose ends . . .

Pete held up his hands, showing off Clara Barton's gloves. "How about we finally neutralize these puppies?"

"Already?" Worry creased her brow. "Maybe you should keep them on a little longer? Just in case they're . . . well, keeping you alive."

"I feel fine," he insisted. "Anything they're going to do, I think they've done." He did his best to alleviate her anxiety. "Honestly, Mykes, I want to get these things off me." He scratched at the back of his hand. "They're starting to itch."

Myka nodded. "Okay. Let's do this." She took out a silver retrieval bag and held it open. "Any time you're ready."

She didn't need to ask twice. He unbuttoned the gloves and peeled them off. Into the bag they went without a second thought. Golden sparks erupted the minute the gloves hit the goo inside. A pyrotechnic flash left his eyes watering—just like usual.

"All right." He punched the air triumphantly. "Now, that's what I call a proper neutralization."

"And none too soon." Myka sealed the bag shut. "I don't know about you, but I'm ready to declare this case closed."

"You and me both," Pete agreed.

Seated on the carpet a few feet away, Nadia sighed ruefully as she watched Myka put the bag away. "It was nice while it lasted, I guess." She gazed at her empty hands. "I should have known it was too good to be true."

Pete didn't want to leave her feeling like she had lost something irreplaceable. "Look, there are still plenty of ways you can help people if you really want to. Do volunteer work, become a doctor, a teacher, a Secret Service agent, whatever. You don't need some spooky Civil War gloves to do good, just a big heart and a willingness to go the extra yard for folks who can use a helping hand." He smiled down at Nadia and Jim. "From what I've seen, you've already got plenty of both."

She looked at him hopefully. "You really think so?"

"I know it. Just don't make yourself sick this time, okay?"

Jim squeezed her hand. "Trust me, I'll take good care of her."

"Take care of each other," Myka stressed. "You'll be okay as long as you have someone watching your back." She punched Pete again. "Even if they scare you to death sometimes."

"Ouch!" Pete said. "Stop doing that!"

■ ■ ■

"Ah. There you are."

Artie found Brigadier General Laverlong's cane lying not far from where Pete had dropped it. To his relief, the artifact did not appear to have been damaged in its travels. He had been uneasy about shipping the elephant cross-country. Past attempts to transport artifacts by post or special delivery had not always turned out well, as in the case of Philo Farnsworth's 3-D TV projector. Handling the cane carefully, he tucked it under his arm. "Back to the Warehouse for you," he muttered. "Safely away from any fault zones."

He peeked at his watch. They needed to keep an eye on the time. Mrs. Frederic could keep the area contained for the present, citing "national security," but they shouldn't linger. The sooner he and the others relocated to a more secure location, the better. Fortunately, the Regents had long ago arranged for a safe house down in the Village, tucked away inside the old Northern Dispensary building. They could camp out there before heading back to South Dakota with the gloves.

Where to shelve them? he wondered, thinking ahead. In the Civil War wing, next to Harriet Tubman's thimble, John Brown's body, and the original grapes of wrath? Or in the medical aisle, alongside the Hippocrates and Florence Nightingale collections? There was always the Dark Vault, of course, but that was getting a bit crowded. . . .

A bitter voice interrupted his ruminations.

"Who are you people anyway?" Worrall demanded. His hands cuffed behind his back, he had been propped up against a convenient tree trunk. Dried goo caked his face and clothes. He strained impotently against his bonds. "This is none of your business!"

"You couldn't be more wrong about that, actually." Artie ambled over to check on their prisoner. He eyed Worrall curiously. "How's your head, Calvin? The migraines still bothering you?"

The question took Worrall by surprise. "How do you know . . . ?"

"I know all sorts of things, Calvin. That's my job." He removed a magnifying glass from his leather satchel and examined the veins beneath Worrall's hairless scalp. They didn't look particularly swollen. "Anyway, about your head?"

"It's fine," Worrall said sourly. He twisted away from Artie's examination. "What do you care?"

"Just testing a hypothesis. And your ulcer?"

"My ulcer?" Worrall paused. A puzzled look came over his face, as though he had just noticed something. "It's not bothering me." A note of wonderment crept into his voice. "Not at all. I feel fine." He tugged on the cuffs. "All things considered."

Interesting, Artie thought. *Just as I theorized.*

"Ironically enough, Calvin, I suspect that wearing both gloves actually cured you of your various ailments. You can probably look forward to a long and healthy life . . . in federal custody."

Worrall frowned. "What do you intend to do with me?"

That was for the Regents to decide. Now that Worrall had been stripped of the infectious left glove, he no longer posed an active threat to humanity, but his ruth-less actions required some manner of retribution. Artie doubted if the Regents would have Worrall bronzed alive, as had been done to many of the most danger-ous individuals in history, including MacPherson and H. G. Wells, but Worrall was going to need to be kept under wraps from now on. There were other hazardous artifacts still at large in the world, after all, and Calvin had already demonstrated a reckless desire to wield them. They couldn't risk him getting his hands on something comparable to Clara Barton's gloves—or maybe even worse.

"Let us worry about that," Artie said. "You just stay put while we clean up your mess."

"But you can't simply hold me like this!" He squirmed indignantly, rattling his cuffs. His once pallid face turned an apoplectic shade of purple. "I demand to call my lawyer!"

Artie chuckled at the notion. "I'm afraid you have us confused with the FBI. We don't work that way." He turned his back on the renegade collector. "Enjoy your migraine-free life, Calvin. At least you got something for your trouble. And ours."

Worrall cursed Artie vociferously as the agent walked away. Artie tuned him out. Calvin was just a minor detail to be disposed of now. What really mattered was Clara Barton's gloves, now safely residing inside a neutralizer bag within his satchel. They had come a long way from the bloody battlefields and disease-ridden infirmaries of the Civil War, but their wanderings, both together and apart, were nearing their end.

He peeked inside the satchel to make sure they weren't acting up.

"No more touring for you," he said. "And no more sideshows."

Their next stop was a permanent engagement at Warehouse 13.

CHAPTER 25

LEENA'S BED-AND-BREAKFAST

"Of course!" Myka finally finished that crossword puzzle she had been working on before. "A six-letter word for 'empty fingers' is . . . 'gloves.'" She triumphantly filled in the final square. "I can't believe I didn't think of that before."

Breakfast was on the patio again. The B&B's grounds and gardens were nowhere near as expansive as Central Park's, but she wouldn't have traded them for all the buried treasures in the Warehouse. It was good to be home.

Coffee, croissants, and fresh-squeezed orange juice were laid out atop the table, alongside the morning papers. Pete wolfed down pastries like there was no tomorrow, clearly making up for lost time. He had already gained back much of the weight he had lost in the hospital. Myka took his healthy appetite as proof that his fever had passed for good. *That's our Pete,* she thought, claiming a croissant before they all disappeared. She looked forward to him annoying her for years to come.

Pete wasn't the only person who was recovering.

According to Vanessa Calder, those afflicted by Calvin Worrall were now responding to conventional treatment. Neutralizing the gloves had not cured Worrall's victims, but now their fevers could be treated by antibiotics and other forms of modern medicine, unavailable in Clara Barton's time. Vanessa expected them all to make a full recovery.

"This is such a waste of my talents," Claudia grumbled as she clipped out newspaper articles for Artie's files. "Doesn't he know print is passé? Digital is where it's at."

"Think of it as a hard copy backup," Myka advised. She suspected that Artie just wanted to keep Claudia too busy to cause any more havoc in the Warehouse. Apparently, there had been an incident concerning a totem pole? "Indulge him."

"Easy for you to say." Claudia worked her scissors like she was digging ditches. Her tongue stuck out of the corner of her mouth. "You're not stuck scrapbooking like a suburban hausfrau. . . ."

"Maybe you'll get time off for good behavior."

Pete stole a copy of the *New York Times* from Claudia's pile. "Hey, check this out," he mumbled through a mouthful of buttery pastry. "Says here that a freak earthquake in Central Park resulted in an episode of mass hysteria." He squinted dubiously at the front page. "You really think anyone's going to buy that?"

"As opposed to believing that Clara Barton's cursed gloves nearly gave everybody typhoid fever?" Myka assumed that Mrs. Frederic or the Regents had somehow planted that story—and covered up what had really taken place. "People want sane, rational explanations. I know I did . . . before."

"Yeah, not even our next door neighbors can handle the truth." Claudia slid a newly excised clipping across the table. "According to the *Univille Unquirer,* a spectacular 'air show' at the street fair this weekend was rained out by an unexpected storm. They're blaming global warming." She took a break from scrapbook duty to pour herself a fresh glass of OJ. "Apparently, somebody vandalized a sculpture in the park too."

"Bummer," Pete said. "I always liked that thing. It was totally tubular."

"Oh, really?" Myka looked askance. "Since when have you been interested in modern art? Your idea of high culture is a *Jersey Shore* marathon."

"Hey, don't diss The Situation" He patted his abs. "Can I help it if you have no idea what cool is?"

Before Myka could fire back with the ideal retort, the screen doors opened and Leena joined them on the patio. She brought a bowl of ripe strawberries to go with the croissants. She smiled wryly at the agents' friendly bickering. "Sounds to me like everyone is back to normal."

"Whatever that means around here." Claudia leafed through the local paper. "Hey, guess what? There's a circus coming to town." Her eyes lit up with excitement. "We should *so* check that out!"

Pete lobbed a strawberry at her head.

"Or not," she amended.

She ducked the fruity missile which flew past her head just as Artie strolled through the door. It splattered at his feet.

He heaved a world-weary sigh. "A nursery. I'm running a nursery."

"Sorry, chief," Claudia said sheepishly. She pointed at Pete. "He started it!"

"Snitch!" Pete accused her. "That's it. I'm not letting you win at Halo anymore."

"Right." Claudia snorted. "Like you ever had a chance. . . ."

Artie held up his hand to forestall any further discussion. "That's enough, both of you." Plopping himself down in an empty chair, he opened his satchel and pulled out a bulging accordion file. "We have work to do." His gaze alighted on the breakfast spread. "Ooh, croissants!"

"Just one," Leena advised. "Remember your triglycerides."

Myka was intrigued by the file. "What do you have for us, Artie?"

"A ping if I ever saw one." Artie helped himself to a single croissant. "Seems the dead are rising in New Orleans. . . ."

That got everyone's attention.

"Marie Laveau's voodoo doll?" Claudia guessed.

"So it would seem." Artie handed Pete and Myka a pair of plane tickets. "Your flight is in an hour."

Myka gulped down the last of her coffee. She nodded at Pete. "Flip you for the Tesla."

"You're on." He grabbed a croissant for the road. "The Big Easy, here we come."

Myka grinned in anticipation.

"The beignets are on me."

ACKNOWLEDGMENTS

Looking back, I wanted to write a *Warehouse 13* novel as soon as I watched the first episode, but it took a lot of people to make that possible.

First of all, I want to thank my editor, Jen Heddle at Pocket Books, for recruiting me in the first place, and my agent, Russ Galen, for making the deal happen. And the real-life proprietors of Warehouse 13—Jack Kenny, Nell Scovell, Drew Z. Greenberg, Ian Stokes, and others—for generously sharing their time and expertise. And Chris Lucero at NBC Universal for making the whole process run smoothly.

Finally, I can't forget my girlfriend, Karen, who put up with me babbling about artifacts and neutralizers and Tesla guns for months, and insisting on watching the episodes over and over. And our four-legged offspring, Lyla, Churchill, Henry, and Sophie, as well as their big brother Alex, who passed away while this book was being written. It feels very strange to be writing this without him sleeping in the background somewhere. He will be missed.

ABOUT THE AUTHOR

GREG COX is the *New York Times* bestselling author of numerous books and short stories. He has written the official movie novelizations of *Daredevil*, *Ghost Rider*, *Death Defying Acts*, and all three *Underworld* movies, as well as novels and stories based on such popular series as *Alias*, *Buffy*, *CSI*, *Farscape*, *The 4400*, *The Green Hornet*, *Roswell*, *Star Trek*, *Underworld*, *Xena*, and *Zorro*. He has received two Scribe Awards from the International Association of Media Tie-in Writers. He lives in Oxford, Pennsylvania.

His official website is www.gregcox-author.com.